Praise for the novels of Susan Krinard

"Susan Krinard was born to write romance."
—*New York Times* bestselling author Amanda Quick

"A master of atmosphere and description."
—*Library Journal*

Praise for Theresa Meyers

"This is an original and well-written story with a fascinating mythology and wonderfully complex characters."
—*RT Book Reviews* on *The Half-Breed Vampire*

Praise for Linda Thomas-Sundstrom

"Linda Thomas-Sundstrom's well-written, action-packed novel will keep readers entertained from start to finish....A compelling page-turner!"
—*RT Book Reviews* on *Guardian of the Night*

SUSAN KRINARD

has written and published more than fourteen novels and written stories for a number of anthologies, and her Harlequin HQN novel *Lord of the Beasts* appeared on the *New York Times* bestseller list. Susan makes her home in New Mexico, the Land of Enchantment, with her husband, Serge, their dogs, Freya, Nahla and Cagney, and their cat, Jefferson.

THERESA MEYERS

was selected in 2005 as a finalist in for the American Title II contest, the *American Idol* of books. She is married to the first man she dated and currently lives in a Victorian house on a minifarm in the Pacific Northwest with their children, a large assortment of animals and an out-of-control herb garden. You can find her online at her website at www.theresameyers.com, on Twitter at www.twitter.com/Theresa_Meyers or on Facebook at www.facebook.com/TheresaMeyersAuthor.

LINDA THOMAS-SUNDSTROM,

author of contemporary and historical paranormal romance novels, writes for Harlequin Nocturne. She lives in the West, juggling teaching, writing, family and caring for a big stretch of land. Visit Linda at her website, www.lindathomas-sundstrom.com, and the Nocturne Authors' website, www.nocturneauthors.com.

HOLIDAY WITH A VAMPIRE 4

SUSAN KRINARD, THERESA MEYERS AND LINDA THOMAS-SUNDSTROM

HARLEQUIN®

entertain, enrich, inspire™

Recycling programs for this product may not exist in your area.

ISBN-13: 978-0-373-88559-6

HOLIDAY WITH A VAMPIRE 4

Copyright © 2012 by Harlequin Books S.A.

The publisher acknowledges the copyright holders of the individual works as follows:

HALFWAY TO DAWN
Copyright © 2012 by Susan Krinard

THE GIFT
Copyright © 2012 by Theresa Meyers

BRIGHT STAR
Copyright © 2012 by Linda Thomas-Sundstrom

THE GATEKEEPER
Copyright © 2012 by Slush Pile Productions, LLC

This edition published by arrangement with Harlequin Books S.A.

For questions and comments about the quality of this book, please contact us at CustomerService@Harlequin.com.

® and TM are trademarks of the publisher. Trademarks indicated with ® are registered in the United States Patent and Trademark Office, the Canadian Trade Marks Office and in other countries.

www.Harlequin.com

Printed in U.S.A.

CONTENTS

Dear Reader,

As we prepare to ring in the New Year, we have some exciting news to share with you. Starting in January, Harlequin Nocturne is unveiling a brand-new look that's a fresh take on our paranormal covers. Please turn to the back of this book for a sneak peek.

Our stories still feature powerful, mysterious alpha male heroes facing life-or-death situations as they battle for the heroine's love. But we will be increasing the page count to allow for a wider breadth of story, subplots and heightened sensual and sexual tension.

New York Times bestselling author Heather Graham gets Nocturne off to a great start with the launch of the thrilling new miniseries *The Keepers: L.A.* And Rhyannon Byrd returns with another title in her popular *Bloodrunners series* about a pack of very alpha wolves.

So don't miss out on your favorite series. Look for the newly repackaged Nocturne titles starting in January wherever you buy books.

In the meantime, be sure to look for this month's reads: *Holiday with a Vampire 4* by Susan Krinard, Theresa Meyers and Linda Thomas-Sundstrom and *Sentinels: Kodiak Chained* by Doranna Durgin.

Happy reading,

Ann Leslie Tuttle

Senior Editor

HALFWAY TO DAWN

Susan Krinard

Prologue

The War began with the Awakening

The first Opiri—those beings that folklore called vampires—had arisen at the dawn of human civilization. Creatures of darkness, the Opiri were nevertheless unlike the legends in many respects. They were not supernatural creatures but a distinct humanoid species with a severe intolerance to sunlight, a dietary need for human blood, indefinitely long life spans, exceptional strength and speed, and senses as keen as those of a true predator.

The first true Opiri civilization arose at the time of the Egyptian First Dynasty when the eldest among them, known as Bloodmasters and Bloodlords, began to convert members of the human population to serve as vassals. Along with vassals, the Freebloods—possessing neither masters nor vassals of their own—made up the larger part of this society, which adhered to a rigid caste system.

But after centuries of coexisting with humans in the ancient world, the Opiri, known as "Nightsiders" in the vernacular of the former United States, learned that they could not survive without decimating the human population, their most vital source of nourishment.

So, the Bloodlords and Bloodmasters gathered from all corners of the earth and sat in council. They determined that only time would provide them with what they required: a human population vast enough to meet their needs, but malleable and divided, ripe to fall under Opiri rule.

They built a vast network of underground chambers where they could never be discovered or disturbed, and all but the Bloodmasters retreated into a sleep humans would call death. They waited while the Bloodmasters roamed the earth and watched, preparing the way, patient and undying as human empires rose and fell.

At last, when the world was teeming with humans and filled with discord, the Bloodlords began to rouse those Opiri who slept. Thousands of so-called vampires emerged in every corner of the world, in every nation, hungry and eager to claim all the earth and conquer its inhabitants.

That was the Awakening, and it began the most terrible war in human history, a war not over territory or ancient hatreds but for survival. Thousands upon thousands of humans fell into death or serfdom or vassalage.

During those terrible years, Homo sapiens retreated into city-states called Enclaves, where they could maintain strong defenses and hold the Opiri at bay. The Opiri formed their own strongholds as the war raged on. Between human and Nightsider territories stretched the neutral zones, where ground troops struggled to claim scraps of land and ultimate victory.

The first Enclave established in California was centered on the city of San Francisco, encompassing Northern California's remaining human population. The city-state established its own Enclave Defense and Intelligence, creating special military forces trained as scouts and agents capable of moving where regular troops could not.

In the sixth year of the Opiri-human war, leaders on both sides of the conflict arranged for secret negotiations. But they faced great opposition, and there was no guarantee that a truce, let alone a lasting peace, could ever be achieved.

—from the Introduction to *A Brief History of the Nightsider War, San Francisco Enclave*

Chapter 1

No Man's Land, Northern California

"Are you warm enough, Ambassador Sandoval?" Fiona asked.

The ambassador's dark eyes peered up at her from the shadow of his hood. "I'll be fine," he said, giving her a brave smile, though he was anything but a soldier. In fact, she doubted the wiry professorial man with the serious face and nervous glances had set foot outside the Enclave of San Francisco since the war began.

That was why she was here, she and her team. They had to get him to the rendezvous alive...and still human.

A wet, stinging wind probed her neck with icy fingers, trying to find a way inside her jacket. She pulled the zipper as high as it would go and exchanged glances with Joel and the other members of her Special Forces team. Their grim expressions mirrored her own.

This was the coldest December any of them could remember, one storm after another lashing a state once known for sunshine and warm winters. Waves of heavy rain, driven by gales strong enough to upend trees, turned the ground to icy mud, and nighttime temperatures were bitter enough to freeze even the toughest native plants.

Some said it was all because of the Awakening. Fiona had heard her own colleagues muttering about it back at Enclave Defense and Intelligence, hardened professional agents and soldiers who should have known better. The belief wasn't rational; even the most powerful vampires didn't have control over the weather.

But there wasn't a lot of rationality going around where the bloodsuckers were concerned. They'd killed too many in their quest for dominance over all life on earth, leaving vast wastelands around them.

Wastelands like the one visible on the opposite side of the Carquinez Bridge. Once a thriving suburb of Vallejo, it was now a maze of overgrown streets and abandoned middle-class houses, schools empty of students, stores long since looted of anything valuable. The former residents of the homes—those who had survived the first Nightsider attacks—had fled, scattering to various refugee encampments and eventually to the Enclaves. Many more had been condemned to a life of slavery, taken as serfs by Bloodmasters or Bloodlords, the highest-ranking aristocracy in Nightsider society.

These days, you seldom saw Bloodmasters or Bloodlords on the battlefield. They had bound vassals and Freebloods—independent Nightsiders who chose their own loyalties—to do their fighting and increase their holdings for them.

But things were starting to fall apart on both sides of the conflict. Fiona knew firsthand that there were plenty of Bloodlords trying to set up their own little fiefdoms instead of working for ultimate victory, and thousands of Freebloods, singly or in gangs, seeking prey among their enemies with no regard to orders from above. Some Enclave scouts had seen Nightsider commanders using serfs as living shields, compelling human forces to abort attacks or kill their own kind.

But that meant the bloodsuckers were getting desperate. To throw serfs away was worse than setting a fortune in paper bills on fire. If no one could control the rogue Bloodlords and Freebloods…

Ultimately good for our side, she thought. *And very bad for* us.

"Us" meaning, in this case, her team, soldiers cut off from their platoons, or other humans unfortunate enough to be out in No Man's Land.

"Captain Donnelly," Commander Joel Goodman said in a low voice, coming up beside her. "Chen and Patterson say we're clear to proceed. No sign of rogues or any recent action in the area."

Fiona nodded acknowledgment, by no means set at ease. Bloodsuckers had a way of popping up when you least expected it. And while it was only morning and the team would have a good eight hours of travel time, daylight was no guarantee of safety. Just because the Opiri had come out of their hidden caverns only six years ago didn't mean they were backward. Or stupid. The Bloodmasters had seen to that.

Less than a week until Christmas, she thought, giving the hand signal to proceed. Last year she'd spent the holidays with her family, her father and cousins, nieces, aunts and uncles, stealing a little peace from the long days and weeks and months of war. She'd made the most of it, laughing and singing carols and enjoying every precious moment.

This year she would have to hold the celebration in her heart. Traveling only by day and at their current pace, they would be lucky to make Sacramento by New Year's.

Maybe that was an exaggeration. But if they were attacked and pinned down…

One day at a time, she reminded herself. *One hour.* That was the way to survive. And she not only intended to survive but make sure Sandoval, his aide and every member of her team survived, as well.

Kane paused to listen, his head cocked to one side as something moved in the low brush.

An animal, he thought. Fox, by the smell of it. They generally fled when they scented an Opir, though only the most desperate vassal or Freeblood would stoop to taking blood from a beast, and then only in the final stages of starvation.

"What's up, guv?" Alfie asked, his gruff voice loud in the near silence.

"Nothing," Kane said. "False alarm."

Alfie scratched his ribs under his black fatigue jacket, his ugly face relaxing in the sheer bliss of relieving an itch. Not that Opiri, even vassals, would be bitten by the mosquitoes that frequented the expanses of marsh north of what had once been known as Grizzly Bay. Vampire blood was as good as the most potent insect repellent for keeping other bloodsuckers at a distance.

"Penny fer yer thoughts, guv," Alfie said.

"Estimating how much farther to the bay," Kane said, staring south through the frigid darkness. They had been following a rough southwestern course since they'd gone beyond the Opiri perimeter, well past the zone they had been assigned to scout. They'd been moving quickly, making good time as they headed toward open water, and the chance to find a boat and a quicker road to freedom.

Freedom. It had been a word without meaning for Kane since he'd died at the Battle of the Somme over a century ago. Died on a muddy field in France, his rifle still in his hand, and been resurrected into a new life of horror and bondage.

In some ways it had not been unlike the life he'd had before. His heart still beat. His body was still warm. He could still sleep, and sometimes even eat the foods humans took for granted.

But in every other respect it had been a nightmare, scavenging and hunting on battlefields instead of fighting on them. Hunting for blood.

It had been many years before he'd been able to accept what he had become, and between his conversion and that acceptance he had fought with everything that was in him to escape.

But there had been no escape from the fate to which he had been condemned. His Sire was not merely a Bloodlord, capable of converting any human into a vampire, but a Bloodmaster—one of the most ancient and powerful Opiri, those who had lived out the centuries awake and aware, while the rest of the vampire breed slept the deep sleep of hibernation in hidden catacombs under the earth. Erastos had been alive when Athens ruled Greece, when Genghis Khan had conquered the better part of Eurasia, during the awakening of the Renaissance and the grand birth of the Enlightenment.

And he had been walking the battlefields of the First World War when he had swept Kane and Alfie Palmer out of death and into eternal vassalage.

"Yer broodin' again, Yank," Alfie chided, nudging Kane's shoulder. "We better get a move on."

Good-humored as Alfie's warning was, the Englishman reminded Kane how much they both had to lose if they were caught. Every day their bond with Erastos grew a little weaker, but their only hope was to put as much distance between themselves and the Bloodmaster as possible. Erastos had been much distracted by the current war, but he would never willingly let one of his vassals slip the leash—least of all two of the Opiri's most valuable scouts.

It had been during the course of their scouting that Kane had become convinced that prolonged physical separation from their Sire was the key to freedom— separation and raw determination. The breaking of the bond was painful, a bone-deep wrenching of brain and gut that had nothing to do with human emotion.

And then there was the hunger. Ever present, sapping their strength, inexorably slowing their pace a little more every day.

Kane was grateful that they hadn't run into any humans. Partly that had been by design; he didn't want to face the temptation, not until neither he nor Alfie had a choice. They had subsisted on the blood of animals, but it did no more than keep them alive. What they would do once they reached the Pacific Coast remained a question Kane knew better than to dwell on.

Unhooking his canteen, Kane shook it to determine how much water was left. They were both running low, and the water around them was unpalatable even to Opiri. Lack of blood made it even more necessary to stay hydrated, but they were nearly at the point where access to fresh water would no longer make any difference to their survival.

Nodding to his friend, Kane plunged into the half-frozen mud and pushed his way forward. Alfie pulled his tattered scarf higher around his scarred chin and followed in Kane's footsteps. Small, hard pellets of snow blew into Kane's face. It was like the winter of 1914 all over again.

"Sometimes I think I'd rather be back on the Western Front," Alfie said, flapping his arms around his chest to keep warm. "What I wouldn't give fer a good cuppa."

Or a flask of whiskey, Kane thought. As if alcohol would do either of them any good. Still, he grinned in answer to Alfie's comment and reminded himself that things could be worse. They could be fighting with their fellow vassals on the front lines of this seemingly endless war, fighting for a cause they both despised.

He and Alfie went south and west through the long night, crossing fallow fields and broken fences, pausing to rest only when the cramps in their bellies and muscles grew too much to bear. Then they stopped wherever they could find dry ground beneath the bare branches of a lone tree, or under the fallen roof of an isolated, abandoned farmhouse.

Kane could smell the bay before they reached one of the sloughs that wound a tortured path through the marshes, heading toward open water. The birds that lived in the marsh—heron and killdeer, rail and duck—huddled with heads tucked under wings or among the brown reeds, waiting for the coming of dawn. Somehow Kane and Alfie found the will to move faster, their boots breaking a thin crust of ice with every step.

"Only a li'l over an 'our left, I reckon," Alfie remarked. "Better find a place ta 'ole up before sunrise."

He was right. Some of the legends about vampires were no more than myth, but this one was all too true. The first rays of the sun to strike an Opir would cause third-degree burns. Even with the protection of heavy clothing, a few minutes of exposure could do more damage than standing in the middle of a raging fire, and another few would cause injuries beyond any vampire's ability to heal.

Kane surveyed the area. There was a house tucked in a small valley among the brown, oak-studded hills to the west, on the other side of an abandoned highway. He had wanted to avoid the crumbling paved roads, though he and Alfie were nearly as exposed crossing the wetlands. It was instinct more than sense, but he had spent too long letting instinct guide him to abandon it now.

"There," he said, gesturing toward the house.

"It'll do as good as any," Alfie said, and they set off again. Soon they were on the road, the hills looming ahead of them. They were halfway across when Kane heard the sounds of struggle, coming from the south and around a bend in the highway.

Without thinking, he dropped flat onto his belly. Alfie fell beside him.

"Rogues?" the Englishman whispered.

"And humans," Kane said, as the scent came to him on the stiff, chilly wind.

Alfie sniffed loudly. "If there was any Opiri scouts out 'ere, we'd know it. But 'umans, this far from the Enclave?"

"The only humans who would be this far into No Man's Land would be Special Forces or Enclave scouts," Kane said. "I count at least a dozen humans and almost as many rogues."

"Bloody 'ell," Alfie swore. He eyed Kane warily. "If them 'umans is so stupid, we don't need ta get involved."

Alfie was right. And yet…

"Yer goin' anyway," Alfie said with cheerful resignation. "Ya can't resist a chance ta take down a few o' them filthy blighters." He shifted the rifle over his shoulder. "Come ta that, neither can I."

Kane almost smiled. As usual, he and Alfie were in perfect accord. "We'll have to go up the hill and around, come down on them from above," he said. "We may not make it before daylight, but the rogues will have to get under cover soon. Maybe we can take them out when they're least expecting it. And if there are any humans left alive…"

He didn't have to finish. Enclave Special Forces might be tough and well trained, but generally even the best of them was no match for a rogue head-to-head.

Rising to a crouch, Kane ran across the highway to the overgrown verge that stretched to the foot of the hills. Dry ground crunched beneath his sodden boots. Immediately he started up the nearest hill, passing to the left of the farmhouse they'd chosen to wait out the day.

The humans didn't have much time left.

* * *

The attack had come without warning, an hour before dawn. One of the forward scouts was dead before Fiona had her M28 in her hands.

They all knew about the rogues, of course. The sixth year of the war had seen their numbers double. No amount of discipline or punishment could hold Freeblood troops together for so long without heavy losses— not only of lives but of loyalty.

This band was on the edge of starvation. Fiona could see it in their wild eyes and gaunt faces as she, Joel Goodman, Johnson and Li Chen took up their places around Ambassador—and Senator—Sandoval and prepared to defend him and his aide. The others, outfitted with infrared visors, met the rogues with bullets aimed for the hearts and heads of their enemies, the only parts of a bloodsucker's body vulnerable to fatal damage.

The battle was vicious. Some of the rogues were also armed, but they had a clear disadvantage: the sun was rising, and they were too weak from hunger to get off many effective shots. But in hand-to-hand combat, they were stronger than the strongest human, and they were fast. They might prefer to take a few prisoners and keep them alive to supply enough nourishment for several days, but they could also drink the blood of the dying and sate their hunger, no matter how briefly.

When Yugov and Tagstrom fell, Fiona knew she would have to bring out the big guns.

"Johnson," she said.

The tall black man stepped forward. "Captain?"

"Go ahead."

Johnson swung the VS120 into his hands and advanced into the fight. It didn't take long for the new weapon to decimate the rogues, and soon half a dozen bloodsucker bodies, certifiably and permanently expired, were lying among the dead and wounded human soldiers. The remaining five rogues fled, leaving their fallen comrades without looking back.

Fiona signaled Johnson to put the weapon away and ran to assess the damage. Yugov and Tagstrom were dead. Of the others, Patterson had been bitten, but not fatally. She wasn't at any risk of conversion; vampires had to *want* to do it, and the rogues certainly hadn't been interested in adding to their number.

Nakamura was struggling to his feet with a bloodied arm, and Cole was limping. D'Agostino and Lefevre had minor injuries, nothing the medic couldn't take care of fairly quickly. Bakhtiar was already kneeling beside Lefevre, binding her shoulder. Li Chen looked over the rogues' bodies one more time, while Goodman and Johnson laid out Yugov and Tagstrom.

"No time to bury them," Goodman said, joining Fiona.

Leaving the fallen was a necessity, but she hated it. Almost as much as she hated the bloodsuckers.

She stared in the direction the surviving rogues had fled. "Joel, keep the team moving as fast as you can."

"Where are *you* going?"

"To scout out the rogue survivors, make sure they've gone to ground and can't give us any more trouble."

"You should stay with the ambassador. I'll—"

"That's an order, Goodman. You know the bloodsuckers will be more worried about finding shelter than ambushing me."

Joel stiffened, his face going blank. "Yes, ma'am."

He remained behind while she started after the

rogues. The bloodsuckers had been clumsy enough to leave clear tracks and a trail of blood heading up into the hills. The tracks split after a quarter mile, two in one group and three in the other.

Wary of a trap, she followed the larger group uphill. The cover here was scant, and if she was lucky she could catch them before they found a place to hide.

She realized she'd made a terrible mistake when one of the rogues stepped in front of her, so silent that she'd never even heard him coming. The other two, one badly wounded in the shoulder, came at her from behind, knocking her down and wrenching the M28 from her hands. Before she could reach for her sidearm, they had taken that, as well.

The two uninjured Freebloods yanked her to her feet and dragged her into a thicket of tangled brush near the base of a hill. It gave barely enough shade to keep the sun out; they would have to huddle together very closely to fit inside it.

After binding Fiona tightly, the rogues left her lying in the dirt while they crawled under the thicket. She closed her eyes and prayed her team would do their duty and go on without her. It would be hard for them, especially Joel—who had once been her close friend and partner—but he and Chen would have no choice but to consider her lost and get Sandoval to Sacramento.

Somehow she made it through the day. The rogues had torn off her heavy jacket, removed her helmet, discarded her boots and left her with only her winter fatigues to stave off the cold. Falling snow melted on her face and hair, but the moisture didn't reach her lips. By sunset her mouth was as dry as the Mojave Desert.

When the sun went down behind the hills, the rogues

began to move. They crawled out of the thicket and untied her hands. Then they forced her to walk to a young live oak farther up the hill.

Fiona knew what was coming when they tied her to the tree. They planned to drain her dry, but the look in their eyes told her they wouldn't make it quick.

One of them—the leader, she guessed—grabbed her chin. "Where are your companions now?" he asked, baring his teeth. "Run off to leave you here to die? I heard humans never abandoned their own dead."

Fiona realized that they didn't know about the meeting in Sacramento. Why should they? They'd willingly cut themselves off from their own kind.

"I told them to go," she said, jerking her chin out of the creature's hand.

"You're their captain?" the injured one asked. His ragged, bloodstained shirt had fallen away from his shoulder, revealing that his wound was already partially healed. "You led them right to us."

"What are you doing this far east?" the third bloodsucker asked. He glanced at the others. "Maybe she'd be worth more to us alive, Kallias. If we take her back to Command HQ…"

"Fool," Kallias spat. "We deserted. Do you think they'd welcome us with open arms?"

Fiona laughed. The injured one grabbed her by the throat with his good hand and squeezed.

"You want her dead, Ianos?" Kallias snapped. "We can get enough out of her to last two days, maybe three if we're careful."

Ianos let go of Fiona's throat. "Who goes first?" he asked.

"You want to challenge me, Ianos?" Kallias asked.

Ianos and the third rogue looked at each other and slowly backed away. Maybe they weren't up for confronting Kallias now, Fiona thought, but the problem with rogues, as with their superiors, was that they achieved leadership through challenge. That was a weapon she could use.

"That's right, Ianos," she said. "Better back off. Don't forget who's boss, even if he seriously misjudged who he was up against and got six of you killed."

Kallias raised his hand to strike her but thought better of it. She guessed that he probably didn't want the others to know how much she'd gotten to him.

"How many of yours did you lose?" he taunted. "You're going to wish you were one of them by this night's end."

She ignored his threat and looked at the third vampire. His face wasn't as hard as those of the other two, and he appeared much younger, hardly more than a boy. He seemed almost reluctant to kill her—or, more accurately, torture her. It might be only wishful thinking, but she decided to take a chance.

"What's your name?" she asked.

The bloodsucker gaped at her, the thin lines of his face drawn in confusion. "Natham," he said.

"Silence," Kallias snapped, but Natham continued to stare at Fiona.

"Mine is Fiona," she said. "How long have you been an Opir, Natham?"

"Shut up," Kallias said, raising his hand again.

Natham ignored him. "One hundred twenty-six years," he whispered.

"Do you know what night this is?" she asked.

His expression relaxed. "Three nights before Christmas Eve," he said.

"Do you remember what it was like back then?" she asked. "Just before the turn of the Nineteenth Century, when people still rode in carriages and greeted each other in the streets?"

Tears glittered in Natham's eyes, giving the lie to the myth that vampires felt no emotion. "I remember," he said. "I remember our tree with all the candles on it, and the presents, and—" He broke off, and his mouth thinned. "The Bloodmaster changed all that. I never wanted this war. *I* wasn't one of the Awakened. Why should I fight for them?"

Kallias backhanded him, and he staggered. Ianos helped him up. "Idiot," he said.

Natham straightened, rubbing his face. "You do what you want to," he said. "I'll have no part in it."

"Then you'll die," Ianos said.

With a last look at Fiona, Natham walked away, his steps uneven. She knew she'd used up her only chance. Once, Natham had probably been a good man, but conversion changed everything. It turned even good men into monsters. And bad men into something unspeakable.

"I admire your courage, human," Kallias said. "But your tricks won't work on me."

She gazed into the darkness, humming her favorite holiday song under her breath as she remembered her own childhood, the warmth, the joy.

Kallias laughed and lowered his mouth to her throat.

Chapter 2

They'd come too late.

Kane crouched over one of the human bodies. She'd died fast, and so had her male companion—victims of the fight he and Alfie hadn't been able to reach before the sun had forced them to take shelter.

But the humans were not the only casualties. Six rogue Freebloods lay scattered on the ground, five of them nearly torn apart by projectiles Kane didn't recognize.

"Good work," Alfie remarked with admiration.

Crouching to read the pattern of boot prints impressed in the muddy ground, Kane nodded. "At least ten humans left here," he said. "Maybe more." He followed several sets of tracks leading in the direction of the highway. "Headed toward the road," he said.

Alfie shook his head. "They won't be foolish enough

ta travel on the 'ighway. They'll move along the foot o' the 'ills."

"They must have urgent business to have left their dead behind," Kane said. He rose and walked in the opposite direction. "Here," he said. "Six others went this way." He crouched again, sifting a pinch of soil between his fingers. "One human, female. Five Opiri."

"Rogues," Alfie said. "Poor lass."

"We're going after her."

"'Course we is, mate."

Kane didn't need to remind Alfie of the risks they faced or the danger they might present to the very human they wanted to save. Even if they took care of the rogues, they would still be confronted with their own starvation…and an easy source of blood right in front of them.

The difference was that the rogues would make the female suffer a very long time.

Signaling to Alfie, Kane took the lead as they began following the tracks. They quickly found the place where the rogues had split up and the woman had followed the larger group.

It didn't take long to hunt down the three rogues. They hadn't taken many pains to hide themselves. One of them was laughing, drunk on fresh blood, and the other was drinking from the woman, noisy as a pig at a trough.

"Only two," Alfie whispered, joining Kane behind a low wall of evergreen shrubs. "Even odds."

Alfie was being optimistic, as he usually was. Freebloods in general were stronger than vassals, just as Bloodlords were more powerful than Freebloods and

Bloodmasters superior to Bloodlords in almost every way. It was a hierarchy an Opir ignored at his own peril.

That didn't mean he and Alfie wouldn't do their damnedest.

The rogue finished his meal and drew back from the woman. Her red hair fell in wavy strands over her forehead and down to her shoulders, and her face was pale as new-fallen snow. Under other circumstances, Kane would have called her beautiful.

But beauty was the last thing on his mind. Very quietly he lifted his gun. Alfie did the same, flashing Kane a wicked grin. The drunken Freeblood looked up, scanning the shrubbery. His nostrils flared. The woman raised her head, her eyes glazed with pain and exhaustion.

"Ready?" Kane asked.

As one they plunged from behind the shrubs, firing as they attacked. The rogue who had just finished his meal spun around and dodged the bullets as if Kane and Alfie were moving in slow motion. He charged Kane, who braced himself for the impact.

Immediately the Freeblood went for his throat. Kane fended off the rogue with all his strength, grabbed the Opir's shoulder and spun around, flinging the rogue away.

By then Alfie was near the human, and the drunken Freeblood was staggering toward him. As big as he was, Alfie was surprisingly agile. He jumped out of the way and took careful aim. The rogue moved to stand directly in front of the woman.

"Shoot me and you kill her," he snarled.

The Opir Kane had temporarily incapacitated attacked again. Driven by the sheer power of rage, Kane grappled with the rogue and threw him to the ground. He drew his knife and drove it into the rogue's chest, piercing his heart. Then he rolled away and jumped to his feet, instantly taking in the deadly tableau.

"Let's get out o' 'ere," Alfie said loudly, backing away. "I ain't gonna die fer no 'uman."

Kane knew Alfie's words were a ploy, and they worked. For a split second the rogue standing in front of the woman was diverted by Alfie's slight retreat. Kane crossed the distance in two running steps and struck the rogue hard at the base of his neck with the side of his hand, unbalancing the Freeblood just long enough for Alfie to get off a single shot, precisely aimed to pierce the vampire's body from the side so the bullet wouldn't hit the human.

While Alfie made sure the Freeblood was out of commission—permanently—Kane cut the ropes that bound the woman to the tree. She collapsed, and he caught her just in time. She was too weak from loss of blood to stand, even with the solid trunk of the tree behind her.

"You're all right now," he said, easing her to the ground and kneeling beside her. "They can't hurt you anymore."

Her chin lolled on her chest, and he thought for a moment that he and Alfie had come too late again. He brushed her thick ginger hair away from her forehead. She opened her eyes, focusing on his face.

She wasn't capable of fighting, but she gave it her best shot, her expression suddenly fierce and her slender body taut as a bowstring. She tried to speak, but the effort was too great. Kane steadied her with one hand, careful not to touch her more than necessary.

Even so, he felt a shock when he grasped her arm, as if the blood she had lost had been replaced by an electric current. The torn, stained fatigues she wore couldn't conceal her athletic but very womanly figure. When she looked at him again, her eyes were defiant and lit with a strength of purpose even her extreme weakness couldn't extinguish.

"Who…are you?" she whispered, blinking in the darkness.

"Easy," Kane said. "You've lost a great deal of blood."

Blood. His hunger was stronger than ever before, but letting it get the better of him now was out of the question.

Alfie crouched beside him. "'Ow's the lass?" he asked.

"I don't know," Kane said. He cupped the woman's chin in his hand. "Do you understand me? Moving will only make it worse."

She looked at Alfie. "Are you…human?" she asked.

Kane exchanged glances with his friend. As a rule, vassals didn't take on the distinct appearance of older vampires. Only once they became Freebloods—vassals released by their lords—did they begin to resemble mature white-skinned, white-haired Opiri, though the process could be slow. Kane and Alfie might almost have passed for human, except for their night-black fatigues, and he doubted she could make out what they were wearing.

"We're here to help," Kane said.

"We can't stay 'ere," Alfie said under his breath. "The poor lass shouldn't 'ave ta suffer this place no longer."

Alfie was right. Kane slipped one arm behind the

woman's back and another under her knees, lifting her
easily. She stiffened again, but her resistance didn't
last.

"We got 'alf the night left," Alfie said. "Them others
she was with won't be travelin' after sundown. We
might catch up with 'em before daylight."

"And what do you think they'll do if we show up with
one of their own in this condition?" Kane asked grimly.
"They'll assume we did it, and I'm still inclined to go on
living. We can follow them, but we'd better make sure
she can walk into their camp under her own power."

He glanced down into the woman's face. Her eyes,
framed by long auburn lashes, were closed again. She
hardly weighed anything in his arms, and her heart was
beating as fast as a frightened bird's. The wounds in
her neck were raw and red.

Kane looked away from the pulse surging beneath
the skin of her throat. "We'll get as close to her team
as possible without attracting their attention," he said,
"and find someplace where she can recover."

"Wonder if they went ta that 'ouse we saw," Alfie
said. "That'd be a good place to 'ole up if they decided
to wait."

"If they didn't try to rescue her, they wouldn't have
had any reason to stop at all."

"If they got enough wounded, they might have. Worth
a try, ain't it? The 'ouse ain't too far north o' 'ere."

"All right. I'll move on ahead. See if you can find the
lady's jacket and boots, and catch up with me as soon
as you can."

He started down the hill, the woman limp in his
arms. Alfie caught up with him fifteen minutes later.

"Couldn't find the stuff," the Brit said. "Either the blighters took 'em, or they left 'em far behind."

Kane knelt, brushed the melting snow aside and laid the woman down gently. He removed his boots and slipped them on over her feet. They were two sizes too large, but at least she would be protected until she was with her own people.

He lifted her into his arms again, and he and Alfie continued toward the house. When they descended the final slope, which blended into the valley floor, they headed north, weaving their way among small stands of oak and low-lying brush.

As they neared the house, Alfie, who had taken point, raised his hand. "'Umans," he said. "Some definitely wounded."

"Then we'll stop here," Kane said. There was just enough cover to keep him and Alfie from getting badly burned, and the area was level enough to provide a decent resting place for the woman.

He eased her down to the flattest patch of ground, removed his field pack and fatigue jacket, and balled the jacket under her head. Alfie shrugged out of his own jacket and laid it over her.

"Her wounds are worse than I thought," Kane said, glancing at the fresh bloodstains on his shirt. "She's hemorrhaging."

"Poxy blighters," Alfie said, his bulldog face going red.

Kane could think of a few more vicious insults. "They meant to kill her—slowly," he said through clenched teeth.

"Question is," Alfie said, "'ow soon'll the bleedin' stop?"

Maybe never. There didn't seem much hope of binding the wounds; the cleanest part of Kane's shirt was mud-splashed and filthy, useless as a bandage. Alfie's was no better. The rest of her people might push on, too, if he and Alfie waited too long, but if the woman moved too much, the bleeding would only increase.

"There's one thing we *can* do fer t' lass," Alfie said softly.

Kane didn't answer. He knew exactly what Alfie meant, and the prospect sickened him. The woman would be terrified. She might wish she'd died instead.

He bent over her, bringing his face close to hers. "Can you hear me?" he asked.

Her lips parted. They were full, ripe for kissing. Vassals were generally converted "young" enough that they still remembered what it was like to kiss, to feel passion. To love.

He drove the thought out of his mind. His body was reacting too powerfully to hers, to her blood, desire and hunger intermingled. At the worst possible moment.

"Yer mind seems to be wanderin'," Alfie said, his gruff voice lightly mocking. "Better try again."

Kane clenched his teeth and drew back. "Can you hear me?" he asked her again.

Her eyes opened. Vivid green, like the springtime that seemed a distant memory.

"Listen to me," he said. "I can't restore the blood you've lost, but I can ease the pain and stop the bleeding."

Without warning she bolted up, and he was forced to pin her to the ground. The wounds on her neck began to bleed even more.

"Won't 'elp ya ta struggle, lass," Alfie said, settling

a little distance away. "We jus' wanna get ya back ta yer own folk."

The woman stared directly into Kane's eyes. "You're like *them,*" she said hoarsely.

"We're not rogues, if that's what you mean," he said. "We don't hunt down humans and tear into them like animals."

She tried to rise again, without success. "Where are the other rogues?" she asked.

"Two of them split off a quarter mile back, but they aren't anywhere near here," he said, speaking to her as he'd once spoken to frightened soldiers in the trenches of the First World War.

"I don't...believe you."

"You don't have much choice," he said. "If we let you go, you'll collapse in a matter of minutes." He hesitated, trying to make her understand. "We're deserters, like the rogues. But we aren't interested in joining a mob of killers. We're heading west, toward the coast."

"Those others...were Freebloods," she said. "Are you—"

"Vassals," Kane said, hating the word as much now as he had when Erastos had revived and converted him.

"'At's what we're tryin' ta change," Alfie put in. "Kane 'as an idea that the farther we go from the Blood-master, the less 'e can control us."

"But that isn't important right now," Kane said. "All that matters is saving your life."

Her clouded gaze was bleak. "Why?" she whispered.

He didn't bother with explanations, none of which she would accept in any case. "What's your name?" he asked.

Her voice cracked in a desperate, throaty laugh.

"What difference does it make?" she said, as if to herself. "Fiona. Fiona Donnelly."

"Shoulda known," Alfie muttered, shaking his head. "Irish."

"My name is Jonathan Kane," he said. "But I go by Kane. My companion is Alfie Palmer." He glanced at his friend. "Alfie, hold her down."

The big Brit moved slowly around to the woman's head. He put meaty yet gentle hands on her shoulders. All her muscles tensed, but she had grown too weak to fight.

"Her skin's cold," Alfie said.

"She's going into shock," Kane said. No time left. He bent over, pressing his lips to Fiona's neck. Blood flowed onto his tongue, stretching his control almost to the breaking point.

Closing his eyes, he ignored his cravings and altered a small but very potent chemical in his body. He couldn't convert her; no vassal was capable of that. But the chemicals could seal a wound, and vassals were often set to healing the injuries of serf soldiers. No Bloodlord wanted his slaves to die, at least not until they had given too much blood to be of further use.

Fiona's eyes widened, then closed to slits as the chemicals did their work. They numbed her flesh and began the process of coagulation, stimulating the platelets and proteins that would seal the wounds from within.

Gradually her rapid heartbeat began to slow. The bleeding stopped.

Kane straightened, rocking back onto his knees. "She'll sleep now," he said.

Alfie ran his hand over his face. "What're we gonna do about *us?*" he asked.

The hunger, he meant. The hunger that the sight and smell of blood made a thousand times worse.

"You're usually the one who sees the best side in any situation," Kane said wryly. "Any suggestions?"

Alfie gave a gusty sigh and shook his head. "You want me ta go look fer a deer or somethin'?"

"No," Kane said. "We should both stay here to keep watch."

"Then it's best we take our rest. We got nothin' better ta do."

Ravenous, wet and cold, as they had been so many times in the trenches, Kane and Alfie huddled back to back next to the woman, shielding her from the worst of the icy rain, and waited out the rest of the night. At dawn they moved into the denser cover of a nearby thicket and watched Fiona wake with the feeble sun.

Fiona opened her eyes.

The first thing she saw was the watery sunlight filtering through the waxy leaves of the live oak above her. The first thing she remembered was the bloodsuckers roaring and staggering around, drunk on her blood.

And then the sounds of violence, followed by quiet and the murmuring of voices. A strong but gentle touch. Faces…

Nightsiders.

She tried to sit up, but a heavy, invisible hand shoved her back down again. Daylight had hardly affected the temperature, and the sky was still a dead, featureless gray save for the one place where the sun valiantly struggled to burn its way through the clouds.

A black fatigue jacket lay over her chest and shoulders, and a roll of sturdy fabric supported her neck. Her feet were encased in hugely oversize boots, and she dimly remembered the owners of the voices putting them there. Somehow they'd saved her from the rogues, and she didn't know why.

No more than a few feet away, the intertwined branches of a small thicket rustled with something other than the wind. Two men huddled under it, curled in on themselves with heads and hands tucked against their chests.

Vassals. That was what they had called themselves. But they were still Nightsiders. They wouldn't try to move until sunset. She could escape. All she had to do was find enough strength to get up.

She tried. The jacket fell onto the dirt behind her. Her muscles strained, and repeated waves of dizziness made her stomach heave. Even so, she pushed herself up onto her elbows and made it to her knees before the invisible hand reached out to smash her down again.

"Fiona."

The voice. The calm baritone that had urged her to be still, to let him…

Her hand flew to her neck. It was tender, but she could feel nothing but a slight scar where the ugly wounds had been.

"Fiona," the voice said again. Firm but easy, like that of a man used to command and too certain of his own masculinity to fear showing compassion. She stared into the thicket. The man emerged halfway, his face barely in the shadows.

He was unquestionably handsome, though there were deep shadows under his eyes and cheekbones—gray eyes, she saw, beneath an unruly shock of dark hair. He was barefoot, and wore only uniform pants and a shirt against the cold, a shirt that had obviously seen better days but revealed the breadth of his shoulders and the fitness of his body. A soldier's body.

"It's all right," he said, raising his hand. The sunlight touched his fingers, and he snatched his hand back into the thicket. "The ones who attacked you are dead, but you shouldn't move yet. Your body needs more time."

"Kane," she said. "Your name is Kane."

He nodded. "How much do you remember?"

Too much, now that she was fully conscious. Pain, humiliation, growing weakness as the Opiri drained the blood from her veins.

"Why did you save me?" she asked.

Kane shrugged, but the big man behind him shifted so that his broad face showed over Kane's shoulder.

"'E's a 'ero," the man—Alfie, she remembered— said with a good-humored grin and a thick Cockney accent. "'Eroes can't 'elp 'emselves. They sees a lady in distress, they've got ta save her."

Kane cleared his throat. "Not all of us are like *them*," he said.

With an effort, she rolled onto her side. "You said you were deserters," she said.

"We want freedom," Kane said, his face hardening. "Just as you do."

Freedom from the Bloodlord or Bloodmaster who essentially owned them. When Fiona had first been told about the vassals, men and women who had been converted in the century before the Awakening and through the years that followed, she had felt only pity and anger, as she did for the serfs who provided Nightsiders with blood. It had taken only a year in the field to rid herself of such illusions. No vassal could escape what he had become, and Kane's kind, along with Freebloods, formed the majority of the troops who fought for the Bloodlords and Bloodmasters.

No matter what these men had done for her, they were still her enemies.

She braced her hand on the trunk of the tree and tried to stand once more, swaying as she pushed herself to her feet. The world spun. Arms caught her again, arms hard with muscle and stronger than any human's.

Kane's face was half in sun, half in shadow, and even as she watched the part exposed to the sun began to redden. He showed no sign of pain, but she knew his skin was burning. His hands were growing hot against her skin, almost scalding her.

She pushed him away. "Get back in the shade," she ordered. "I won't be responsible for your death."

But he didn't let her go. His face had begun to blister as he snatched up the fallen jacket, grabbed her wrist and dragged her with him, supporting her when she almost tripped in her oversize boots. Once he was in the shelter of the thicket, he pulled her down again, keeping his hand locked around her wrist.

"You're staying here until nightfall," he said. "Then we'll lead you back to your people."

"You've seen them?" she asked. "Where are they?"

"We found the bodies," he said. "We tracked you and the rogues to where they tied you up. The others from your unit went on ahead." He searched her face. "You're their leader, aren't you?"

"I'm a soldier," she said brusquely.

"I've commanded men to the brink of death and over

it," he said. "I know when I meet someone who's done the same."

She tried to yank free of his hold. "I don't want your help, 'hero' or not."

Her biting words seemed to have no effect. Kane looked into her eyes, and she could see the red reflection shining behind the gray, framed by the ugly blisters on his face, which were just beginning to heal.

Why did those gray eyes have such a powerful effect on her? It was as if she had known him all her life.

She dropped her gaze. "You shouldn't have come out," she said.

"I'll survive," he said. "But *you* won't if more rogues show up."

"Kane 'ealed you," Alfie said, his voice serious. "'E gave ya what ya needed ta make the bleedin' stop."

Fiona remembered the touch of lips on her neck— not biting or rending, but gentle. The pain was gone.

She met Kane's eyes again. "I'm grateful," she said, "but I have a duty to my own people."

He tightened his grip on her wrist. "I assume you're Special Forces?" He went on when she didn't answer. "I don't know what your mission is, but you haven't got a chance if your team keep going in the same direction they're heading. If you make it past the bands of rogue Freebloods, you'll be facing seasoned troops under the direct command of Bloodlords. And if they don't kill you, they won't bother to hold you hostage. They'll make serfs of you."

"We'll get past them," Fiona said. "Just as you did."

"It weren't easy," Alfie said. "We got away 'cause we was scouts, and we could move beyond the lines."

"You said the farther you go from the Bloodmaster,

the less he can control you," Fiona said. "I've never heard that before."

"I believe it takes prolonged separation," Kane said. "If we're caught, we die. But death is better than slavery."

She knew he meant it. He would sooner stand in the sun and be consumed than be taken. She respected him for that far more than she would have thought possible.

But she saw something else in his face, and Alfie's. Hunger. Starvation, more likely. A slower death than any they would get from their master.

And still they hadn't touched her.

"Let me go," she said. "I can take care of myself if you point me in the right direction."

Kane released her. "If you're afraid," he said coldly, "if you won't accept my word, then go."

Abruptly he retreated deeper into the shade, only his eyes visible. Fiona contracted her muscles and tried to stand. She could just make it, but only if she stayed completely still.

Afraid, he'd said. But she wasn't. For reasons incomprehensible to her, these two men had saved her life and demanded nothing in return. They were enemies, but they deserved better than she'd given them.

She knelt, grateful to take the weight off her rubbery legs. "Where will you find blood?" she asked. "Will you attack the next human you meet?"

Once again his eyes met hers. Eyes that had seen years far beyond her mere twenty-eight, and suffering she could hardly imagine.

"We will not kill," he said. "We've been living on

the blood of animals, but that won't sustain us much longer. We'll take only the blood we need, no more."

She lifted her chin. "Then I'll stay. And when I'm recovered enough, you can have mine."

Chapter 3

"No," Kane said.

Fiona's green eyes sparkled—not like sunlight on the green leaves of summer, but with an emerald fire of defiance.

"Why not?" she said. "I offer it freely. If I can save some other human from becoming your prey, I'll consider it no more than my duty."

"Duty above returning to your own people?"

"They can do without me a little while longer."

Kane knew she was bluffing. It wasn't that she was afraid…not in the way most humans would be. But after what had happened with the rogues, he couldn't blame her for hating the idea of any vampire feeding on her, even if she donated her blood willingly.

That was why he admired her. They'd met under the worst of circumstances, as natural enemies, but she was prepared to pay the debt she thought she owed them, even though she would find the method repulsive.

He studied her more carefully: the spatter of freckles across her nose; the lightly tanned skin, not yet aged by constant exposure to the elements; the delicate lines of her face that belied her courage and determination; the long curve of her neck; the full lips that could set so stubbornly when she was intent on holding her ground.

Hunger rose in him again—hunger for Fiona's body, as ferocious as the hunger in his belly and his veins.

Maybe it would be beyond his power to control himself. Maybe he would be no better than the rogues.

"No," he repeated. "If you lose any more blood, you'll be dead in an hour."

"We'll make do," Alfie said. "We been through a lot worse than this, eh, Lieutenant?"

"Lieutenant?" Fiona asked, her brows lifting.

"A long time ago," Kane said. "Long before you were born. Before your parents were born."

"Converted together, we was," Alfie said. "I protect 'im, see. 'E gets 'imself into trouble, 'e does, stickin' 'is nose in other people's business."

Kane bowed his head. He didn't deserve Alfie's dogged devotion. He'd put the man in danger more times than he could count.

From the time he and Alfie had been chosen to act as advance scouts for the Opiri, they had begun to work against the interests of their masters. They had helped dozens of human prisoners—soldiers and civilians— escape their Opiri captors, and all the while Alfie had stood by Kane's side and risked his own life for people who hated what he and Kane had become. Each and every time the Englishman had told Kane he was crazy, then cheerfully thrown himself into the fray.

"'At's what 'eroes do," he'd told Fiona. But in his own mind, Kane was no hero. He just didn't know any other way than to protect people who didn't have the strength to fight from those who wanted to destroy them.

Once the enemy had been the Germans. Now it was his own kind.

He pushed the memories back into the shadows deep in his mind and shook his canteen. Just enough left for Fiona.

She had fallen into a sudden deep sleep, her chin on her knees, her tangled hair veiling her face from his gaze.

"Miss Donnelly," he said.

She jerked awake, instinctively scrambling away from him and reaching for a sidearm that wasn't there. Kane extended the canteen toward her.

She shook her head. "I don't need it," she said. "You're the one who was burned."

"And you lost so much blood that every drop of this will help you," he said. "Take it."

She hesitated, then reached for the canteen. Their fingers brushed in passing, and she jerked her hand back, sloshing the water inside the metal container. After a long moment spent studying Kane through narrowed eyes, she drank.

"Thank you," she said, careful not to touch his fingers as she passed the empty canteen back to him. She looked up at the sky, where the faint glow of the sun was sinking toward the west. "It'll be night soon. Have you changed your mind?"

The blood, she meant. "No," he said. "But we will see you to your people before we go."

She scraped her hair behind her head, tore a strip of fabric from the hem of her shirt and tied it back. "They won't be anywhere near here by now," she said.

"Perhaps," Kane said. "But we may catch up to them during the night."

"For your sake," she said, "I hope we don't. I may not be able to stop them from trying to kill you."

"They won't even see us, if all goes well," Kane said.

"You'd better not let them. Unless you strip naked, they'll recognize your fatigues." She looked down at her feet. "If you hadn't given me your boots and jacket, I'd be practically naked myself," she said with unexpected humor.

The image her words put in Kane's mind didn't help his concentration. "Where are your boots?" he asked.

"The rogues threw them somewhere out in the bush, along with my helmet and jacket. I think they took my weapons."

"Do you want to go back for them?"

"It's not important. They can be replaced."

Kane nodded and watched the sun descend until only a glow of fading light limned the hill. He signaled to Alfie. They emerged from the thicket, leaving their field packs next to their temporary shelter, and moved to either side of Fiona to help her up.

She flinched when they touched her, holding herself stiffly upright. Kane was just as stiff, though in a way Miss Donnelly would not appreciate. Touching her like this was painful in every respect, and there was no easing either source of discomfort.

He and Alfie led her toward the house where the

human troops had bivouacked, keeping alert for any sound or movement. They had reached the last hill above the shallow valley, where the trees were thickest, when Kane heard the footsteps. The approaching soldiers were nearly as quiet as Opiri, but no human could quite match the silence of a vampire who chose not to be heard.

Kane unslung his rifle. Alfie followed suit.

"Your men?" Kane asked Fiona in an undertone.

Fiona glanced at him, frowning, and then noticed the movement among the trees. "They must be," she said. "Put those guns down. Stay still. If they see you, don't try to fight."

Suddenly the soldiers emerged from the deeper shadows under the trees—two men dressed in the same camouflage fatigues Fiona wore and in not much better condition, though they still had their helmets. Two other humans moved up behind Fiona, Kane and Alfie, encircling them.

"Captain," said one of the soldiers facing them. "We thought you were—"

"Why did you stop, Goodman?" Fiona demanded, stepping in front of Kane and Alfie. "I ordered you to keep moving."

"I judged it best to let the injured rest. Who are these men?"

"Friends," Kane said, keeping his voice calm and low.

"Look at their uniforms," said the female soldier behind Kane. "They're bloodsuckers." Kane felt the muzzle of a gun punch into his back.

"Captain Donnelly," Goodman said, "are you hurt?"

"Put your weapons down," Fiona said. "Commander, these men saved my life."

"Men?" Goodman said. He removed his helmet, revealing a stern face and contemptuous brown eyes. "They're rogues, like the others."

"They're vassals," Fiona said. "They're heading south to get away from their Bloodmaster."

Goodman raised his rifle.

"Commander Goodman," Fiona said. "I gave an order."

The man—Fiona's second-in-command, judging by his rank—lowered his gun. The others followed suit.

"You want them taken alive?" Goodman asked.

"I want them free to leave," Fiona said. She swayed a little, but her firm expression and steady voice never wavered. "They insisted on helping me get here, but they have to keep moving if they want to stay free."

Goodman's expression remained tight, revealing what he thought of her explanation. "Captain," he said, "if these bloodsuckers have deserted, they may be able to provide us with vital information. We can't just let them go."

"I won't break my word," she said. "You four go back to camp. I'll catch up."

"You're hardly able to stand," Goodman said.

As if to prove his assessment correct, Fiona began to fall. Kane moved to catch her, but Goodman swung his rifle out of the way and got to her first. The other three soldiers closed in with weapons at the ready.

"If you make one more move," Goodman said, "we'll kill you."

"You won't succeed," Kane said, though he couldn't forget the state of the Freebloods' bodies when he and

Alfie had found them after the rogues' attack on the humans.

"They…*can* kill you," Fiona whispered, trying to pull free of Goodman's hold. "We have a…new weapon. It's—"

Goodman covered her mouth with his hand, and she struggled furiously. Kane lunged at the commander. The woman to his left shot him in the shoulder and the knee. His leg crumpled as Alfie dived for the woman and snatched the rifle out of her hands.

The man who had come from behind Kane shifted and pressed the muzzle of his rifle into Kane's forehead hard enough to leave a mark.

"A bullet to the brain *will* kill you," Goodman said, his hand slipping from Fiona's mouth. "Down."

"No, Joel!" Fiona cried. "You have to…" She slumped, silenced by her own exhaustion.

Alfie glanced at Kane, threw down the rifle and dropped to his knees. Kane stared at Goodman and raised his hands. The man with the rifle stepped back, and the woman retrieved her weapon. Goodman nodded to her and the remaining male soldier.

"Get Captain Donnelly back to camp and bring the shackles," he said. He passed Fiona to the male soldier and kicked Kane in his wounded leg. "The captain said you didn't hurt her," he said, "but she's obviously lost a lot of blood. You could have forced her to lie."

Kane laughed, hissing at the pain. "Vassals don't control minds, Commander. Your intelligence is faulty."

"Maybe you'll help bring us up to date."

Kane watched the two soldiers carefully lift Fiona between them and carry her down the hill. Alfie growled. Goodman slammed his weapon into Alfie's chest, knocking him back. Kane struggled to get up and collapsed onto his injured knee.

"Now, that ain't nice," Alfie chided, rolling onto his side. "Not nice at all. By my reckonin', it's comin' on Christmas Eve. Maybe a bit o' charity is in order."

"Opiri don't celebrate our holidays," Goodman said, his lip curled in scorn.

"We did once," Alfie said. "Remember, Kane? The winter o' '14 it was, when all o' us—"

"Quiet," Goodman said. "No more talking."

Kane gave Alfie a pointed glance, and they held their peace. He didn't trust the man who had silenced Fiona when she'd been warning him about a new weapon. What if Goodman thought Fiona was a traitor for letting Opiri come so close to the human camp and for nearly telling their enemies about something the humans obviously wanted to keep hidden?

Maybe it was his imagination, nothing more. But if Fiona needed him to stay alive, he planned to stay that way. And if she was in any kind of danger, he planned to save her again. Even if he had to pretend he and Alfie were defeated.

A very unpleasant hour later, as Kane's injuries began to close and his flesh knitted itself back together— far more slowly than it would have if he hadn't been starving—the soldiers Goodman had sent back to camp returned with two sets of heavy shackles. While they kept their weapons trained on their prisoners, Goodman pulled him up by the back of his shirt, jerked his arms behind him and shackled his wrists together.

Kane worked his hands. The shackles were clearly designed to hold Opiri. He could get out of them eventually, if only by deliberately breaking every bone in his hands, but Alfie's hands were so big that he couldn't get free even by such drastic and agonizing means. Kane knew that once he was free he could find a way to release the big Brit as well, but first he had to make certain that Fiona was safe. And would stay that way.

Alfie gave him a lopsided grin as Goodman bound his wrists and dragged him to his feet. Then the commander and his subordinate pushed the two of them down the hill, tensely alert for resistance that didn't come.

The house huddled in on itself like a rabbit surrounded by a pack of wolves, collapsing walls dull white like fungus in deep shadow. Once they reached the floor of the valley and entered the house, Kane and Alfie were herded along a hallway off the central area where the remainder of the human troops had gathered in conference. Fiona was not among them. A man with very dark eyes and black hair, his arm in a sling, glanced up, his gaze meeting Kane's for the briefest instant.

The soldiers shoved Kane and Alfie into a room and closed the door. The walls here were stronger, nearly intact, but even so, it would take little effort for him to knock them down.

"Well?" Alfie said. "This is a bit of a fix, innit?"

"A temporary one," Kane said. "Did you see Captain Donnelly?"

Alfie shook his head. "Ya still worried 'bout the lass, guv?"

"I don't like the way they silenced her. And I don't trust Goodman."

"Yer instincts was always good," Alfie said. He looked sideways at Kane. "You likes 'er, don't ya?"

"She's got a great deal of courage," Kane said, looking away.

"And she's more 'n just pretty," Alfie said, trying to ease his shoulders. "'Aven't seen ya look at a woman that way since 'e brought us ta America."

Kane leaned against the wall, trying to ignore the pain in his wrists and his ravening hunger. The smell of the humans, of their blood, was more torment than any wound.

"My feelings are irrelevant," he said. "Once I'm sure she's safe, we'll get out of here."

"Not without somethin' ta keep us alive," Alfie said. "We can't go on like this. It's not like we'd really 'urt anyone."

As much as he hated to admit it, Kane knew they didn't have any more choice in the matter. They would have to take human blood within the next few hours... or die.

He tested the shackles again. "We'll get out of the house while it's still dark," he said. "They'll either send men to hunt for us or keep a scout on watch in case we return. Either way, we'll get what we need."

"Good a plan as any," Alfie said. "Too bad we can't—"

He broke off as three soldiers opened the door and walked into the room. One was Goodman, another a tall, dark-skinned man with a rifle, and the third bald and heavily muscled. The tall man closed and locked the door behind them.

"We better make this fast," he said. "The captain won't go for it, and neither will Sandoval."

"It won't take long," the bald man said, flexing his

fists. "They're half-dead anyway, or they would've gotten away by now."

"We need to keep them alive until they talk," Goodman said. He stared at Kane. "We might even let you go—if you cooperate."

"We always cooperate," Alfie said. "We're right friendly when we 'as reason ta be."

"Then you'll tell us who's waiting for us."

Kane held the officer's gaze. "Since I don't know what your mission is," he said, "or where you're headed, I can tell you only what I told your captain. If you continue on your present course, you're going to meet more rogue Freebloods and eventually advance columns under Opiri command. Isn't that what you expected?"

The man with the rifle advanced on Kane. "We never expected the bloodsuckers to agree to the talks," he said. "We know the opposition sent you ahead to look for us."

"You may have fooled the captain with your sob story about running from your Bloodmaster so you can be free," Goodman said, "but it won't work with me. I know that kind of bond is unbreakable."

"The talks?" Kane said, focusing on the tall man's words. "What talks?"

"Don't pretend you don't know," Goodman said. "You're going to tell us how many are waiting and where they are."

"I have nothing to tell you," Kane said. "We found Captain Donnelly being held prisoner by rogue Freebloods. We freed her and brought her here. We know nothing more than that."

"You're lying," Goodman said, showing his teeth. "Maybe it wasn't rogues who hurt the captain. Maybe you planned to take her hostage."

"You're a fool," Kane said. "If we'd intended to take her, we would have done it and been gone long before you found us."

"Like I said before, maybe you *forced* her to cooperate."

"Captain Donnelly?" Kane said with a laugh. "Do you believe she can be so easily manipulated?"

"That's another thing we intend to find out." Goodman looked him over, his gaze lingering on his healing wounds. "We can make things very unpleasant for you. In your condition you won't heal so fast, and you're going to be a lot more sensitive to pain. You may have tolerated these wounds, but eventually we'll break you."

The bald soldier crouched in front of Kane and withdrew a knife from a sheath at the back of his belt.

"Talk," Goodman said.

"I said I have nothing to tell you," Kane said.

There was a brief moment of stillness, when all Kane heard was his own slow heartbeat. Then the bald man plunged the knife into Kane's knee joint.

Alfie roared and surged forward. "Bloody cowards," he snarled. "If yer too scared of a fair fight—"

The tall man reversed his rifle and knocked Alfie down. Goodman nodded, and he swung the rifle around again, aiming at Alfie's chest.

It was a type of weapon Kane had never seen before, heavier in the barrel and equipped with features he couldn't identify.

The weapon that had slaughtered a half-dozen rogue Freebloods? The one Fiona had tried to warn him about?

"If you don't cooperate," Goodman said, "Johnson will shoot your friend. Rest assured that he'll stay dead this time."

"Stop!"

Fiona's voice was as bright and clear as a bugle call on the battlefield. She strode into the room as if she'd never been ill a day in her life, fixing the bald soldier with a stare that could fell an elephant. Immediately the man dropped his knife, and the other two jumped to attention.

"Did you think I wouldn't find out about this?" she demanded, taut with rage. "Whatever the Nightsiders may do, *we* don't torture. Not for any reason." She strode up to the tall man and snatched the weapon out of his hands. "Now get out of here. All of you. I'll deal with you later."

The three men left the room in haste and closed the door. Fiona propped the weapon against the wall, knelt before Kane and swore softly.

"My God," she said. "If I'd been in my right mind, this never would have happened. Are you badly hurt?"

The mere sight of her made him forget the pain completely. "I'll mend," he said.

Her eyes told him that she didn't quite believe him. "I'll call for the medic."

"The medic isn't necessary," Kane said. "But Alfie and I wouldn't mind getting out of these shackles."

Pale with worry, she returned to the door, issued a few sharp commands and stood aside as a different pair of soldiers set Kane and Alfie free. The soldiers lingered, but she dismissed them with a sharp word.

"I'm sorry," she said, crouching in front of Kane again. She turned to Alfie. "Are you all right?"

"Right as rain," he said, still wearing his irrepressible grin.

Kane gazed at Fiona, amazed at the strength of his

own long-suppressed feelings. He could hardly avoid noticing that she was dressed only in loose-fitting pants and an undershirt that revealed taut nipples through the clinging fabric. With her hair loose around her shoulders and each strong, slender curve of her body revealed, she sent every spare ounce of Kane's blood surging to his cock.

If she sensed his reaction, she refused to show it. She laid her palm on his forehead. "You're freezing," she said.

Her touch made his sluggish heartbeat accelerate to a dangerous speed. "Cap'n Donnelly," Alfie began, "it ain't good—"

But Fiona had already drawn away. "I gave the—" She hesitated. "I told the leader of this expedition the whole story of how you saved me. He trusts my judgment of you, and he's not a man to be easily deceived."

"The leader?" Kane asked, searching her face. "I thought *you* were the captain of this team."

"Of this unit, yes. What did Goodman want from you?"

"He thought we might have controlled your mind or come to stop you from completing your mission."

"Our mission?" She swore. "He told you what it was?"

"Only that there were to be talks between Opiri and humans, and that you expected some Opiri opposition."

"He wasn't authorized to say anything. He'd only have done that if he thought he could get away with killing you or convince me to order it." Her jaw set. "He'll be broken in rank for this."

If Kane's instincts about Goodman were right, the

human deserved much worse. "Do these talks concern a truce?" he asked.

"If he didn't give you the details, I can't." She let out her breath. "I'm sorry, Kane. More than I can say."

"As long as you're safe, it doesn't matter."

She met his gaze with a frown. "Safe? Why shouldn't I be?"

"Goodman didn't want ya to tell us 'bout this 'new weapon' o' yours," Alfie said. "And he weren't too gentle about it, neither."

"In that one thing he was right," Fiona said, flushing a little. "But now you've seen it."

"I'm under the impression that it kills Opiri," Kane said. "Permanently, and without the need to hit the heart or brain. Evidently Goodman felt that particular method would induce us to tell him what we don't know."

Fiona swept her hand over her hair. "I'll take care of him and make sure you get what you need."

"What in God's name is going on here?" an unfamiliar masculine voice said from the doorway.

Chapter 4

"Senator Sandoval!" Fiona said, rising too quickly. She steadied herself, taking great care not to wobble.

The ambassador surveyed the room, his eyes couched in deep hollows of exhaustion. "Why are these men still here? I thought you said they were free to go?"

Fiona considered how much to tell him. She couldn't forgive what her men had done to Kane and Alfie, but she still needed Goodman and the others to get to Sacramento. In spite of her very personal anger, she had great difficulty believing the commander's behavior hadn't been based on concern for her and the mission rather than his hatred for Nightsiders. He and his accomplices would be subject to disciplinary action, likely severe, when they returned to the Enclave, but before then she had to remind them who was in command in no uncertain terms.

And find out what the hell Joel had been thinking, telling the Opiri about the talks and letting them see the new weapon.

"Unlike you," she said to Sandoval, "some of my men didn't believe my story. They took it upon themselves to find out if Kane and his friend were lying about saving me or whether they'd been sent to lead us into a trap."

The senator raised a quizzical brow. "Is there a problem I should know about, Captain?"

"I'll inform you if there is, sir."

Sandoval seemed satisfied. "Are you hurt?" he asked, looking from Kane to Alfie. His gaze lingered on the holes in Kane's uniform. "Do you require a medic?"

"As I told Captain Donnelly," Kane said, probing his knee with a barely perceptible wince, "it will heal soon enough." He smiled crookedly. "I can hardly blame them for suspecting us, if your mission is so important."

"What do you know of our mission?"

"Very little."

The senator glanced at Fiona, then turned back to the Opiri. "Captain Donnelly says you were bringing her here before her troops apprehended you, and that you never attempted to take her blood. If she trusts you, I'm inclined to do so, as well."

"Right generous o' ya, guv," Alfie said.

Fiona's legs chose that moment to go wobbly again, and she staggered. Bracing his arm against the wall behind him, Kane pushed himself to his feet, favoring his injured leg.

"Senator," he said to Sandoval, "I think Captain Donnelly still requires treatment."

"Indeed she does," Sandoval said. "Captain, I believe the medic is waiting for you."

"I'm all right," she insisted.

"Fiona…" Kane said.

"I'm fine," she said. "Senator—"

"Go," Sandoval said. "That's an order. I'll see that these men are given what they need."

Fiona hesitated, retrieved the prototype weapon and then reluctantly walked toward the door. Lefevre and D'Agostino, who had been waiting outside, looked at her inquiringly.

"The senator will be all right," she said, handing the gun to Lefevre. "Put this away and make sure Johnson, Cole and Commander Goodman don't get anywhere near this room."

"Yes, Captain," Lefevre said.

Fiona glanced down the hall. She didn't like the idea of waiting to deal with the insubordinate soldiers until after her treatment, but she wasn't going to be able to stay on her feet much longer.

"Is that all, Captain?" D'Agostino asked, concern in his voice.

"Have one of the others bring blankets, water and Mr. Kane's boots to the Opiri," she said. "Dismissed."

The men glanced at each other and headed for the living room. Fiona hesitated for only for a moment, then pressed her ear to the door and listened.

"Will the lass be awright?" Alfie asked, his deep voice muffled through the wood.

"She's a strong woman," Sandoval said. "She has a very powerful instinct for survival. I'm sure she'll be fine once she's given a transfusion. The unit carries a certain amount of blood for situations like this one." He hesitated. "I apologize for your treatment. I know the captain wouldn't have permitted it if she hadn't been unconscious, but I should have seen the problem earlier."

"Why?" Kane asked. "Who are you?"

"I'm sure you heard Captain Donnelly speak my name, though I doubt she intended to do so in your presence," Sandoval said in a dry voice. "I'm Carlos Sandoval."

"And you're involved in some kind of talks? Negotiations?"

Sandoval sighed. "Under other circumstances I would consider this mission compromised and return to the Enclave. But I have been told I have a certain talent for reading people, and as I said, I'm inclined to trust you. Yes, there are to be negotiations. Between your people and mine."

"The Opiri," Kane said, "are not our people."

"Captain Donnelly mentioned your feelings about that, Mr.—"

"Kane. Jonathan Kane."

"Alfie Palmer," Alfie said.

"Mr. Kane, Mr. Palmer, Fiona tells me you're heading west to escape the influence of your Bloodmaster. I appreciate the difficulties you must be facing. Once you've sufficiently recovered, you're free to go…if that is what you choose."

"Why would you let us go when we know so much?" Kane asked.

"We can't take you with us and watch you every instant, and I won't authorize your—"

"Execution?" Kane interrupted,

"Yes. We cannot expect peace to begin with more violence. That is my sincere belief. That is why I ask if you also believe in peace."

Alfie made a snorting sound. "Peace don't believe in *us*," he said.

"Nevertheless, we could use your help—if you choose to stay."

Fiona closed her eyes, trying to remember to breathe. She wanted Kane to stay, but she couldn't blame him for a second if he chose to leave them. Leave *her*.

"I realize it's a lot to ask," Sandoval said. "But if you'll hear me out—"

"How could we 'elp?" Alfie asked.

"I've been chosen to represent the San Francisco Enclave and the NorCal District in negotiations for a cease-fire. Captain Donnelly's team has been tasked with getting me to Sacramento, where the talks are to take place."

"An armistice," Kane said with a short laugh. "Was it the Opiri commanders who suggested this meeting?"

"It was a mutual decision."

"You can't trust them. The Opiri believe they can win this fight and ultimately subject all humanity to their will. Why should they agree to a truce?"

"Because their losses have been heavy, too," Sandoval said. "As you must know. They've even lost Bloodmasters. They may be able to sacrifice thousands of Freebloods and vassals, but sooner or later they will find themselves without the means to ensure their own survival."

"Then why would you negotiate with them?" Kane asked. "Your people despise the Opiri, because any of you could become like them."

"No," Sandoval said quietly. "*I* don't despise you. I want you to be free as much as you want to be free. I also have faith in the worthiness of our cause. It may be that in this season, at this time when we most think of peace and the brotherhood of all peoples, we will have the best chance of succeeding."

"'At's right," Alfie put in. "Ain't the first time enemies 'ave put down their weapons, 'oping fer the day when war'll be over fer good."

"The war we fought a century ago didn't end because of a temporary truce," Kane said. "Many more good men died before it was over."

"Perhaps," Sandoval said. "I have no doubt that there will be sacrifices. But your friend's optimism may well turn out to be justified. And you can help us make certain that more of you will have a chance at freedom. If nothing else, if our negotiations are successful it may lead to the release of hundreds of human prisoners before they become serfs or vassals like yourselves."

A long silence fell. Fiona tensed, waiting for Kane's reply.

"You face a major obstacle before any of that can happen," Kane said at last. "You know that some important Opiri will be strongly against these talks, and you could be ambushed anywhere along the way to Sacramento." He took a deep breath. "Even if none of the enemy knows where you are now, you have miles of abandoned cities and open ground to cover, all of them swarming with scouts and rogue Freebloods."

"We understand all this, Mr. Kane," Sandoval said. "Captain Donnelly has said that you may have recently traveled the country we will be crossing over the next several days…that you might be willing to be our guides."

"I'll be a bloody monkey's uncle," Alfie said. "Looks like we awready volunteered."

"We backtracked to see that Captain Donnelly was safe with her own people," Kane said. "We have no reason to trust you or your soldiers. Why should we put our lives on the line for any of you?"

Alfie laughed. "'E's just makin' noise," he said. "Like I told the lady, Kane ain't got no sense when it comes to savin' people. Always 'elping 'umans, 'e is. Rescuin' 'em whenever 'e can, even if 'e might die 'imself. Been like that since I can remember."

"Alfie," Kane growled.

"That seems in accord with Captain Donnelly's opinion of you, Mr. Kane," Sandoval said. "I guarantee that you will receive the nourishment you need and the freedom to go your own way, whatever your decision. I will donate my blood. As much as you require, until something more convenient can be arranged."

Fiona released her breath. She should have known that the senator would be willing to do whatever was necessary himself.

But *she* wanted to make the offer, too. She wanted to feel Kane's lips on her neck…not only taking her blood, but exploring her body with his hands and mouth and tongue, caressing her, entering her…

"We'll do as you ask," Kane said. "For the captain's sake."

"You care for her," Sandoval said.

"I thought that humans believed Opiri have no emotions."

"I never believed that, Mr. Kane. You are proof of it."

Another silence fell. Fiona tried not to let her own emotions overwhelm her. Even if Kane agreed, she would never get a chance to know what they would be like together. Once Kane and Alfie had done what they'd agreed to do, they would continue south and she would never see Kane again.

She moved away from the door just before Sandoval emerged.

"Captain!" he said. "Are you finished already?"

"Senator, I wanted to make sure—"

He gave her a knowing look. "You heard?"

"I can't permit you to give your blood, Senator. You—"

"It is my choice. Though I *was* hoping you might find a volunteer or two among your people."

"I'll ask, sir."

"I'll do the asking. If you don't go to the medic now—"

He didn't finish his threat, nor did he need to. Fiona felt herself becoming dizzy again. "Yes, sir," she said.

She staggered to the cot the medic had set up in the master bedroom, passing D'Agostino, who had a canteen slung over his shoulder and Kane's boots lying on a pile of blankets in his arms. With a reproving glance, Bakhtiar inserted an IV into her arm and began the treatment. Well before it was finished, D'Agostino, Chen and Sandoval entered, looking a little pale but otherwise unharmed.

"The bloodsu—the Nightsiders got their blood, ma'am," he said. "Me and Chen volunteered, but the senator insisted on helping, too."

Fiona tried to sit up on the cot. The medic shook her head and gently pushed her back down.

"Easy, Captain," Bakhtiar said. "We're not finished. I suggest you try to sleep."

Fiona nodded, closing her eyes. Her final thought

was of lying in Kane's arms, feeling him move inside her for the first and last time before they marched into battle.

When Sandoval and the soldiers left, Kane was still hungry. He and Alfie had taken as little blood as possible, and it would be enough to keep them going for at least a few more days.

But there were other kinds of hunger still unsatisfied, a desire for something more than mere survival.

There was only one human whose graceful neck he wanted under his mouth, whose body he wanted under his.

"It weren't enough, were it?" Alfie asked quietly from his seat on the rickety chair.

Kane rested his hands on his knees and stared at the cracked ceiling. No. It would never be enough. Not for the rest of his life.

"The way the lass looks at ya," Alfie said, "I think she feels the same way, and not because ya saved 'er life."

"Your imagination was always stronger than your sense," Kane muttered. "If she—"

The door opened. Kane jumped to his feet without considering the lingering pain in his knee, expecting to see Fiona. But it was only D'Agostino, still a little pale but clearly undisturbed by his unusual experience. He had Kane's and Alfie's rifles in his hands.

"The senator wanted to make sure you're all right," the soldier said. "And to return these."

Kane took the rifles and passed one to Alfie. "How is Fi—Captain Donnelly?" he asked.

"Resting." D'Agostino fixed Kane with a probing gaze. "The senator wants you to look over some maps, if you're up to it."

Kane glanced at Alfie. "Of course," he said. He and the Englishman followed D'Agostino out the door. The living room was crowded with soldiers, including Johnson and Cole, who avoided his gaze. Goodman was nowhere in sight.

Fiona, however, was. Kane could see her through a door to an adjoining room, lying on a cot and apparently asleep. He reassured himself that she was resting easily and accompanied Sandoval to the kitchen, where maps were spread across a table.

Kane and Alfie consulted with the senator and his aide, a woman named Radha, going over the safest route to Sacramento. When they were finished, Kane went past the soldiers to the sagging front door. Alfie joined him.

A whole day and half the night had passed, and Kane realized how unaware he had been of the passage of time. He stepped outside, breathing air untainted by the smell of human perspiration and hostility. The sky was clear, but icy snow still lay in patches on the ground, and he could smell another storm on its way.

"Let's go up the hill," he said. "We need to go back for our packs anyway, and I want to have a look around."

"Yer knee okay?"

"Good enough. Let's go."

They climbed the hill behind the house, watching and listening. Once they had retrieved the field packs they had left behind near the tree where they'd moved Fiona, they returned to the hilltop to survey the open land to the east.

"Nothin'," Alfie said.

"So far. But we aren't alone." Kane readied his rifle, listening to the tread of boots climbing to meet them.

"Goodman," he said, rising. "To what do we owe this dubious pleasure?"

Goodman stopped. He was empty-handed, but his mouth was twisted in disgust. "Put that down, bloodsucker," he said, "or you won't like what happens."

"Threats, Commander?" Kane said. "Hardly effective, under the circumstances."

"It's not my life that's in danger," Goodman said. "The senator may trust you, but I know better. I've been with the captain a long time. I don't know what you've done to her, but she's lost her judgment where you're concerned."

"So, apparently, has your ambassador," Kane said coldly, lowering his weapon.

"Sandoval," Goodman said. He spat inches from Kane's feet. "He's too softhearted for this. They could both jeopardize the mission."

"And you would be more suited to lead it."

"I don't have a problem getting rid of anything that stands in our way."

"Or yours," Kane said. "What do you really want?"

"What should have been mine." The commander dragged his hand across his lips, as if even the act of speaking to Opiri left a bad taste in his mouth. "I've come to give you a final warning. Leave now. If you stick around, I'll arrange for the captain to have an accident. I'll take command, and I'll finish the job I started with you two."

A red veil fell over Kane's vision. "You'd kill your former partner?"

"We haven't been partners in a long time," Goodman said. "Whatever happened in the past doesn't matter now."

"Why do you think I'm concerned with the captain's fate?"

"You must think I'm stupid. You saved her life at the risk of your own. You'd do anything to save her again, and that's why you'll do what I say."

"The captain won't believe we've left of our own volition."

"You'd better hope I convince her."

Only Alfie had the strength to hold Kane back. "You oughtn't talk ta the lieutenant that way," the Brit said pleasantly, keeping a powerful grip on Kane's arm. "'E might get mad and tear yer 'ead off."

"He'd better not try if he wants the captain to live," Goodman said. "You understand, bloodsucker?"

"I understand," Kane said through his teeth. "Now I warn *you*—"

"I have men to back me up. One of us'll always be able to take care of the captain if I don't return or you refuse to cooperate. If you behave, she'll be all right."

"Why should I trust your word?"

"You have no choice. You've got your blood. Keep going the way you were before, and be glad I didn't bring the VS120."

"Your new weapon?" Kane asked.

Goodman grinned. "We call it the 'Vampire Slayer.'"

"Very appropriate," Kane said. "But I doubt you'll ever have a chance to use it again."

"Lieutenant," Alfie whispered behind Kane, too quietly for Goodman to hear. "We better do what 'e says— fer now."

For now. Kane stared into Goodman's eyes. Wisest to let the human think he had won.

"We'll go," he said.

"If you try to follow us," Goodman said, "we'll know it. Get moving."

Turning their backs on the commander, Kane and Alfie descended the hill and headed south, away from the house. Once they were out of the range of human hearing, they crouched amid a stand of oaks and waited until they were sure Goodman had gone back inside.

"What now, guv?" Alfie asked.

"We aren't leaving Fiona in that house."

"'Course not."

"Goodman won't let her keep command. He'll find a way to remove her and make the others think it was an accident. I won't let that happen."

Alfie sighed and rested his thick arms over his knees. "She won't thank you fer it."

"I know. I'll be stealing her honor as surely as if I'd made a serf of her."

"'Onor?" Alfie said. "We don't 'ave that luxury no more."

Kane turned to face Alfie. "No," he said. "I'm not honorable. Not where she is concerned." He scraped his hair back from his forehead. "All I can think about is tasting her blood."

"I don't think that's all, guv," Alfie said, laying his hand on Kane's shoulder. "I was wrong about 'onor. You 'ave it, 'n' you'll 'ave it till ya die."

"I hope you're right, my friend." Kane rose. "We'll have to get her outside, where we can take her without alerting the others."

"What's yer plan?"

Kane told him. Odds were the humans wouldn't fall for it, but it was the best he could come up with.

He and Alfie worked their way carefully back toward the house. Alfie climbed the hill behind it, while Kane continued north to hide inside a small wood of frost-damaged eucalyptus trees. He waited for Alfie to get into position and then opened fire on the house.

His shots were deliberately angled to hit the roof and not the walls, but that wouldn't matter as far as the people inside were concerned.

"Humans!" Kane shouted, altering his voice to a higher pitch. "We know who you are, and we outnumber you. Send your commanding officer out unarmed, or we'll cut you to pieces."

Nothing happened for several minutes, and Kane was about to open fire again when Fiona walked out of the house, hands raised. Her hair was in braids tightly pinned around the top of her head, and she was dressed in heavy winter fatigues. She still wore her sidearm.

"Come into the trees alone," Kane called. "If anyone follows, you'll be shot."

Fiona walked toward him, her expression grim. When she reached the trees, Kane set down his rifle, grabbed her and pulled her into the deeper shadows.

"Fiona," he said, dropping his voice back to its normal register. "Listen—"

"You ran!" she yelled, wrenching her arm out of his grasp. "Goodman made a serious mistake in trying to question you, but maybe he was right."

Kane realized then that Goodman had already gotten to her, convinced her that he and Alfie had abandoned her and the senator.

"Have you forgotten we saved your life?" he asked, matching her coldness.

"How do I know you didn't do it just to get a look at our plans?" she asked. "I let myself believe I owed you a debt. I deserve to lose my command for making the mistake of trusting you."

"Has it ever occurred to you that you're playing right into Goodman's hands?"

She laughed. "He's made mistakes, but he's a good soldier. You want to turn me against him for reasons of your own."

It was as if she was parroting someone else's words. Something wasn't right. "Believe what you want," he said. "I can't stop you."

"But *I* can stop *you*." She pulled her gun and pointed it at Kane's chest. "I knew it was you out here all along," she said. "I decided to gamble that you wouldn't shoot me. But *I'm* not so merciful. I can hit your heart before you can move. Give me a reason not to."

She was bluffing. If she really thought he and Alfie had betrayed her, she knew her odds of getting back to the house were slim to none.

And now he would have to make her believe that he and Alfie were exactly what Goodman had told her.

Chapter 5

Kane lunged for Fiona, squeezed her hand until she was forced to drop the gun and then shoved the weapon under his belt.

"You're coming with us, Captain Donnelly," he said.

She rubbed her hand. "I'm no good to you as a hostage," she said, her voice still pitched to a level anyone near the door to the house could hear.

"We don't want a hostage," Kane said, looking away from her accusing eyes.

"I'll kill myself before I let you take my blood," she spat.

Alfie strolled into the grove. "D'ya think we can't stop ya?" he asked.

Kane nodded to Alfie. "Bind her."

The Englishman took a rope from his field pack and tied Fiona's hands. She didn't struggle, but her expression was stark as she tried to resist showing any sign of emotion.

"Let's go," Kane said.

"They'll come looking for me," she said.

"You said yourself that they won't risk the mission, not even for their captain," Kane said, picking up his rifle. "Remember?"

She said nothing more until they were in the hills southwest of the house. Kane took her arm when he thought she might stumble in the dark, feeling the tension in her muscles. Her rejection.

"Where are you taking me?" she asked when they stopped to rest.

"I know you won't believe me, but our only purpose was to get you away from Goodman."

"Because he wants to take command of the mission?" Kane stared at her. "You know?"

Her laughter held an edge. "That's why I came out to you. Why I said the things I did."

"What?" Alfie said, coming to join them.

"Goodman knew that was you out here shooting, too," Fiona said. "He got me alone and said I couldn't be trusted, that I was going to pass command to him. He said he'd kill you if I didn't find a way to get rid of you, even if I had to leave with you."

"Because 'e knew 'ow ya felt about Kane," Alfie said.

"He thought he knew," Fiona said, looking away, "but it wouldn't have mattered if he was right about that or not. He wanted it to seem as if I believed you'd betrayed us, for the sake of the other troops. But sending me out here was only a trap. He was watching all the time, and he planned to kill you the second he got the chance."

"With the 'Vampire Slayer'?" Kane asked.

"Who told you that name?"

"Goodman did, when he politely asked us to leave."

Fiona's jaw hardened. "He met with you again?"

"Didn't bother to 'ide 'is plans, neither," Alfie said.

"He said he'd kill you if we didn't go," Kane said.

"He believed you would protect me from him and his supporters," Fiona said, "but I think if things had gone as he planned, he would have killed *me* out here, too, and blamed it on you. There was just no good way to handle this except hope that, between us, you and I could keep him from shooting. I don't know how he got hold of the weapon again, but keeping it out of his hands was my responsibility."

"Ya did what ya could," Alfie said gently.

She shook her head. "I never knew he hated me so much. He thinks he should have been promoted to captain years ago. He believes I'm too soft, that this mission should have been his."

It wasn't as if Kane hadn't seen men kill each other for lesser reasons. "If you go back," he said, "he'll find another way to get rid of you."

"But I can't leave the mission in his hands. He's too reckless, too angry. He'll fight instead of think. Now that he has the weapon, he'll keep it. Sandoval can't stop him, but he'll have a hard time murdering me in front of the team." She pulled on her bonds. "You can let me go now. I'll take care of Goodman the way I should have before."

"No," Kane said. "You're still coming with us."

She stared at him. "I'll be all right. Go. Take your freedom."

"I'm sorry, but I can't let you leave," he said quietly.

He got up and turned his back to her, listening as Alfie moved closer and began to speak.

"'E won't do it," Alfie said, well knowing Kane could hear every word. "Ya see, 'e cares too much about ya. 'E just won't admit it out loud." He chuckled. "Same thing with ya, ain't it? Too proud. But ya tried ta save each other anyway."

"I owed him," Fiona said stiffly. "I owed both of you. That has nothing to do with—"

"Ya can't fool ol' Alfie. I been watchin' both of ya. Ya think 'e let your soldiers take us because 'e's weak? He coulda killed all of 'em before they could move. But 'e wanted ta make sure *you* was safe. 'N' you did the same for 'im when Goodman said 'e'd kill 'im."

"No," Fiona said. She moved to stand behind Kane. "Don't do this, Kane. If I ever…cared about you, I'll despise you if you don't let me go back."

"There are only a few hours' travel time left before dawn," he said, ignoring her.

"And where will you take me?" she demanded. "Have I become your serf now, Kane?"

"No. Never."

"But you'll take me against my will anyway. If you're headed southwest, you'll be very close to the Enclave borders. The first chance I get, I'll run to the nearest outpost and send them after you. They won't take any chances with you. They'll kill you."

It wasn't her threat that cut into his heart but her desperation, her determination to get away from him.

"I'll let you go as soon as we're far enough away that you can't rejoin your team," he said, turning to face her. "Or if you're prepared to accept our help… The Opiri who are against any move toward peace will have sent scouts to pinpoint your position and assess your strength before a direct attack. They'll likely be coming from the northeast. If we find them first, we can warn your people."

Her breath quickened, loud in the silence. "You're still willing to scout for us?"

"If *you* stay with us," he said. "If you give your word you won't try to go back until I let you leave."

"Are you sure my word is sufficient?" she asked bitterly.

"Yes," he said. "And I promise your people will receive any intelligence we obtain."

"But not through me."

"Alfie and I will make sure word gets to them." He looked past her in the direction of the house. "You don't have your pack with you, but we have enough rations for you."

"Not hungry?" she asked, her voice sharp with mockery.

"Our field rations are supplementary. Without blood, we can't digest them. But you must know that." He met her gaze again. "We need to get going. I expect another storm to arrive sometime in the next twenty-four hours."

Fiona folded her arms across her chest. "If we're heading back toward the lines, how likely is it that you'll fall back under your Bloodmaster's influence? What will you do then? Will you forget you ever 'cared' about me?"

She was right. That was a danger, and he had known the risk from the moment he offered his compromise. He and Alfie could both be caught again. That would be enough to put Fiona in grave peril.

"If that happens," he said, "we'll know it. If I so

much as begin to feel his influence, I'll tell you. You know how to kill an Opir, especially if he isn't fighting back." He untied her hands and then pulled her handgun from his belt. "Keep this with you."

She took the gun from his hands and stared down at it as if she'd never seen it before. "You'd let me kill you?"

"Not only for your sake." He glanced at Alfie, who was pretending to be absorbed in rearranging the supplies in his pack. "For ours, as well. Neither one of us is willing to be taken again."

"You think I could do it?" she said, slowly looking up at him again. "You think I could kill you in cold blood?"

"If it becomes necessary, yes. I would demand it."

Her eyes were suspiciously moist, but she holstered the gun and said nothing more.

Shrugging into his pack, Kane started down the hill again, listening for her footsteps behind him. Every part of him ached with need. He kept on walking so he wouldn't turn around and pull her into his arms.

Kane moved quickly away from her without looking back, and she knew he trusted her to follow.

She had given her word. Admittedly, she had pretty much been coerced into giving it, but even so, she knew she couldn't break her promise. Just as she knew Kane wouldn't break *his* promise to get word of any Opiri presence back to her people.

But he was putting her entire mission in danger because of his desire to protect her. Alfie had told her why. *"'E cares too much about ya. 'E just won't admit it out loud."*

Of course he wouldn't. She wasn't deceived into

thinking he wasn't every bit as much the soldier as she was—nor any more inclined to express his feelings openly, whatever they might be. Alfie had said that Kane had let himself be taken by her men because he had wanted to make sure she was safe, and she didn't doubt him for a minute.

But had Kane somehow sensed that Goodman was a threat even before the commander had tried to interrogate him? If Goodman hadn't compelled Kane's cooperation by threatening to kill her, would Kane have killed *him?*

It was very possible. Even likely. Because Kane *cared* about her.

And Alfie, at least, knew the feeling was mutual. *"Too proud,"* he'd said of her. Too proud to admit she wanted Kane the way she'd never wanted another man. With her entire body. And her soul.

A soul that would begin to wither and die if she had to do what Kane had demanded of her. If she had to kill both him and Alfie to save them. And herself.

Fiona realized she'd been lagging behind and caught up with Kane, taking care not to stumble lest he feel compelled to reach out and steady her. Alfie brought up the rear. They moved carefully north and east across the wetlands, intending to avoid the suburban communities at the junction of the old Highway 680, which passed by the house, and the major artery connecting the San Francisco Bay Area to Sacramento.

The new storm Kane had expected hadn't yet arrived, so they only had to contend with the marsh itself. Fiona's boots soon became waterlogged from wading through the sloughs. Kane called a halt to give her his jacket, and she didn't object. She had work to do, and she couldn't get it done if she died of exposure.

They'd nearly reached dry ground when the sun began to rise. There was little enough shelter in the area, but Kane and Alfie had deliberately aimed for a small, isolated stand of trees anchored on a low hill. They removed and unrolled tarps they'd fastened to their packs and stretched them between the lowest branches.

Almost immediately Alfie fell onto his back, covered his eyes with his arm and sank into a heavy sleep, snoring like an old-time steam engine. Kane crouched beside him, staring toward the northeast.

Fiona followed his gaze across the open ground toward the old community of Fairfield and the abandoned Travis Air Force Base east of the city. A perfect place for light-averse Nightsiders to hide.

She knelt to face him, staying outside the small rectangle of shadow cast by the tarps. "I'm going to scout ahead," she said.

"No," he said, hardly glancing at her. "It's too dangerous."

"You trust me to keep a gun but not to do what we came out here to do?"

He looked into her face; his gray eyes were like finely polished daggers. "Will you come back?"

She jumped to her feet. "If I wanted to, I could walk away right now, and you couldn't follow me."

"You're right." He rose and glanced at Alfie, who was still blissfully asleep. "But if there are any Opiri scouts out there…"

"They'll be under cover, too."

"There's one thing I failed to mention when I told you we have to stay together," he said. "Some of the scouts have been outfitted with new protective suits, impervious to sunlight for a certain length of time. If you run into any of *them*..."

"You think we didn't know? I was given that intelligence, and so was Sandoval. We also know they haven't been widely distributed among the Opiri ranks."

"Any scouts looking for the ambassador would be given such equipment."

"I can handle them. It's what I'm trained to do."

"The way you were trained to deal with those rogues?"

She couldn't help flushing at the reminder. "I know it's a risk. But it's part of my job. I've always accepted that."

"I didn't take you out of Goodman's reach to let you throw your life away now."

"You said I wasn't your serf. Have you changed your mind?"

Kane's jaw clenched. "Where are you going?" he asked.

"Toward the old air-force base. That's a likely shelter for any Nightsider scouts in the area."

"If you see anything," Kane said roughly, "if you *feel* anything, come back immediately."

"Is that an order, *sir?*"

He gave her a dry half smile. "I believe you outrank me, Captain."

She snorted. "Then this is an order. Get some shut-eye. I have a feeling you haven't had much in the past couple of days."

"Opiri don't need—"

"Then why is Alfie fast asleep? You did get *some* blood, but I doubt it was enough to sustain you for long if you wear yourself out. I'll be sure to wake you when I get back."

"Take the rifle," he said, his face rigid. "And be careful."

She took the weapon and turned to leave. But before she'd gone a single step, he had her by the wrist and jerked her back under the tarp. He pulled her against his chest, lowered his face to hers and kissed her.

The part of Fiona that had longed for this since he had healed her—the part she had tried so hard to fight—melted against him and leaned into the kiss, opening her mouth to feel the push of his tongue, the graze of his teeth on her lower lip. His tautly muscled arms held her still as his mouth pressed against the corner of her lips, her chin, her neck. She felt him growing hard against her thigh, and she thought again of lying naked in his arms, feeling that hardness thrusting deep inside her.

It was too much. For both of them. Kane released a shuddering breath and let her go just as she pushed him away. She scrambled into the sunlight where he couldn't follow, panting and furious with shame.

"Don't ever do that again," she snapped.

"Not even if you ask me?"

"Don't count on it." Without another word, she turned on her heel and left the Nightsiders to wait out the day, thinking to herself that she would be glad to shoot Kane if he forgot her warning.

Who are you kidding? she thought as the sky began to cloud over again. She would far rather shoot herself. Even if he kissed her a thousand times. Even if they lay together and shared everything their bodies had to give.

But that would be all they would share. Even assuming they both survived, there could never be anything else.

Kane woke to the moan of the wind.

The tarp flapped above him, one corner beginning to work loose from its anchor on a low tree branch. Sleet gathered in the tarp's folds and melted almost immediately. In a few hours, when the sun went down, the slow drip of water would turn to ice.

"Alfie," Kane said, pushing at the broad back turned away from him. "Have you seen Fiona?"

Alfie rolled over, blinking heavy-lidded eyes.

"She's gone?" he asked, sitting up and running blunt fingers through his sparse blond hair.

"I think you heard our discussion," Kane said.

With a false expression of chagrin, Alfie peered at the sky. "Been about six 'ours, ain't it?"

Six hours, Kane thought. She should have been back long since. "I should never have let her go," he said grimly.

"That lass 'as a mind 'o 'er own," Alfie said. "You woulda 'ad ta tie 'er up ta get 'er ta stay once she got the notion ta go."

But that didn't give Kane any comfort. Either she was in some kind of trouble, or...

Or he had driven her to stay away as long as possible. He hadn't intended to kiss her, and he had known as soon as he'd started that he had to put an end to it or he wouldn't be able to stop.

Neither would she. She might fight it with every fiber of her being, but he knew now that she wanted him as much as he wanted her. In every way.

"Don't worry just yet, guv," Alfie said, heaving himself to his feet. "Still got about three hours o' daylight left. She'll turn up."

"I'm going after her."

Alfie grunted. "Sure ya is," he said. "Go on 'n' get yerself a nice suntan while yer at it."

Kane held out his hand. "Give me your jacket."

"Yer mad," Alfie said, his face darkening with real anger. "Ya know our fatigues ain't much use against sunlight."

"Your jacket, Alfie. And your shirt."

"Can't let ya," Alfie said. "It'll be sure death." But even as he spoke, the Englishman was pulling off his jacket and passing it to Kane. "The lass is prob'ly fine," he said. "Ye think she'll thank ya fer gettin' yerself kilt?"

"If rogues have her—"

"Ya think she'd be fool enough ta let 'em catch 'er in the shadows?"

"And if she's run into Opiri scouts?" Kane said, arranging Alfie's jacket over his head and tying the wide sleeves around his shoulders. "The new daysuits remove any advantage she has."

"If they have 'em," Alfie said, his long face giving the lie to his hopeful words. "I care about the lass, too. Let *me* go."

Kane draped the tail of Alfie's shirt over his forehead for extra protection. "You know *I* have to do it, my friend. I need you to stay here, in case she returns."

"'Eroes," Alfie grumbled. "They gets tiresome sometimes."

"I'm no hero."

"But ya care for 'er."

"Now you're the mad one."

"I tol' the lass no one fools ol' Alfie," the Brit said, wrapping his huge arms around Kane. "Ya bloody well better not get yerself kilt, 'ear me?"

Kane stepped back and grinned. "Trust me, Alfie. I've found I have something to live for."

Alfie turned his face away. "Yer not back 'ere by sunset with that woman o' yers, ye'll 'ave me ta answer to."

Knowing there was nothing left to say, Kane plunged into the sunlight. Not that there was much light; the thinner patches of cloud cover were beginning to fill in with a heavier gray. That gave him a small advantage as he picked up Fiona's faint tracks and headed across the empty brown fields toward the base.

Dim as they had seemed at first, the sun's diffuse rays began to penetrate Alfie's jacket before Kane had gone more than a hundred yards. By the time he had come to the end of his second mile, his fatigues and Alfie's jacket were no longer providing much protection. His skin had begun to burn, though at first it felt no worse than the kind of sunburn he had occasionally suffered in the trenches.

Ignoring the pain, he focused on the long runways and low buildings that rose up from the fields approximately three miles to the north. He was staggering when he reached the perimeter of the base and pushed through the fallen fence, his boots tracing a crooked path across the broken surface of the runway with its handful of abandoned aircraft. He had found no trace of Fiona, nor any sign of Opiri troops. He didn't dare call out for her, though every instinct told him that she was in trouble.

So was he. His heart had begun to race so fast that he

couldn't catch his breath, and his muscles were cramping with such force that he could no longer stand, let alone walk. He fell to his knees on the concrete, aware that his skin was beginning to blister and crack beneath his clothing.

And his mind…his mind began playing tricks on him, replacing the modern jets with the primitive biplanes that had performed their deadly aerial dances above the battlefields of France over a hundred years ago.

Somehow he dragged himself across the runway and into the high grass on the other side, losing Alfie's jacket in the process. If he could reach the nearest building, he might recover enough to look for Fiona again after nightfall.

He didn't make it. The last of his strength gave out, and he lay facedown in the grass, his darkening mind oddly fixed on one irrelevant thought.

Tonight would be Christmas Eve. And he would never see Fiona again.

Chapter 6

The sun had nearly set when Fiona found Kane. She didn't have to look closely to know how badly he had been burned. The only question in her mind was whether or not he was still alive. And how much she would be forced to hurt him if he was.

Let him be alive, she prayed silently.

"Kane," she said, lying flat on her stomach beside him. "Kane!"

His burned eyelids twitched. Offering up another prayer, this one of thanks, she rolled him onto his side, crouched and maneuvered him across her shoulders in a fireman's carry, pushing herself to her knees and then to her feet. He was heavy, his body dense with muscle, and she knew that if she let herself think about just how heavy he was, she would collapse under his weight.

But it never occurred to her to give up. Saving him

was all that mattered—more than the presence of Nightsider scouts waiting to make their move, more than the knowledge that her team's entire mission was in danger of failing.

Far more than her own life.

The sun was sinking below the horizon by the time she got Kane into the nearest building, the hangar in which she'd set up a barricade against the bloodsuckers. She dropped to her knees behind the wall of crates near the back corner of the vast, nearly empty interior, letting him slide to the floor.

He rolled onto his back, and she examined his face. Her heart rose into her throat.

God help her.

"Fiona?"

His voice was a raw croak, as if even his vocal chords had been seared.

"I'm here," she said. She bent over him, gently arranging his arms at his sides. He flinched but made no sound to indicate the extremity of his pain.

"They're out there, aren't they?" he whispered.

"I don't know. I think there were about a dozen of them when they pinned me down. They were wearing those special suits you mentioned, and they only stopped shooting when there wasn't enough daylight for me to get back to you."

Speaking softly, she told him how she had run across a troop of Opiri scouts, obviously on their way to head her people off. Believing she had the advantage of daylight, she had tried to get past them and return to Kane and Alfie's shelter before dark.

"You're faster than me," she said. "I knew once night

fell I could send you back to warn Sandoval that they would be walking into an ambush."

But the Nightsiders hadn't let her get more than a few hundred feet outside the hangar where she'd taken shelter. "I don't know why they didn't stop me from getting you now," she said. "Maybe because the daysuits only prolong the time Opiri can stay in the sun, not allow indefinite exposure."

"Very likely," he said, closing his eyes.

"Where's Alfie?" she asked.

Kane must have heard the worry in her voice. "Safe," he said. "But he won't…stay where I left him. He'll come after us."

Of course he would, she thought. Even though he had little chance of getting past the scouts outside.

"You should go," Kane said. "Try to…get back to your people. Maybe…I can keep them occupied."

"How? You can't hold a rifle, and I won't let you die here alone."

He reached up to touch her face, though the effort must have been agony. "Fiona…if we'd had more time…"

"I know."

"I've…wanted you since the moment I saw you."

Bending over him again, she touched her mouth to his cracked lips with infinite tenderness. "I know. Yesterday I would have said it was only the blood, the hunger. But when you kissed me, I knew it wasn't just instinct. And I *wanted* you to bite me. I wanted you inside me, taking my blood right there under that tree."

He shivered, and his body stirred, his erection straining under his pants in defiance of his terrible injuries.

With utmost care she laid her hand over the hard ridge beneath the heavy fabric.

"Fight," she whispered. "Fight, damn you. I won't let you die. I want you. If you live, you can have me in every way a man can have a woman. Even if that man is a vampire."

He tried to smile. "Is that a…promise, Fiona?"

"Yes. And I don't break my promises."

At that moment she almost said words that shouldn't be possible between a human and a Nightsider. But she swallowed them down, more afraid of those three syllables than of a whole army of bloodsuckers.

"Sleep now," she said, bringing her face as close to Kane's as she dared. "Sleep will help you get better. If you heal enough to walk, maybe we can make it out. Together."

Kane closed his eyes, too exhausted to argue. The last feeble rays of the sun striped the floor of the hangar, then vanished. Fiona could almost feel the Nightsider forces preparing to come in after her.

"Human!"

The slightly accented voice was amplified, carrying easily across the distance to the hangar from the building where the Opiri had waited out the day.

Fiona shifted position to rest her rifle on top of the highest crate, aiming between the abandoned refuelers and tractors that no longer served any purpose save to give her a slightly better chance of holding the bloodsuckers at bay. Thick snowflakes began to fall like a curtain across the open door.

Strange, Fiona thought, that such a feeling of peace could come over her now.

"I'm here!" she called back.

"Give yourself up," the voice said. "We won't harm you."

"You won't harm me?" she said. "Isn't that what your kind do to us when you take our blood?"

"You know that is not why we are here. If you cooperate, at least your ambassador and his escort can live."

His response told her all she needed to know. They were here to stop the mission.

"You'll let us live?" she asked. "As serfs? Vassals?"

"You cannot stop us. We will take you *and* them," the voice said. "But we will permit you to offer your people the chance to surrender without bloodshed."

Surrender? That was something her team would *never* do. Giving herself up wouldn't change a thing.

"Forget it," she said.

"We know you have a vassal in there with you. Send him out."

Fiona tightened her grip on the rifle. They *had* seen her rescue Kane. Did they think she was holding him hostage, or did something more sinister lie behind the demand? Was it possible that Kane's Bloodmaster was actively hunting him and these scouts had been able to identify him before she'd dragged him into the hangar?

"There is no vassal here," she called. "Only a free man. And he's ready to fight to stay free."

The only response was a brief laugh. "Why are you protecting him, human? Why did you save the life of an Opir when we are your enemies?"

"We all act according to our natures," she said. "Human or otherwise. Your nature is to seek blood by any means possible, and ours is to trust those who have proven themselves our friends."

"You place your trust foolishly, human. Do you think he won't turn on you if *he* has need of blood?"

"He's already taken what he needs."

"But he has been badly burned. He will require more blood to heal, and you are the only human there."

Fiona cursed. They knew how badly Kane was injured, how little help he could be to her in a fight. It was only a matter of time now until the first Nightsider soldiers came charging into the hangar.

If they wanted Kane, they would have to get past her first.

"Listen to me, human," the Nightsider said. "We will give you two hours to surrender before we come after you."

Two hours. Two *centuries* wouldn't make her change her mind, but at least she could be with Kane a little longer. Even if he didn't know it.

Every sense alert for the first sign of attack, she settled in to wait. When she heard the sound of scratching and the creaking of bending metal behind her, she spun around, ready to fire.

Alfie pushed his head through the opening he had punched through the hangar wall, his fingertips bloody and his face split in a wide grin. "Would've been easier with a can opener," he said.

Fiona lowered the rifle and spoke softly. "Alfie, how did you make it through?"

"Kane 'n' me, we learned in the Great War 'ow ta move across battle lines without bein' seen. We di'n't lose them skills when we was converted." He glanced down at Kane, and his grin vanished. "Bloody idjit. 'E 'ad to get ta ya, knowin' 'e'd kill 'imself doin' it."

"He'll get better," Fiona said fiercely. "Right now

you have to get back to the house and warn the others. Just remember that Goodman will try to kill you, and be careful. If they've already moved on, I know you can find them."

Releasing an explosive sigh, Alfie pushed the metal flap back into place and sat against it. "Can't go now. Them scouts're patrollin' the area, 'n' I'm gonna have ta wait a bit."

"How many are there?" she asked.

"'Round ten, I think. Usual scout patrol." He looked toward the hangar door. "Prettiest snowfall I ever seen. Snowed sometimes in Lunnon, but never so nice. Peaceful. Like Christmas should be."

Fiona resumed her position at the barrier. "How did you and Kane meet?"

"Kane joined up early. Not too many Yanks enlisted back when it started in the summer of '14. Adventurous, 'e was, and one o' the most 'onorable men I ever known. He joined me Division, 'n' we went over ta France ta fight the Hun. The Germans."

"So, the two of you were together in the war until…?"

"Until we was taken by the Bloodmaster," Alfie said. "More 'n' a few o' us, though most o' the others we never saw again." He blinked, and Fiona saw tears in his eyes. "I don't like ta talk 'bout them days, what the bloodsucker made us do, no matter 'ow much we tried ta fight 'im. But we'd seen most everythin' that could 'appen on a battlefield even before then. Bad things."

Bad things always went with war, she thought. "I'm sure you would have stopped it if you could," she said.

He wiped at his face with the back of his hand. "Funny," he said. "There *was* one good thing that 'appened, one day we never forgot. The day of the

Christmas Truce." He smiled, his eyes focused on something Fiona couldn't see. "It were cold that day, too. No snow. Just ice 'n' fog. But it weren't like no day I ever seen, before or since."

She looked down at Kane's face. "Tell me," she said.

"Christmas Eve," Alfie said, "the Germans started out by puttin' decorations with lights at the tops o' their trenches, and then in the trees around 'em—them trees that still 'ad branches. They sang 'Stille Nacht'...'Silent Night.'

"Well, we didn't know what ta make o' it at first. Then someone on our side started singin', too. Before ya knows it, we was all yellin' 'Happy Christmas' ta each other, 'n' pretty soon some o' us was out in No Man's Land, givin' each other snouts—cigarettes to you Yanks—and chocolate. We gathered our dead 'n' read verses over 'em. Not one bullet, not one cannon, was fired all that night, nor Christmas Day, neither."

"A miracle," Fiona whispered.

"That night, we knew all men was brothers, no matter what 'appened after."

Men. Not men and Nightsiders. But as she gazed over the crates at the softly falling snow, she wondered. Most of the Opiri out there had probably been human—if not recently, then sometime during the centuries when the Bloodmasters had walked the earth, preparing for the Awakening.

Would these Nightsiders recall a time like Christmas 1914, when men had remembered they were brothers?

She didn't speak the thought aloud, and she and Alfie lapsed into a waiting silence. He cocked his head, listening to sounds she couldn't hear. Kane lay still.

"What can I do for him, Alfie?" she asked when the stillness had grown too deep.

The Englishman met her gaze. "I think ya knows, Cap'n. But 'e's very sick. Ya don't know what 'e'll do or what'll 'appen to ya when the thing's finished."

"I'm not afraid. If he dies, I won't much care what happens to me."

"Awright." Alfie hesitated. "'E ain't up to doin' it 'isself. Ya got a knife?"

Slowly Fiona pulled her knife from the sheath at her belt. Alfie touched the side of his neck, above the external jugular vein. "Right 'ere," he said. "But ya gots ta be careful. Best let me do it."

She held very still while he crouched beside her. "Don't move," he said and pressed the sharp point into her neck.

He was so gentle that she hardly felt the prick, but the blood begin to flow almost immediately.

"Now," he said, "lean down. Yeah, like that."

Closing her eyes, she bent over and rested the small wound against Kane's lips. He reacted almost at once, his body jerking to life, trembling violently.

"Just stay there," Alfie said. "Let 'im take what 'e needs."

While she knelt over Kane, Alfie took her place at the barricade. She felt Kane's mouth open, his lips close over the cut, his tongue slide over her skin. There was no pain, no discomfort. She lay down beside him, careful not to press him too hard.

She could not have said when she began to feel his strength returning. Perhaps it was the growing tension in his body, his muscles hardening, his mouth demanding more. His arms closed around her, holding her immobile, his fingers lacing through her hair and loosening it to fall around her shoulders.

All at once she was back under the tree where the rogues had bound her, slowly coming alive again under the caress of Kane's lips on her throat. This was a hundred times more potent. He wasn't saving her life. He was exchanging something incredibly precious for her blood, mingling the very essence of his being with hers.

When she lifted her head to look at his face, the burns were nearly gone. His breath was coming fast, but not because he was ill. He rolled onto his side, and she could feel the hard length of his erection against her thigh.

Her own breath quickened. They didn't dare risk it. He wasn't strong enough. Over an hour had passed since the Nightsider scout leader had set the deadline for her surrender. And Alfie...

Alfie was gone. He had slipped out while Kane was feeding, closing the hole in the wall behind him.

He had left her alone with Kane. He had known it would be all right.

More than all right.

Kane took her by the arms and shifted her gingerly, pulling her face to his. He kissed her lips as he ran his hand over her stomach to her breasts, working at the buttons of her shirt. His fingers found her nipple, erect beneath her undershirt.

Fiona didn't know if he was fully aware of what he was doing. She only knew he was still in need—in need of *her*—and she wouldn't deny him. If he could find strength in joining their bodies, there was nothing she wanted more.

If they were to die in this place, first they would share everything life had to give.

Without waiting to remove her undershirt, Kane lowered his mouth to her breast and sucked at her nipple until the material over it turned transparent. She gasped and arched into him, tangling her fingers through his hair.

But soon it wasn't enough. She wanted to feel his mouth and tongue on her naked skin. She urged him to pull her undershirt above her breasts and whimpered as he teased her nipple with the tip of his tongue. She began to ache almost unbearably, growing wet with the need to have him inside her. She gasped as he loosened her pants and slipped his hand past her belly into the nest of curls below. When his fingers found her most sensitive area and began to circle around it, she was sure she wouldn't be able to control her response.

Somehow, though, she did. She undid the buttons of his shirt and pushed it away from his chest. His skin was warm and firm underneath. Somehow between them they managed to remove her shirt. He slid his hand back up over her belly and ribs, and pressed her breasts together, burying his face between them, then began suckling. She dug her fingernails into his shoulders and bent her head back, urging him to take her blood again.

His mouth moved to her neck, but he didn't bite or attempt to open the wound that had already closed. He braced himself on his arms and looked down into her eyes.

"Be sure, Fiona," he said hoarsely. "Once I begin…"

"I don't want to stop," she whispered. "I want *you*."

He hissed through his teeth and closed his eyes as she reached between them and cupped his erection.

"I can make you pregnant," he said abruptly.

She laughed without meaning to. No one had ever seen a child of a Nightsider and a human. No matter what he thought, it couldn't be possible.

But even if it *had* been, it didn't matter. This was their one and only chance to be together. With growing urgency, she shimmied out of her pants. Kane shed his. The length of his body covered her, his cock nestled between them. She opened her thighs and wrapped her legs around his waist, too hungry to wait a moment longer.

She didn't have to. He eased into her, almost as if he were afraid she had never been touched before. She moaned, feeling him hard and full inside her as he began to move. At the same time his mouth came down hard on her neck, and she felt the slight prick of his teeth as they punctured her skin. She clawed at his back, feeling the flex of his muscles as he pushed deep inside her and began to drink her blood in an ecstatic rhythm of erotic bliss. His own hunger seemed to consume her, burning outward from the very core of her body along her sensitized nerves to her neck and back again.

She knew he could have killed her then if he'd chosen to, and she would not have fought it. This was the peak of her existence, a pinnacle of joy that could never be reached again.

But she was wrong. A great wash of overwhelming sensation began where their bodies joined, shuddering, quivering, forcing her to cry out as the wave engulfed her. Kane groaned as she pulsed around him, and a moment later he stiffened and reached his own completion. His teeth closed on her skin once again, a slight pinch she hardly felt in the midst of her euphoria. A healing warmth flowed into her as he withdrew, easing her down from the heights.

He kissed her lips, her forehead, her chin, her cheeks, her eyelids, murmuring her name. Contentment she had never known erased every fear, every doubt she had borne since she had met him. He rolled onto his side, carrying her with him. She tucked her head into the crook of his arm, and he held her close.

It was part of the miracle of that special night that nothing interrupted them until, by unspoken agreement, they gathered their clothes and dressed again. They both knew that nothing had changed outside the hangar walls; the only difference lay within themselves.

Kane, his skin unblemished and his body strong again, crouched behind the crates and stared toward the door. The snow continued to fall peacefully.

"They'll be coming soon," he said.

"I know." She knelt behind him, resting her cheek against his back. "Let's make the most of the time we have left."

He turned to meet her gaze and smiled. They knelt facing each other, and he took her face between his hands. He didn't speak, but his eyes told her everything he couldn't say aloud.

Fiona kissed him. "I love you," she said.

Chapter 7

Kane and Fiona lay together, their bodies entwined as the snow drifted down, piling up around the hangar entrance like a mother wrapping her child in a blanket of white.

He took a deep breath, holding her scent in his lungs as if he would never need to breathe again. It was no more than an hour, maybe two, until dawn, and he knew the Opiri forces would have to attack soon.

Why they hadn't done so remained a puzzle to him. Fiona had told him of the scout leader's offer after they had made love, but the two hours had already passed.

If Alfie had escaped, he might still reach Fiona's team. But there would be no rescue. Two lives meant nothing against the hope of an enduring peace.

But if those two lives could be put to good use by continuing to distract the enemy…

Maybe one life would be sufficient.

He bent over Fiona, who was just beginning to stir. She reached for him with a sleepy murmur. He pulled away carefully.

"Kane?" she said, opening her eyes.

"Forgive me," he whispered. He bent over her, sank his teeth into her neck and altered the chemicals in his body just enough to achieve the necessary effect. Her head rolled to the side. He covered her with his jacket and kissed her forehead, begging her silently to understand.

"Human!" a voice shouted. "Your time is up!"

Kane walked out the doorway and stopped. He could see several Opiri waiting a few yards away, their pale daysuits almost blending with the carpet of snow. One of them had marks of rank on his helmet, the insignia of a Freeblood scout *dekarchos,* a leader of ten.

Kane held up his hands to show them empty of weapons.

"Where is the human?" the officer demanded.

"Dead," Kane said. "I killed her."

The *dekarchos* looked past Kane to the hangar. "Why, when she seemed so eager to protect you?" he asked.

"For mercy," Kane said. "To spare her a life of servitude."

"The life you have tried to escape." The leader shook his head. "You should have killed *yourself,* deserter."

So the Opir knew who he was. Perhaps he'd been told to look out for a vassal matching Kane's description.

"While you were occupied with us," Kane said, "my comrade has gone back to the humans to warn them."

"Your fellow deserter? Did you think he actually escaped us? He is leading your ambassador to us."

Kane laughed. "If you expect the humans to come to you, you badly underestimate their intelligence. They won't endanger their mission for their captain's sake, and certainly not for mine."

Or at least so he and Fiona had believed. But he knew he didn't dare assume anything now. All he could do now was prevent the Opiri from entering the hangar and finding Fiona while she was unconscious.

"What will you do with me?" he asked, already knowing the answer.

"It seems the Bloodmaster Erastos took a particular interest in your disappearance," the *dekarchos* said. "He promised a substantial reward for your capture and return."

"I'm honored by his interest," Kane said. "What am I worth? A few prized serfs? Elevation to Bloodlord?"

The leader removed his helmet. Kane felt a moment of utter disbelief. He *knew* this man. Not his name, nor anything about him save that they had once faced each other across a field of mud and blasted trees over a century ago.

"You were once a fine soldier, Kane," the Opir said. "I regret the necessity of taking you back to die in torment rather than on the battlefield."

"I remember you," Kane said, swallowing his shock. "Were you taken during the War or after?"

The Opir's sharply cut face revealed nothing. "Does it matter?" he said.

"It can't have been long after," Kane said. "You're no vassal. You must have served your master well to have won your freedom."

The Opir's mouth thinned. "One does what one must to survive. Apparently you did not serve well enough. If you were a Freeblood, you would have had some control over your own fate."

"Would I?" Kane smiled wryly. "I've seen the rogues, like animals squabbling over any human they can find because they see no reason to serve any lord. I've made the same choice, but I've elected to keep my dignity and strive honorably for what I want."

"Like the female?" The leader cocked his head. "Did you not pause in your flight to help her and her kind, when you might have obtained your freedom by moving beyond the bounds of your Bloodmaster's influence? Why would you sacrifice so much for humans?"

"The strange thing is that I continue to remember what it was like to be human. To fight for what you believe in, no matter what the odds."

"You have fought and lost," the leader said. "And if other humans come, they will quickly find themselves surrounded." He nodded to his followers. "Take him."

"Stay where you are!"

A blinding streak of light cut across the ground between Kane and the Opir like an ancient warrior's blade. A human soldier appeared, the light blazing from the top of his helmet. Two others came up behind him, weapons trained on the Opiri. Kane didn't need to see their faces to recognize that one of the humans was Commander Goodman.

They had come after all. And they had walked right into a trap.

Fiona woke alone and shivering under the weight of Kane's jacket. She touched her neck, aware of a faint throbbing under the skin, and shook herself out of her stupor.

Kane was gone. But it wasn't only his absence that told her that something was terribly wrong.

She scrambled to her feet and checked her weapons. The rifle was still propped against the crates, her side-arm within easy reach. She holstered the gun, shouldered the rifle and started toward the hangar door at a run.

The shouting stopped her in her tracks a few feet from the entrance.

She knew the voice: Joel Goodman's. Her heart clenched.

No. Whatever he'd done, he was the only hope the ambassador had of reaching Sacramento. He would have no reason to try to save her, much less Kane. If anything happened to the senator because of *her*...

Where in God's name was Kane?

More shouts, more voices she recognized. She ran half-crouched out the door and flattened herself into the snow just outside, preparing to fire. She could see a half-dozen Nightsiders—there had to be more out of sight—and three of her own soldiers facing them from the west.

The Opiri leader had removed his helmet, and she could just make out his pale, craggy face. No one was moving. Lights bobbed in the air behind the human soldiers, and she could see—reinforcements, God knew how many.

If she had been less of a soldier, she might have wept. For her own foolishness, for her people, for the senator and the peace he might have brought.

For Kane.

But Kane was there, too, standing between her and the Opiri troops. What in hell was he hoping to accomplish? He would be caught in the cross fire, and even a vampire couldn't survive a hail of bullets from every side.

She stood up, shaking the snow from her fatigues. The Opiri nearest Kane saw her and aimed their weapons. She threw her rifle aside.

"Captain!" Goodman's voice called. "Are you all right?"

Fiona advanced slowly, arms raised, to stand beside Kane. "Commander," she called, "go back. Retreat."

"I think it is too late for that now," the Opiri leader said. He gestured at Kane with his rifle. "You see, we anticipated the arrival of your underlings. They are now surrounded by my troops."

"You think we're that stupid, bloodsucker?" Goodman shouted. "We have a soldier for every one of yours, and two of yours are already dead. All we have to do is wait until sunrise. I'd say you've got about half an hour. Your suits may buy you a little more time, but all we have to do is pin you down and wait for them to fail."

"Then we will all die," the Opiri leader said, "my troops and yours. But others will come after us to find your so-called ambassador, no matter where you have hidden him."

"If you think you can stop negotiations," Kane said, "you're wrong. Even if you kill or capture this ambassador, those on your side who favor peace will eventually succeed. Too many want an end to this war."

"He's right." Senator Sandoval stepped into the blaze of the lights, hands raised. "You can kill me, but your victory will be temporary."

Ignoring the Nightsider guns, Fiona turned to the ambassador. "Why did you come?" she asked. "Why did any of you come?"

"He insisted," Goodman said, a strange note in his voice.

"No," Sandoval said. "The commander said he would go after you alone. I refused to let him."

Fiona closed her eyes. In the end, Goodman had remembered *his* honor, but at a terrible price.

"Not for my sake," she whispered.

Kane took her hand. "Your senator wouldn't trade even a single life for his," he said. "He once told me he knew there would be sacrifices to achieve a lasting peace, but I think he believes that peace cannot be bought with more death." He squuezed Fiona's hand and met the Nightsider's gaze. "I would say that's the difference between your kind—*my* kind—and humans. But I believe there are some Opiri who haven't forgotten."

The leader was quiet for a long time, staring at Kane with a quizzical expression on his angular face.

"I am curious," he said at last, "whether you would give yourself to us without struggle and make no attempt to escape should I promise to let your human friends go."

Kane must have known that the Nightsider was merely playing a game, but he answered without hesitation. "Yes," he said.

"Even though you know you will suffer a painful death?"

"Yes."

"Would you sacrifice this female for the ambassador?"

"Yes," Fiona said. "He would."

Kane looked at her. "No. Never."

"You would do it," she said, gazing into his eyes, "because you fight for more than your own freedom. Because you are a soldier. Because you believe in what the ambassador is trying to achieve." She faced the Opiri leader again. "A friend told me a story about a war when his soldiers and the enemy came together on Christmas Day in the name of peace…because they recognized their common humanity."

"*We* are not human," the leader said.

"But you were once. Maybe *you* remember, too."

The Nightsider stiffened. "You presume too much. Just because Kane and I—" He broke off, but Fiona knew he'd been about to say something important. Possibly something that could save all their lives.

"You what?" she demanded.

"He and I faced each other across that battlefield on Christmas Day," Kane said. "As I recall, I gave him chocolate, and he gave me a pack of cigarettes." He looked into the Nightsider's dark blue eyes. "You know my name. It seems only right that I should know yours before we finish this."

"There can be only one end," the Opir said.

"Victory for one side and humiliating defeat for the other?" Kane asked. "Or an endless stalemate until no one is left to fight?" He took a step toward the leader. "Neither you nor I saw the end of that war. But we can help put an end to this one. Not just a truce for this single day, but an armistice that will let us all, human and Opiri, share this world in peace."

The hush was profound, as if the whole world were holding its breath. The first blush of dawn lightened the sky over the hills to the west.

Slowly the Opiri leader removed his right glove. His hand was pale, fine-boned, like that of a man who might play the violin or caress the fragile pages of antiquarian books.

"Von Grunwald," the leader said. "My name was Leutnant Hermann von Grunwald."

He offered his hand. Kane took it.

"Jonathon Kane," he said. "Lieutenant, British Expeditionary Force."

"American," von Grunwald said. "You joined the fight before your countrymen."

"It seemed like the right thing to do at the time."

"And this female?"

"Captain Fiona Donnelly, Enclave Special Forces."

Fiona felt something change in the air, a subtle shift from open hostility to a sense of…not friendliness, but acceptance.

It felt like hope.

"We lost much in the War," von Grunwald said, dropping Kane's hand. "More than our humanity."

"Yes," Kane said. "The future we could have had."

"True death, too," the Nightsider said. "But that, at least, would have been honorable."

"We can still find our honor again," Kane said.

Von Grunwald glanced at Fiona. "You truly care for this woman?"

"I love her."

The German smiled sadly. "You are fortunate. She is most extraordinary."

"Dekarchos!" one of von Grunwald's Opiri said. "It's nearly dawn."

Looking toward the east, von Grunwald nodded. "It is true that we could fight in daylight, for a while. But it seems those we sought have disappeared." He sighed and tugged his glove back on. "We will have to return empty-handed."

Fiona could hardly believe what she'd heard. Were the Nightsiders giving them up?

"The ambassador?" Fiona asked.

"He escaped us." Grunwald signaled to his men, who began to fall back. "So, alas, has the rogue vassal we hoped to locate."

Kane inclined his head. "If your lord finds out what you've done," he said, "you'll suffer for it. I'm still prepared to go with you."

"No!" Fiona said.

"It is not necessary," von Grunwald said. He shrugged. "We are very good at what we do. The Bloodmasters and Bloodlords can hardly afford to kill every vassal or Freeblood who displeases them. And perhaps, I, too, have not forgotten what it is to have free will. And honor."

Joel Goodman and his men rose from their defensive positions and moved toward the Opiri with lowered guns. Fiona immediately saw that Goodman was carrying the VS120.

"What is this, Captain?" Goodman asked. "Did you authorize a cease-fire?"

"I'm doing it now," Fiona said, facing him. "There will be no fight today. The ambassador is safe."

Goodman stared at von Grunwald. "Why should we trust them?"

"Because they could have killed us, and they didn't," she said. "We will continue north to Sacramento."

"And we will continue looking for our elusive prey," von Grunwald said with an ironic lift of one eyebrow. He pulled on his helmet. *"Auf wiedersehen,* Lieutenant. I hope you succeed in winning your freedom." He bowed to Fiona and clicked his heels. *"Hauptmannin."*

He signaled his men again, and they began to retreat, backing away from Fiona's troops.

Suddenly Goodman moved, aiming the Vampire Slayer at von Grunwald. Before she could move to stop him, Kane flung himself in front of the Nightsider.

"Kane!" Fiona shouted. She tried to push him out of the way. "Goodman! Joel! Stand down! Remember what we're fighting for!"

Everything stopped. The rest of Fiona's troops had moved into position behind Joel. Von Grunwald's scouts aimed their own weapons more quickly than Fiona's human sight could follow.

Senator Sandoval walked up fearlessly behind Joel and laid his hand on the commander's shoulder. "We have all lost too much in this war," he said. "Let there be no more pain, no more sorrow. On this day of all days, let us be at peace."

"Joel," Fiona said softly. "Will you be the one who destroys that peace?"

Slowly Goodman lowered the VS120. In the growing light of dawn, she could just make out his features through his visor. His face was racked with pain, shame and the memory of losses he had never quite put behind him.

"Peace," he said in a broken voice. He threw his weapon to the ground and looked at Fiona. "I betrayed you," he said. "Captain, I wasn't right in my head. All I could think of—" He broke off. "There are no excuses." He came to attention. "I stand ready to face a court-martial when we return to the Enclave."

She went to him, stepping around the VS. "We'll deal

with that when we come to it," she said. "Right now we still have work to do."

He bowed his head. She heard a faint sound behind her and turned. The Opiri were melting away like winter fog, retreating to the shelter of the hangar while their long shadows stretched over the pink-tinged snow.

And then they were gone.

Kane joined her, hovering protectively behind her as if he expected Goodman to threaten her again.

Goodman looked over her shoulder at Kane. "What I did…" he began.

"Your captain has accepted your apology," Kane said. "But never threaten her again."

"No," Goodman said. "No."

Kane nodded and followed Fiona as she went to meet the senator. "That was very foolish of you, sir," she said sternly.

"I know it," Sandoval said with an apologetic smile, "but I'm glad I came. I witnessed something extraordinary today."

"Because of Kane," Fiona said, reaching behind her for Kane's hand.

"No, Fiona," Kane said. "Because of you."

"You gonna keep thankin' each other," Alfie said from the direction of the hangar, "or d'ya think a poor body could get a li'l rest?"

Kane and Fiona turned to see Alfie wading toward them through the snow, grinning from ear to ear.

"Alfie," Kane said, grabbing his friend's arms and giving him a shake. "Where the hell were you?"

"Keepin' a bead on the Hun," Alfie said. "Just in case 'e decided 'e wanted ta take you along with him."

"But he didn't," Kane said, releasing the other man.

"Just like the Truce all over again," Alfie said. "But that time we went right back to fightin' the next day."

"Maybe we will, too, for a while," Fiona said. "But perhaps *this* time we can stop it before it ends in tragedy. For everyone." She searched Kane's face. "What will you do now?"

He stared at her as if she'd spoken in a language too ancient for even the Nightsiders to remember. "Go with you," he said. "Protect the ambassador. And protect *you* from your own foolhardiness."

"You're one to talk," she said. "You were trying to move away from your Bloodmaster's control. You have a second chance now. If you come with us, you may become trapped. You could turn back to *them,* because you won't have any choice."

"No," he said. "There's something stronger than any Bloodmaster's influence." He hesitated. "Did you mean what you told me in the hangar?"

"Did you mean what you said to von Grunwald about your feelings?"

In answer, he took her into his arms and kissed her with her soldiers, the ambassador and Alfie looking on.

She pulled away, a little embarrassed at her lack of professional control. It was a pity there were so many witnesses, or she might have committed a real indiscretion.

"You'd better move on," Kane said, letting her go.

"Not without you," Fiona said.

"I can catch up after sundown. Not all the Opiri looking for us are likely to remember the Christmas Truce."

"But *we* will," Fiona said, her heart expanding with almost unbearable joy. "For the rest of our lives." She gave him a stern look. "You know the direction we'll be heading. I expect you to catch up with us by midnight at the latest."

"Yes, Captain."

"And you're never going to take blood from anyone but me. Is that clear?"

He saluted her, his expression grave but his eyes sparkling. "Yes, Captain."

"I love you, Lieutenant," she whispered.

Kane took her hands and kissed them.

Alfie rolled his eyes."Well," he said, "looks like I'll 'ave ta come along ta look after ya both. Never trust people in love, 'at's what I say." He gave a long-suffering sigh and looked at Kane. "Ya needs yer rest, guv, 'n' I don't want ta sit up listenin' all day ta ya moonin' over the lady." He met Fiona's eyes. "As fer you…ya better get movin'. Ya got a lot o' ground left ta cover."

Kane grinned at Fiona. "More than you can possibly imagine."

The baby was born nine months from the night Fiona and Kane had spent together in the hangar.

She looked completely normal by human standards, with Fiona's red hair and Kane's gray eyes. He had been completely unsurprised, but Fiona had been in a state of blissful shock from the moment she'd learned she was pregnant.

Kane sat on the couch in their apartment, holding Fiona while she held the baby. He couldn't decide which of the two of them was more beautiful. It was a pointless exercise.

Little Jenna began to whimper. Fiona laughed.

"Hungry again, you little monster?" She glanced back at Kane, flushing. "Sorry. Sometimes I forget…"

"That I'm not human?" He nuzzled her hair. "Your mayor and congress managed to forget. I am grateful for their poor memories."

It hadn't been easy at the beginning. When Fiona and her troops had returned from the peace mission—minus the ambassador, who had remained in Sacramento with his aide and two personal guards—Kane had hardly faced a warm welcome, especially when he declined to provide Defense and Intelligence with information they could use to prolong the war if negotiations were to fail.

But Kane had faith peace would prevail, and in the end, DI had let him go. For his part in aiding the ambassador's mission, he had been permitted to take up residence in the City and marry Fiona. It was the first such marriage known since the Awakening.

Fiona opened her blouse to let Jenna take her breakfast. When the baby was asleep, she and Kane would retire to the bedroom, where she would give Kane what he needed and they would give each other what they never tired of.

"She still seems like a miracle to me," she murmured, stroking the baby's wispy hair. "Do you think this is the first child born to a human and a Nightsider?"

There were still so many things Kane couldn't tell her. But now that peace was so close, the time would soon come when there would be no more need for secrets. He had a feeling Fiona wouldn't be content to stay safely ensconced in the City once she knew there were innocent lives she and Kane might be able to help.

"Even if Jenna isn't the first," he said, "she'll still be important, a living link between our peoples."

"Yes," Fiona murmured. "But we can't ever let her believe she has to be anyone but who she wants to be. She'll never go through what you did."

"I'm grateful now," Kane said softly, kissing her temple. "If I hadn't been converted, we would never have met."

She looked up into his face. "Funny how things work out in the end," she said with a tender smile.

There was a brisk knock on the door. Fiona covered herself and shifted the baby into the crook of her arm. Kane took Jenna from her and made noises he never would have believed he was capable of making. Fiona went to the door and opened it just as Alfie walked in.

"Awright," Alfie said, glancing from Fiona to Kane and the baby. "'Bout time ol' Uncle Alfie got a chance with the li'l mite." He took Jenna from Kane's arms, and the baby gurgled contentedly.

Alfie cooed and made a series of ridiculous faces, even though Jenna was already falling asleep again. "Go on," he said without looking up. "I'll take 'er for a li'l walk. You get on with—" He tilted his head toward the bedroom.

Fiona blushed. "Alfie—"

"Cap'n," Alfie said, walking toward the front door, "time you 'n' the lieutenant get workin' on more o' them li'l peacemakers."

Before Fiona could protest, Kane had her in his arms. He kissed her neck, grazing her skin gently with his teeth.

"The sergeant always did have good sense," he murmured.

Fiona laughed and took his hand.

* * * * *

THE GIFT

Theresa Meyers

This book is dedicated to my readers.

Whoever you are, wherever you may be, know that
you are greatly appreciated, for without you,
I wouldn't have a reason to send my stories out into
the world. Thank you.

Chapter 1

He had to find her.

The last holder of the locket had passed away almost a month ago, and Cullen McCormack had to find the new owner as soon as possible. Time was running out.

He knew her name, Angelica Edwards. He knew that she lived in New Harmony, Pennsylvania. But beyond what he could dig up on the internet, he knew little else save she was Tamara Edwards's only daughter and his entire existence hung in the balance. Not that he called continually hiding in the shadows and constantly living in fear that a single woman's whim might be your demise an existence.

Being immortal had sounded like the greatest gift when he'd been young and brash, but if Cullen McCormack had learned one thing in the past two hundred years, it was that being immortal hardly ever turned out the way you expected.

For one, he never anticipated how tiring it would become to try to convince one woman after another to give him back a locket that held his immortal soul. Especially when his efforts always failed. For another, he'd never considered how lonely it would be to live without love.

Not the physical sensation, mind you, but the warm feeling deep in one's bones—that utter certainty that another person made the sun rise and set just by their sheer presence.

The weight of his morose thoughts matched the fat snowflakes falling from the leaden sky. Cullen pulled the lapels of his black wool coat tighter about his throat as he sniffed the air fragrant with the scents of wood smoke, evergreens, mulled apple cider rich with spices, and wet wool. Normally shadows stretched luxuriously along the walkways and streets of New Orleans at this time of day. But not here.

He couldn't wait to get out of New Harmony and return home to the warmth of New Orleans. Every time the locket changed hands, he came close to being damned for eternity, thanks to the scorn of Marie, the voodoo priestess he'd crossed so long ago.

The twinkle of holiday lights in the trees lining the street reminded him of the fireflies that had danced in the thick, humid heat of the night he'd last been mortal.

That night, crickets had hummed a chorus in the darkness as he'd climbed the steps of Marie's rickety gray cypress plank cabin, the shake roof draped heavily with the pale green of Spanish moss from the trees all around.

"Der's dat Cullen." The way Marie had stared at him with her dark, smoldering eyes should have told

him that she'd discovered his tryst with the plantation owner's flirtatious daughter, Lisette. But he'd been too stupid to see the signs. Too confident in himself and his prowess with ladies to believe he was in any danger.

He'd reached out to hold Marie's hand and pressed a kiss to it. Her eyes burned with black fire.

"*You have betrayed me, Cullen.*"

"*Betrayed? Don't be silly.*"

"*Dat porcelain French doll been worth it?*"

Cullen pulled Marie into his arms, pressing her womanly curves against him. "*Lisette was nothing but a dalliance. I don't love her, as I love you.*"

Marie plied her long fingers through his hair, her nails dragging along his scalp as she skimmed her lush lips over his. "*You don't know what love is. But you going to learn.*" *She gave a vicious tug and pulled out some of his hair.*

Cullen shoved her away from him, massaging his scalp. "*What the devil was that for, woman?*"

"*Exactly. De debil you be, de debil you become.*" *The heated words cut quickly to his core, like a searing knife melting butter. She tossed the dark strands of his hair into the small fire she had burning in the brazier on her worktable, and the flames turned green.*

Cullen realized the flame danced on the surface of a black liquid. Perhaps it was port or something stronger. He couldn't smell any alcohol coming from the pot, only the dank, fetid smell of the bayou and the musty odor of dried herbs that hung in shriveled bunches from her cabin's rafters.

From her pocket she pulled an oval gold locket and swung it through the greenish flames. The locket's shining surface reflected the oddly colored flames.

"Cullen McCormack, you always asked me how to make de magic dat make you immortal. Now you going to find out." Her husky voice chanted in her native tongue, the rhythm of it vibrating straight through him so that he felt it as deeply as his own beating heart.

"Da girl dat takes dis locket holds your soul. If she love you wit all her heart, den she may give you de locket. If she does not, you will be at her beck and call her whole life, but never her love.

"When de time come and you can truly love in return, you'll have but one chance to make tings right, Cullen. If you miss dat chance, de gods will take your soul to the deepest reaches of Hell."

Her words disturbed him deeply, so he resorted to making light of it to ease his discomfort. *"Is that a threat or a promise, Marie?"*

Her dark eyes bored into him, making his stomach shrivel with certainty. *"Dat be a promise."*

Damn.

A searing pain pierced him, like the white-hot sting of a bullet, the heat of it burning through his veins. He tried to scream, but nothing came out as he toppled to the floor.

Marie took a battered tin cup, dipped it into the black liquid and poured the scalding mixture down his throat. *"Till de day you have de locket freely given back to you, you will roam de Earth a vampire who feeds on life, but never knows it."*

Cullen choked against the vile warm liquid but could neither sputter nor spit it out.

The bitter memory made Cullen stop in his tracks before he forced himself to move forward. Just a block ahead lay the tree-lighting ceremony in the quaint downtown of New Harmony.

Four times he'd already been through this ridiculous process. First had been Charlotte, who'd chosen the richest man in town, only to find that once he died in the Civil War, she was a penniless Southern widow. Next had been her daughter, Anne, who'd married herself into high society and found her husband preferred his mistresses. Third had been Anne's daughter, Catherine—Kate—whose flashy beau passed away in World War II, leaving her heartbroken. And last with Kate's child, Tamara, who'd wanted her high school boyfriend so badly that she'd wished for him, gotten promptly pregnant and then found herself at his funeral after an unfortunate motorcycle accident had taken him before the baby was ever born. Each time it had turned out the same. While their chosen love died, he stayed on to serve them—opening doors to opportunities and giving them the benefit of a mysterious yet powerful benefactor, but never love. The connection between them perpetuated the cycle of loneliness, spreading it like a cancer he couldn't control, which gave him little hope for this current case. Somehow these women had known the power of the locket and kept it from generation to generation.

He'd offered them all the same choice: the man of their dreams or immortality. All of them had picked the man, but not once had he been that man. It was a simple enough process to go out and glamour whatever beau had attracted their fancy. But it grew increasingly harder and harder for Cullen to stomach the loneliness. Any physical relationship he had was short and brief. He could make promises to no one because his existence teetered on uncertainty, tied to the locket and the women who owned it.

Most inconvenient and annoying.

He dug his frigid fingers deeper into the pockets of his coat as he scanned the gathering of locals. The mingle of their heartbeats was like the roar of the ocean. *Focus,* he told himself. One woman, her brown hair caught into a twist at the back of her head, her elegant profile lit by the sudden brightness emanating from the tall tree in the town square, caught his attention. From the angle it was hard to tell if it was Angelica Edwards, but the intense pull in his gut gave him the confirmation he needed.

Cullen edged his way toward her, trying not to attract undue attention. Several female gazes lingered on him, but Cullen didn't return them. What he needed now was to gain Angelica's interest…and her trust.

Chapter 2

The cold wind whipped against Angel's hair, sending damp wisps lashing at her cheeks. She took a deep breath, the cool air piercing her lungs, then exhaled slowly to hold back the tears. Coming to the holiday tree lighting had always been a tradition she'd shared with her mother ever since she'd begun singing in the choir. But now her mother was gone.

The colored lights, seen through a veil of softly falling snow, looked beautiful against the black sky. Even though the love and support she'd received after her mother's death four weeks ago had helped, she still felt too sad to mingle tonight and stood apart from friends and acquaintances. The clear, pure voices of the New Harmony High School choir soared in the cool air. Her eyes burned, welling with tears at the thought of her mother being gone.

The last gift from her mother, the oval gold locket around her neck, had only arrived that morning via a big brown delivery truck.

The words from the note still swam before her eyes.

Dearest Angel,
It is time for me to pass on to you something very special. This locket has been handed down from mother to daughter for generations in our family. It is a talisman of sorts. Keep it close at all times and pass it down to your daughter after you pass. A man will come asking for the locket. He'll offer you a choice of a lifetime, but whatever you do, don't give him the locket. It's your key to keeping the good luck he'll grant you and your children, and their children. Know that I miss you, more than even you miss me. You were the most wonderful part of my life.
Love Forever and Always,
Mom

Her mom had worn the locket for as long as Angel could remember. She's seemed so sad whenever Angel would ask about it that she hadn't pushed her mother for more information. She'd only ever opened it once.

Her mother had been in the shower and left the locket on her dresser. Angel had been fourteen when she'd snuck into her mother's room and opened it to find the image of a searing blue eye staring back at her. It was a man's eye, not anyone she recognized. Her father had had brown eyes. She'd thought it was strange her mother didn't have a picture of her father or her in the locket. But whenever she'd asked about it, her mother had said it was merely an important family heirloom.

Angel clicked open the locket and the same blue eye stared back at her, making her breath catch. She had the oddest sensation of being watched, as if the owner of the blue eye was able to see her just as clearly as she could make out the flecks of silver in the iris.

She'd never gotten answers from her mother about the locket and only had the cryptic note as consolation. She pulled off one of her red knit gloves to brush back the tears, then let her fingers slip over the cool metal of the locket.

"It's beautiful, isn't it?" A husky male voice spoke just over her shoulder. She didn't recognize the intriguing Irish accent and turned to see who he was, her fingers reactively tightening on her locket.

No. She'd never seen him before. If she had, his was a face she'd never forget. His dark brown hair acted as the perfect foil for the brightest blue eyes Angel had ever seen. *Stunning* was the word that came to mind. Snowflakes stuck to the thick rim of his dark lashes. The brilliant blue of his eyes softened features that were a little too intense and harsh. Or perhaps it was the play of colored Christmas lights and shadows that gave the appearance that he wasn't having as much fun as the small crowd listening to the choir.

A little breathless, she pulled on her glove and forced a smile.

"Yeah, they are. Claimed to be New Harmony High School's finest choir in thirty-five years." Her smile widened a little at the humor dancing in his eyes.

"Which tells you just how small New Harmony really is. Every year is their best year. Still, it's the best show around during the holidays." She stuck out her hand to shake his. "Angel Edwards. Choir of '03."

His lips lifted in a casual smile that made her stomach somersault as he clasped her hand in his much larger one. A charge of electric current raced right through the knit of her glove and up her arm. "Cullen McCormack, nice to meet you. Sorry I missed your operatic performance. I'm sure 2003 was the choir's pinnacle."

Even though they'd only briefly touched, it left a profound impression on Angel. She shook her head. "That's kind of you, but as you can tell I'm here, not singing opera somewhere, so it can't have been that good."

There was an indefinable allure about him. Something she couldn't put her finger on. Cullen was hot. That wasn't in question. But it was more than that. He seemed to radiate sex appeal on a level she'd never seen from a guy. And it wasn't the cocky, I-know-I-could-have-any-woman-I-want kind of appeal; it was as if he'd been a male model for the statues of Greek gods. He was comfortable in his own skin, which stirred up a little bit of envy inside her.

She'd never been one of the popular kids. She was too fascinated by history and art to really fit that mold. She'd dreamed of getting out of New Harmony, traveling, seeing the world and historic places, but it had never seemed to materialize. Her mom counted on her too much at the shop. But with Mom gone, there wasn't much to hold her here any longer—except the shop.

She stuck her hands deeply into the pockets of her red wool coat. "So, what are you doing in New Harmony, other than stopping to watch them light the tree and hear the best school choir this side of the Great Lakes?"

"Stick out that badly, do I?"

Angel smothered a small laugh and tilted her head back, watching the snowflakes drift down like magic from an endless dark sky. "No, *stick out* isn't right." She slid her gaze to meet his. "*Overshadow,* maybe?"

He chuckled, and the warmth of it seeped away the tired ache in her bones, if only for a moment.

Cullen caught her gaze. "I'm in town on business. I saw the flyers for the tree lighting and thought it would be an interesting way to pass the evening." He paused for a second, shifting his weight as if he were working through what to say next. "Would you like to go for a coffee?"

For a second she just stared mutely at him, mesmerized. Why, out of anyone here, would he pick her? Given her current morose mood, she wasn't exactly the best company. And he was a total stranger. She had no business going with him anywhere. "Thanks, but I don't drink coffee."

"Hot chocolate?" The dark brow over his right eye lifted, making him look impossibly hopeful and charming at the same time.

Angel grinned. Perhaps she was making more of it than she should. The note her mother had enclosed with the locket had shaken her, that was all, she told herself. He was simply a good—no, gorgeous—looking stranger asking her out for hot chocolate at a public place. It wasn't as if it could lead to much. And it being the holidays, why shouldn't she show a little warmth and kindness to someone as obviously alone at the moment as she was? "Now, that I can do, once the lighting is finished."

He smiled and it went straight through her.

Chapter 3

Once the crowd gathered around town hall began to disperse, they headed for The Beanery—the small coffee shop on Main Street that was still one of the few places open at this time of the evening.

Apparently half the people at the tree lighting had the same idea. The Beanery was packed. The bell over the door chimed merrily as they entered. Warmth and the heady smells of hot coffee and a hint of cinnamon hit Angel in the face, tempting her to pull off her gloves. She flexed her stiff fingers, then grasped Cullen's sleeve, afraid she'd lose him in the crowd.

In the bright lights of the small coffee shop, he looked bigger and even more handsome than he had in the shadowy lights outside in the square. Bigger and more handsome, and even more unlikely to be escorting plain Angel Edwards.

Should she just tell him she changed her mind? Instead, she said, "There's a small table over there," nodding toward a table barely big enough for the two chairs on either side of it. Considering the former occupants had only just left, the seats were probably still warm.

He nodded. "Why don't you hold down the table and I'll brave the counter?"

Angel glanced at the line. He was brave. It stretched all the way across the shop back to the door.

"What do you like in your hot chocolate? Wait. Let me guess. Hint of cinnamon and whipped cream?"

Angel could tell her mouth had dropped open slightly because she could taste the coffee-saturated air on her tongue. It was as if this total stranger had reached in and read her mind. "Yeah. How'd you know?"

He gave her an enigmatic smile. "Good guess." He pulled out a chair for her at the table.

Angel sat down, her brain spinning and her gaze lingering on his broad shoulders encased in a tailored black wool coat as he headed for the end of the line. No one, not even Alex Sterling, her on-again, off-again boyfriend, had ever read her that quickly before. And if anyone should have been able to read people, it should have been Alex. He was the county's district attorney, for pity's sake. It was his job to peel people apart and reveal their secrets. Angel pulled off her gloves one at a time, setting them on the table, then unbuttoned her jacket, wrapping it around the back of her chair.

Mom had had high hopes for her and Alex. She had, too. But Angel hadn't had the heart to tell her mother the truth once she'd figured it out: Alex wasn't interested in her as more than a friend with benefits. Marriage wasn't likely. Not when he thought he had much better prospects than Angel and far greater aspirations than just becoming district attorney. He wanted a wife that could take him to the governor's mansion, perhaps even further, not a small-town antiques-shop owner. She didn't stick out enough, or rather parts of her stuck out too much. She wasn't polished and attention grabbing.

Unlike Cullen.

Cullen commanded attention—kind of the way a Secret Service agent might. Gina Wiggins, who worked at the post office, turned to give him a good long look, then swiveled around and whispered to Connie Parsons right in front of her. Angel watched the news spread, person by person. She thought he'd created such a stir because he was taller than people around him, but it was more than that. He had an elusive movie-star quality to him that drew attention.

He moved a step forward in the line and turned, glancing back at her. Angel sucked in a startled breath, her cheeks flushing with heat and her heart pounding hard. He'd probably sensed she'd been staring at him. She broke the visual connection between them and worried the knit of her gloves between her fingers as she re-arranged them on the table. Who was she kidding? Just the cut of his expensive coat, suit and red silk tie spoke of wealth, and his commanding presence bordered on aristocratic. Men like Cullen McCormack didn't date or fall for girls like her. Alex was proof of that. And Alex didn't even hold a candle to Cullen McCormack.

Angel sighed. For once she wished a guy like Cullen could see past the extra fifteen pounds on her frame, her plain brown hair or her less-than-chic wardrobe. Per-haps take a moment to get to know her as a person, not as someone to assist them with whatever they wanted.

"Be careful. It's hot." She glanced up to find him holding a plain, cream-colored paper cup, the mound of glistening whipped cream on top wavering slightly.

"Thank you." Her fingers grazed his lightly as she took the cup, and Angel's heartbeat bumped up a couple of notches at the zip of electrical current between them.

"My pleasure." Cullen settled himself into the chair opposite her, his large hands dwarfing the cup he held. "Thank you for being so welcoming to a stranger. It's not often I get to have a hot drink with an equally hot woman."

Angel about snorted her sip of hot chocolate. "I sincerely doubt that. Based on the reaction in here, you look like you'd have no end of female company."

He chuckled and took a sip of his coffee. He had nice lips, well sculpted, perfect for kissing. Angel shook the thought from her head. Why on earth should she care? And why even think about him this way? He was a stranger. A beautiful stranger, and she was just being… kind. Or perhaps he was the one being kind to an obviously plain woman.

Cullen nodded toward her. "That's a beautiful necklace you're wearing."

The chatter of customers and the hissing sounds of the cappuccino machines faded away, becoming nothing but a buzz in the background as Angel focused in on his voice. Her fingers touched the warm metal of the locket.

"Yes. A gift from my mother." She cleared her throat at the last word.

"So, a family heirloom?"

She nodded.

"Do you mind? I'm a bit of an enthusiast about antique jewelry."

It was an odd request, but she wasn't sure she could deny him—anything. Cullen leaned forward, close enough that Angel could smell the clean scent of soap mingled with a spicier fragrance of cloves that lingered on his skin.

Angel's throat swelled shut. She couldn't do more than hold still, even as her whole body trembled while his hand reached toward her. His fingertips gently skimmed the base of her throat, sending a throb of awareness through her body. He grasped the locket and flipped it open.

She swallowed hard. Had this been a different situation, he'd have been close enough to kiss her. And Angel was all too aware of how his nearness spiked every female fantasy she had. Her lips tingled as if she'd just slicked on a mint lip balm.

She heard the locket click shut. His intense, heated gaze flicked up to meet hers. "This is very unusual. I've never seen anything like it." His fingers once more brushed her skin as he lay the locket back again just below the hollow of her throat. Even in the middle of a crowd, he managed to create a sensual haze that made her feel as if there was only the two of them. She struggled to pull together a string of coherent words.

"Are you an antiques collector?"

"Of a sort."

His answer didn't satisfy her curiosity. "Personal or for retail?"

He smiled. "More of a personal collector. Occasionally I'll find items of particular interest to a client."

"So, more like a picker."

He raised a brow and picked up his coffee, taking

a sip as if considering her comment. "A high-end one, I suppose."

Gorgeous, mysterious and totally unattainable. Definitely what she didn't need.

"Now that you've gotten to ask me a personal question, it's only fair if you let me ask you one in return."

Angel shrugged. "I'm not all that interesting. Go ahead."

His eyes sparkled. "What's the story behind the necklace? You said it was a family heirloom?"

Angel took a fortifying sip of her hot chocolate, letting the creamy texture and rich flavor fill her mouth. "My mother always wore it. She passed away recently and left it to me."

Cullen raised his cup of coffee in salute. "My condolences on the loss of your mother. That can't have been easy. The way you talk about her, you two must have been close."

Angel worked hard at blinking back the heat gathering in her eyes. She did not want to cry. Not here. Not now.

"Did she ever say where she'd gotten it?"

Angel took a deep breath and shrugged. "My grandmother. But she passed away before I was born, so I didn't get to know her."

Cullen nodded. "Well, you've been more than fair in your answer. Your turn. Ask me a question. Anything."

In her chest her heart double-bumped. "Have you been in a serious relationship before?"

"Oh, yes." He cast his gaze down to his coffee cup, a crease forming between his brows as they drew together.

"I take it from your expression it didn't turn out

well." The brilliant light that had been in his eyes before had dulled. Angel winced. She wanted to take the words back the second they'd slipped out. *Smooth move,* she derided herself. Perhaps this was why Alex was reluctant to take her anywhere in public. Her annoying habit of speaking first and thinking later meant there were plenty of times she found herself wishing she could take her words back. "Sorry, that was really none of my business."

Cullen waved away her concern with a flick of his hand, then leaned back in his chair, his fingers scraping across the sweep of hair lingering over his eyes. "Let's say the split was a mutual thing." Mutually destructive. Marie had sought to destroy him with her curse of immortality, and he'd sought to avenge himself by burning her cottage to the ground.

Angelica's pretty mouth trembled into a half smile full of insecurity. Of any of the women he'd met, she needed his help more than most. She was fragile inside, either from the recent loss of her mother or the rejection of the clod who'd clearly broken her spirit. A sour feeling swirled in Cullen's gut. He'd bet it was the man who made her insecure. The scent of pepper spiked the air around him. He sincerely hoped only he could smell it. As a vampire he could scent the emotion on the air, but occasionally so could a perceptive mortal.

"So, what's your best relationship advice, then?" she asked, her voice cracking.

He could tell her to never cheat on a voodoo priestess, but it wouldn't make a bit of sense. So, he chose the next best thing.

"Know precisely what you are getting into."

Angelica nodded, her lips closing around the edge of her cup. When she was done taking a sip, the soft pink tip of her tongue swept over her top lip, removing the trace of whipped cream lingering there. His body tightened.

"Good advice," she said.

Too bad he couldn't give himself any. This wasn't at all going how he'd planned. And he'd been so certain this time could be, would be, different, but already he was finding himself far too interested in Angelica. It was always harder to make a mark of someone if one knew them too well. One started to have feelings. Messy things, feelings. Always muddling one's judgment.

"You sound like you've had a serious relationship that didn't go as planned," he replied easily, his tone smooth and unruffled.

She sighed, her fingers absently swizzling the thin red stirring straw in her cup. "Let's just say I was more into him than he was into me."

"He's a stupid bastard," Cullen said without heat. "Men usually are. We often don't know the value of what we have until after we've lost it. You're smart and beautiful. I'm sure he regrets it."

Angelica's eyes widened slightly. Her throat moved reflexively as she swallowed the words, but Cullen heard them all the same, echoing in the thoughts he read. *He's already had me. Alex's never going to be interested in anything else. I'm not suitable for a politician's wife.*

"You can tell all that just over a cup of hot chocolate?" Her voice held a slight tremor.

Cullen hadn't met the man and already hated him. Whoever this moron was, he certainly didn't deserve her, and it angered Cullen that this nameless cad had so thoroughly compromised Angelica's confidence. "So, is it over between you—or are you still hoping he'll come around?"

She offered him a weak smile and deftly changed the subject. "So, you're in town on business?"

Cullen leaned back, taking a long drink of his coffee as he contemplated how to respond. He was certain she still had affections for this Alex chap. The thought both irritated and depressed him. Like the other women he'd met since the curse, it was clear Angelica would give anything to be with the man of her dreams, without even a thought about what her life could be like if it spanned centuries. And the situation was all the more unfortunate since it was as clear as ice to Cullen that Alex didn't deserve her.

"This area is an antiques dealer's playground," he replied, not missing a beat. It was close to the truth. He did collect antiques. It didn't matter that at the time of their original acquisition they'd been new or that he still had an eye and affinity for things from his mortal past.

Her smile widened a bit. "I know. That's why I have a shop here."

"You deal antiques, as well?"

Angelica shrugged. "It's more like the family business. I simply inherited it." Her hand absently strayed to the locket.

She'd just handed him the opening he needed. Cullen ruthlessly held himself in check, not daring to stare at the locket. But the knowledge that he might be getting his hands on the locket infused the dark ichor in his veins with the buzz of anticipation. If she appreciated antiques, perhaps she could be lured by immortality. Considering he liked her, acting as her mentor through the change into a full-fledged vampire wouldn't be too troublesome.

"I'd like to see your shop while I'm here."

Her gaze connected with his. "You would?" The slight tremor in her voice belied the glint of interest in her eyes.

"Of course I would. Can we go now?"

"It's the middle of the night."

"Eight is hardly the middle of the night," he said drily. "I must admit to curiosity, and I've never been good at waiting. Unless you have something else to do tonight…?"

She shook her head. "I'll take you now if you don't mind a short walk."

He gave her an encouraging smile. "I think I can re-arrange my schedule for that."

A pretty blush infused her skin, making his fangs ache. He'd made a conscious effort not to feed from any of the women who held the locket, but he was damned tempted to make an exception in Angelica's case.

Angelica pulled on her red wool coat and mittens, then grabbed her cup of hot chocolate. "Ready?"

Cullen didn't bother to comment. Really he had no choice. Now that he'd found Angelica and obtained her interest, it was just a matter of timing about when to approach her about the locket.

They left the warmth of the coffee shop and strolled side by side, hot drinks in hand, down Main Street. "Elegant Artifacts is up here half a block."

"You said you inherited the shop?"

"My mother and I were business partners."

He smelled her heat and the faint flowery scent of her

soap on the frigid evening air. "That certainly makes her passing even more of a burden for you."

Angelica bit her lip. "It definitely put a strain on things."

They stopped in front of a darkened storefront. The hand-painted sign had a Victorian flourish, the curves of the letters accented with sweeps and curling bits that marked it as one of a kind rather than some average font.

"Elegant Artifacts. That's charming."

Angelica smiled. "I came up with it when I was twelve." She dug in her purse for her keys, then opened the door. Cullen glanced through the wide window-panes. Dark forms hid in the shadows of her shop. But as the lights flickered to life, he could see they were no more than furniture and statuary.

They stepped inside. The smells of lavender and rose, aged wood, lemon oil and that certain mustiness that clung to old things saturated the air. The floors were hardwood, the high ceilings had embossed brass tiles and the walls were exposed brick. He had to give her credit for being both a businesswoman and some-one with a good eye. She'd arranged the shop in little vignettes, each area showcasing not only the furniture but also the smaller knickknacks and more fragile items to their best advantage. "I like the layout. You've done a lovely job with arranging the shop."

Angelica locked the door behind them and checked the closed sign hanging in the window. "Don't want anyone thinking we're still open just because the lights are on."

Cullen smiled. He didn't want to be interrupted, ei-ther. "Surely they know you have business hours?"

Angelica shrugged. "It's a small town. Sometimes

those things don't always matter. People around here heavily rely on personalized customer service."

She followed on his heels as he slowly strolled through the store, his fingers grazing the smooth, elegant carved curves of a settee or the cool marble edge of a tabletop. "You have some excellent pieces here. Do you get much business from out of state?"

"A few tourists mostly. There's a few designers that come on shopping trips once or twice a year."

He nodded. Staying afloat as a small business had to be difficult enough, but being one that specialized in older, more valuable pieces had to be almost impossible when people labored under the impression that new pressboard atrocities would function just as well to grace their homes.

"Would you mind if I tagged a few pieces? There are several that have caught my eye that I know my clients would appreciate."

The air around Angelica fairly hummed with excitement. "Of course!" She hurried back to her office area at the back of the shop and came out with a sheet of stickers. "Mark anything you'd like."

He spent the next half hour marking more than a dozen items for purchase. Cullen took his time. He knew the worth of what she had, probably better than she did, which should have made quick work of his purchases, but he didn't want to appear rushed.

Angelica made notations on a pad of paper of each item he selected and drew up a bill of sale. "Will there be anything else?" She smiled.

Cullen purposely gazed about the shop before coming back to her and the golden locket that lay tantalizingly just above the creamy swells of her cleavage.

"Since you buy and sell, I don't suppose you'd be willing to sell that locket to me?" He tried for nonchalance, making it prosaic enough to be passed off as easily as a comment on the weather.

Her hand closed reflexively on the locket. "No." She trembled a bit. "Sorry. Um, it's not for sale."

Cullen wasn't taken aback. He'd expected her to balk at the suggestion. "What about for ten thousand dollars?"

Angelica blinked, her eyes turning round and mouth dropping open slightly. "What?"

Cullen waved his hand. "I can see that hasn't swayed you. Too low. Fifty thousand?"

"I said—"

"Seventy-five."

"It's not—"

"One hundred." She just stared at him as if he'd grown a second head. He knew he was bordering on the insane, but he wanted to know how far he could push her. Not everyone could wrap their brain around the idea of being offered a huge sum of money, let alone immortality. "Come, now. Everything has a price. Five hundred thousand dollars."

Her mouth snapped shut and she gave a slight shake to her head, making the tendrils of her hair sway about the edges of her oval face. "Not this."

"I see." Cullen leaned in closer and flashed her a smile. He was enormously pleased when he heard her breath catch in response. "That's precisely what I was hoping to hear."

Angelica's brows drew together in confusion. "Why? Is being told no some kind of novelty for you?"

Cullen tilted his head to the side. "Yes and no. I've

had plenty of people tell me no. But not when passing my test."

"Test? What are you talking about? Did you really intend to purchase all those antiques or were you here for something else, Mr. McCormack?"

"Ouch. Back that quickly to Mr. McCormack. I'd rather hoped we were past that. I am purchasing the pieces. They're good pieces. I just am rather more interested in other things, as well."

Her shoulders dropped a notch as she sighed. "I'm sorry. You just caught me off guard. So, what kind of test are you talking about?"

"I've come to grant you a wish."

Angelica stared, then let out a mirthless burst of laughter. "You're not some reality-show producer, or fairy godfather or genie, or something, are you?"

Cullen simply smiled. "Or something. It is true I've sought you out because you hold something very powerful. The locket. And I'm prepared to grant you a wish in exchange for it." He flicked his gaze upward, locking it unflinchingly with hers. "What I am is a vampire."

Angel leaned back from him, folding her hands tightly together on the countertop. "Vampire." She rolled her eyes and sighed. "You know that pickup line is for someone half my age, don't you?"

"Not from where I'm standing. Being two hundred years old can warp your sense of age slightly. And it does not change the matter. I can offer you your fondest wish. The man of your dreams and a lifetime of good fortune or immortality."

"Immortality without love sounds pretty…empty. And just because I like someone doesn't mean it would work out between us, but a lifetime of good fortune sounds good." She paused for a moment, nibbling her lip in a most distracting manner that caused Cullen to wonder what it would feel like to kiss Miss Angelica Edwards perfectly senseless. "What if I'm not interested in either?" she said quietly.

Cullen kept his face neutral although he felt like frowning. "Everyone around you is striving to stay looking young. Diet. Exercise. Are you absolutely sure you wouldn't like to just have all those things, endless youth and beauty, with all the cheesecake you could want and without a gym membership?"

Angelica bit her lip, her even white teeth sinking into the fleshy, rose-colored softness. Temptation, even more encouraging, hope, flared to life in her eyes. "And in exchange I sell you the locket, is that it?"

"Are you willing to trade?"

Angelica's eyes narrowed slightly. She tucked a strand of her glorious chestnut-colored locks behind the dainty shell of her ear, stirring the air with her scent. Honeysuckle and the silky spice of warm, female skin. Thirst gripped Cullen with a raw need.

"Trade, huh?" she said, her tone faraway, as if she were deep in thought.

Cullen smiled and took a sip of his coffee, the warm, fragrant brew swirling over his tongue. It did nothing to abate the parched sensation in his throat. He should savor this moment. He'd never gotten as far as this with the others, but it was difficult when his concentration was slipping. Angelica distracted him on more than one level.

"And what do you get out of this deal?"

Her question took Cullen off guard. He smiled, hoping to distract her as much as she was distracting him from his mission. "Who says I'm in this for me? Perhaps I'm just fated to find you. Perhaps the locket is your lucky charm." From the curiosity sparking in her cinnamon-colored eyes, perhaps he had a chance at victory after all.

Chapter 4

There was no way Angel believed he was a vampire. They didn't exist. But he was gorgeous, obviously well-off, and he was at least interested in antiques, unlike Alex. She smothered the urge to burst out laughing at the absurdity of his offer. Eternal youth. A relationship with the man of her dreams. Good luck. No one could offer such things.

It wasn't that she was a glass-half-empty kind of person. It was more that she was simply practical. Life was what it was. It wasn't going to get better. Her mother wasn't going to come back. If she were lucky, in ten, maybe fifteen years, she could save enough to do some of the traveling she'd always dreamed of, but dreaming beyond that was foolish.

She peered up at the man across from her. He'd purchased more antiques than she normally sold in a month, and he was trying to get her to believe he was something out of this world. Offering her things he couldn't possibly deliver to get her attention. Why?

Even with her mother's note, Angel was skeptical. People just didn't drop out of nowhere offering you things without wanting something in return. "First things first. I don't believe in vampires. And even if you were a vampire, the answer would still be no."

He pinned her with a gaze that held her immobile like a rabbit too stunned to move in the presence of a predator. "And what if you're wrong? What if vampires are real?"

"It would take a lot of convincing, and I'm a bit on the practical side."

"And if I could convince you?"

Angel cupped her hands around the warm cup of hot chocolate she'd left on the counter and stared down into the soft brown depths, swirled with the remains of white whipped cream. Her mother had warned her about Cullen, without naming him. *A man will come asking for the locket. He'll offer you a choice of a lifetime, but whatever you do, don't give him the locket. It's your key to keeping the good luck he'll grant you...* She peered up at him, masking her features so she wouldn't betray herself. "I don't think you could."

"That sounds like a challenge."

Angel pulled his receipt out of the receipt book and handed it to him. "It was nice meeting you, Cullen. Give me your address, and I'll make sure everything reaches you safely by next week."

He drew his dark brows together. "Wait. I've scared you, haven't I?"

Not hardly. If anything he'd scraped along a raw

nerve. She had a taste of being truly alone and didn't like it, and then out of nowhere comes a guy who's not just perfect but *too* perfect. As if someone had carved out the thoughts in her brain and sculpted them into the person standing across from her. Angel shrugged. "No, really. It's more that I just don't believe in fairy tales. You're not a vampire, a genie or Prince Charming. And I'm just not that lucky."

It was time for him to go. The more time she spent with Cullen, the further she sunk into an impossible fantasy where she could see herself with someone like him. She pushed back from the counter and walked around it, making a beeline for the front door, but Cullen grabbed her hand. That electric arc of awareness she'd experienced when he'd shaken her hand shot up her arm again, this time more powerfully as his skin touched hers. Angel gasped, then locked gazes with him.

"Who are you? Really?"

With the force of a lightning bolt, Cullen realized something. Angelica wasn't going to give him the locket in exchange for a gift, nor was she going to make her wish. He was going to have to do something he'd never had to before.

He was going to have to woo her.

Marie's words echoed in the back of his skull. *When de time come and you can truly love in return, you'll have but one chance to make tings right, Cullen.*

Perhaps he'd been going about this locket business all wrong for generations. He'd thought getting the woman to fall in love with him had been his key. But then, that didn't make any sense. To regain his soul, Marie expected *him* to fall in love? Was that even possible? For so long he'd been fixated on getting the last remaining vestige of his soul back from the locket that he hadn't contemplated an existence beyond that moment.

Cullen pulled Angelica closer. "If I can prove to you I'm speaking the truth, and it's not just some elaborate pickup line, will you reconsider my offer?"

Angelica pulled her hand from his grasp and tucked it in the crook of her arm as she crossed them over her chest. "You'd have to be pretty convincing. I'm not promising anything, but I'll at least think about it."

He stood and held out his large hand to her. "I'll need to hold your hand."

Angelica peered at his hand for a moment. Cullen's chest contracted with discomfort, unsure of her response. He could think of only one thing that would convince her thoroughly and gain her trust. He was going to have to show her what it meant to be a vampire.

She glanced around, but they were completely alone in her shop. Angelica uncrossed her arms and put her hand into his. Their palms touched, her skin warm and dry against his. Cullen reached down to his core to gather the power to transport them.

The world became a blur around them as they moved. A flash of panic crossed her features. It had been such a long time since he'd transported a mortal, he'd forgotten how unsettling the experience could be. He quickly pulled her into his chest.

"Close your eyes for a moment. It'll help."

She squeezed her eyes tightly shut and shivered against him, placing her cheek against his chest. Even through the bulk of her jacket he could feel the curves of her female form pressed against him. The scent of honeysuckle, intense and alluring and utterly feminine, drifted up from her hair just beneath his chin. His gut contracted in response and his fangs throbbed.

It was a damn good thing transporting only took mere moments. She was already breathing hard and he didn't want her to hyperventilate before he'd even got to show her around. He couldn't wait to see her reaction.

"You can open your eyes now."

Angel blinked. It took only an instant to realize they weren't at Elegant Artifacts anymore. Hell, they weren't even indoors any longer.

Over the mirror surface of the dark water rippled the pale image of a nearly full moon. Dark trees crowded in on either side of a low bank, and the grass—or was it moss?—was springy beneath her feet. The air was warm, almost balmy, and filled with the fetid smell of verdant foliage, stagnant water and damp earth. The chirping chorus of insects was far louder than the crowd at the coffee shop had been earlier. Angel pushed back from him, and rather than maintain his hold on her hand, he let it easily slide from his loose grasp.

Her head spun as she looked around at the unfamiliar surroundings. How had he moved them so quickly to a place that clearly wasn't home? Had he somehow drugged her hot chocolate? It had only seemed like less than a few seconds. Angel balled her hands by her sides and glared at him. "Where are we?"

"You demanded proof." He held out a hand and gestured to the bayou night. "This is the start of our tour. We're in Louisiana. Welcome to Belle Eau, my ancestral home." He gave a slight bow from the waist.

"Loui-Louisiana?" she stammered. The light-headed

feeling came back in a rush and Angel reminded herself to slow her breathing down. "You abducted me."

"You did demand proof. I could hardly reveal myself as a vampire in the coffee shop or at your shop without causing a scene or having you calling the authorities, now, could I?" He peeled off his long, heavy wool coat from his shoulders and folded it neatly over his thick forearm. "I'll be happy to take you back as soon as we've finished with the tour."

Perhaps she ought to take her coat off, too. "How?"

"The same way we arrived here, unless you really want to take a plane back."

She stood up and waved her hands around. "No, how did we get here?"

"We transported. One of the more banal of my skills as a vampire, I assure you, but useful."

"You can just zap from place to place?" The second the words were out of her mouth, she felt ridiculous. Of course he could. He just had with her in tow. Angel shook her head. "This isn't real. None of this can be real. I must have passed out or be dreaming or this is a hallucination."

"We can only transport to places we've been before." He took a step toward her, his hand extended.

Angel immediately backed away a step.

He laughed. "I'm not going to hurt you. I merely wanted to show you what you'd be giving up if you didn't take my offer of immortality."

"You were serious about that?"

"Deadly," he said with a million-watt grin that made her knees weak all over again. "Now, give me your hand. Among other amplified senses, I can see better in the dark than you can, and I'll help you avoid any rodent holes in the field until we can get to the big house."

"Rodent holes?"

"Nutria. Persistent things. Massive orange teeth. Look like a beaver with a rat's tail."

Angel shuddered and took his hand. The last thing she needed was to twist an ankle or get bitten by a beaver-size rat thing. It was pitch-black as they moved away from the edge of the bayou. On the dirt road, the oaks overhead formed a massive canopy, their large branches swathed with hanging hanks of Spanish moss.

Beyond the swamp odor of the bayou, she picked out the scents of wet wool, from his coat and her own, and the spicy, aromatic hint of cloves. Angel glanced at him. While he hadn't asked her permission to bring her here, she had asked for proof. And while Cullen was a stranger, she felt herself compelled to hold on to him in the unfamiliar surroundings.

"Belle Eau. Sounds old."

Cullen chuckled. "It all depends on who you're talking to. To me, it's simply home. My family plantation." He glanced at her, his eyes bright twin sapphires in the dark of the night. "To you and the local historical society, yes, it's old. Since you were kind enough to show me your shop, I thought you might enjoy viewing my collection."

Deep in her chest, a warmth unfurled. He'd been thinking about her interests when he'd chosen to bring her here. Her interests weren't even on Alex's radar. Cullen didn't think antiques were just old junk. He understood her passion and shared in it.

They strolled along the dirt road in the moonlight, the white shell path crunching beneath their feet. A light breeze ruffled through the leaves and tousled the edges of his neatly cut hair. He didn't look like a vampire. Far from it. But then, there wasn't any way she could explain how he'd zapped them from one place to another, so she was willing, at least at this point, to reserve her judgment.

"Have you lived here your whole life?"

He nodded, holding his coat over his arm and placing his other behind his back as they walked. "Well, nearly my whole life. We only came here during the summers at first, but once my nurse took sick with yellow fever, we remained here."

"Were you alive before the Civil War?"

He smiled. "Oh, yes."

"And you don't have a problem with me being a Yankee?" she teased.

He laughed softly. "Time gives you the luxury of learning which things are important. Right now you're neither Yankee nor mortal to me, but simply my beautiful guest for the evening."

Perspiration gathered on her skin, and Angel realized she was far too warm. She pulled off her wool jacket and tucked it over her arm, just as he had.

Curiosity won out over trepidation. "So, what else can vampires do?"

Cullen slid a gaze in her direction and gave an enigmatic smile. "Now you believe me?"

Angel shrugged. "Not completely, but I'm willing to consider it a possibility. It explains the…" She flitted her hands about. "You know…beam-me-up-Scotty thing."

He chuckled. "You're very much a see-it-to-believe-it person, aren't you?"

She twisted the chain holding the locket around her

fingers. "Let's just say I don't trust everything people tell me."

"Other powers…" he mumbled as he kicked a rock and sent it skittering down the road in front of them. "What kinds of powers were you thinking of?"

Angel swiveled her head, gazing at the dark woods around them. "Well, obviously you got us here. That's not in the movies. So, what else can you do?"

"We can flux."

She frowned in confusion.

"Turn invisible for a time."

"How?"

Cullen shrugged. "We blend in with the air around us. Really that's about as technical as I can be."

Well, that was no help at all. She still didn't see how he'd done it. "But what do you do—is it some sort of spell or something?"

He shook his head. "Frankly I discovered it myself quite by accident. A fire-and-brimstone traveling preacher came at me with a stake, and I simply fluxed and stepped out of the man's way. I looked down to see that I couldn't view my own hands or any of my own body, for that matter."

"I can see where that might come in very handy, especially if you were trying to sneak out on a girl the morning after a one-night stand."

Cullen stopped midstride and pressed a hand over his heart. "I'm crushed you think so little of me."

Angel slid him a sideways glance. She might have believed him if it weren't for the coy smirk that played along his well-formed mouth. "I doubt that. If you're as old as you claim to be, I'm sure you've had a fair share of women trailing after you."

Regardless of her words, Angel decided to just go along for the ride, however short or long it lasted. For once, she would try to enjoy herself.

Chapter 5

They rounded the bend in the road and the massive front of the plantation house came into view. Two-story and square, its row of columns formed stark white bones. The dark windows looked out from the red brick-work—almost like empty eyes with no soul.

"It looks frighteningly beautiful to you, doesn't it?"

His words echoed her thoughts. Angel stared at him for a moment. How had he done it?

"I'm not frightened," she lied. It was more of a half-truth, really. She wasn't frightened, just wary. Cautious. Who knew if the floorboards were too rotten to walk on and might give way or if the old lath-and-plaster ceilings would cave in? No. That wasn't what scared her. No one knew where she was. He could do anything to her, and no one would ever know. A full-body shiver traveled from her head to her toes, and she slowed down.

"You're shivering."

"Temperature change," she muttered. "Are you sure it's safe?"

He laughed. "I assure you, my home is hardly in disrepair. In fact, once I light a few candles, you might find it quite—"

"Romantic?"

His eyes sparkled. "I was going to say *endearing,* but if you prefer *romantic,* I'll go with that."

As they mounted the wide set of steps leading to the portico, the double doors swung wide open on their own. Angel gasped.

"Sorry, I do tend to have a bit of dramatic flair in me. Probably the Irish side coming out. Welcome to my home." He snapped his fingers and the house came ablaze with light. Hundreds of candles, some in chandeliers, others in wall sconces, gave a warm glow to the sand-colored marble floor in the entryway. It was streaked with veins of rust-red and white. Just ahead of them stood a black table, liberally adorned with golden filigree embellishments and topped with a huge blue cut-crystal vase of enormous pure white Casablanca lilies. Their heady, sweet fragrance increased with the heat of the candles. A heart-shaped, double curving staircase swung upward, and the two staircases joined at a central landing overlooking the entry hall.

Everything looked pristine, as if the cleaning staff had only been there minutes before. The black banister gleamed, and nothing marred the yellow watered silk on the walls.

"It's like, like a…"

"Mausoleum?" he suggested.

"I was thinking more like a museum. It's beautiful. I haven't seen anything like it."

A fierce gleam of pride filled his eyes, his shoulders pulling back a tad more. "I've never brought anyone here before."

Angel didn't know if she believed that or if it was the Irish blarney in him making an appearance.

"Where shall we start?"

"Start?"

"You are here for a full tour, are you not?"

A giddy sense of delight made her limbs tingle. "Yes!"

"Here—let me just get rid of our coats and we shall begin." He lightly pulled her jacket off her arm and together with his tossed it off to the side where they disappeared in a poof of smoky particles.

"No way. Now how did you do that?"

"Materializing objects. Another useful, if somewhat boring, skill. A vampire simply concentrates the energy at their core and either calls the object into being or dissipates it."

"Will I get my coat back?"

"Oh, most certainly. That is, if you want to leave." His words sent a tremor through her, causing her belly to swoop and tighten. Everything Cullen said and did was sexy times three with whipped cream and a cherry on top. He just did something that managed to turn all her good common sense inside out and upside down.

"How about the parlor or the dining room? Shall we start there?" Angel mutely nodded, still too stunned to get the words to form properly with her tongue. He grasped her hand in his, sending another shock of awareness into her system of not only how right her hand felt in his but how much she liked him holding her hand.

Chapter 6

Each room was more spectacular than the last. Hanging on the damask-covered walls, and grouped on exotic handcrafted wooden tables, were precious works of art and priceless museum-quality antiques spanning centuries. The luxurious burgundy wool carpets were thick and plush beneath her feet, covering gleaming, highly polished wide-plank wood floors. And every shiny surface reflected their passage down the long hallway. There was no indication in the massive house that anyone else was present.

A frisson of alarm reminded her once again that she was alone with a stranger, thousands of miles away in a place that no one would think to look for her. And yet, foolishly she felt no fear, only a rising excitement as she followed Cullen from room to room.

"That enormous, ornate glass monstrosity once belonged in the palace of the Medicis," Cullen said, a tinge of pride to his voice. They both gazed at the elegant curves and fantastic hues in a handblown Venetian chandelier crafted to look like a twist of vines, leaves and flowers. His comment was an understatement that hardly conveyed the chandelier's delicacy and beauty.

Cullen didn't seem to be one to exaggerate anything. In fact, if anything he undersold the qualities of what he talked about, which made her think. If he truly believed the locket was important enough to offer a half million for it, perhaps she ought to take him seriously and find out why it was worth that much for him to possess it. Not that she was tempted—even for a million—but curiosity ate at her.

"I have to confess I'm a bit envious," Angel said softly. "Your collection is very impressive." She glanced at his profile. Cullen was handsome, but he was masking something deeper. Like his collection, he kept the truth about himself hidden. While he'd told her he was a vampire, he was still keeping something else from her. Something that mattered more to him than revealing who and what he was.

He caught her staring at him. "Not nearly as impressive as the gardens. But it is difficult to fully appreciate them in the dark."

"Could we go and see them anyway?"

Cullen gave her a genuine smile. "Of course."

Angel couldn't help but return his smile. He took her hand in his and led her through a set of French doors and down the stone steps of the veranda. They meandered along the graveled paths until they came to an ancient magnolia tree with a marble bench at its base. Moonlight filtered through the leaves, creating dapples of shadow even in the darkness. The warm night air was rich with the heavy, sweet scent of orange blossoms.

"This is one of my favorite spots in the garden. From here you can see the sun rise over the water."

Angel tilted her head. "I thought vampires burned up in sunlight."

Cullen shook his head. "Just a fabrication of the entertainment industry. If we did burn in sunlight, we'd never be able to blend into the population so well. It simply gives us a headache if we're out in it too long without eye protection. Why else do you think it's fashionable to wear big sunglasses in Hollywood?"

They sat on the marble bench in the garden. The tinkle of the water from the fountain spilling into the reflection pool below blended with the crickets in a kind of magical music.

It all seemed very lonely to Angel: the enormous museum-like house that looked as if no one lived there, the big wide bed that no one slept in, the bench on which they sat, which was perfect for two. What was the point of living an eternity if you were doomed to end up alone anyway? Her heart squeezed in discomfort. Cullen might be smooth and charming, but he had to be lonely. Damn lonely. Angel couldn't believe it, but she actually felt sorry for the vampire.

"Belle Eau is amazing."

"Thank you," he said softly. "It's been a long time since I've shared it with anyone who could appreciate it as I do."

"You truly do love it here, don't you?"

"It was my last mortal home."

"Is that why you like antiques, because they remind you of a happier time?"

He leaned forward, bracing his elbows on his knees, and stared at his clasped hands for a moment. "I enjoy them because they are beautiful, like you."

Part of Angel wanted to be flattered, but the cautious part of her wanted to know what he was hiding and couldn't let the matter rest. "What was your life like before you became a vampire?"

"Really nothing of consequence," he said ruefully and with self-deprecating charm. "A rural plantation owner steeped in his own amusements and convinced of his superiority."

She looked at his aristocratic profile limned by the dappled moonlight and asked softly into the breeze, "And who changed that?"

He whipped his head up to face her, his eyes narrowing. "You're a perceptive little thing, aren't you?"

Angel shook her head. "No. I just know how to spot heartbreak when I see it."

His lips thinned. "Not so much heartbreak as a rude awakening."

"So, there was someone who escaped even your powers of seduction?"

He leaned back, sliding his hand about her wrist. "Is that what I am doing, seducing you?" His thumb rubbed an arc along the sensitive underside of her wrist.

Angel liked this teasing side of him. "You're changing the subject and it won't work. You'll find I can be very determined."

"Very well." He didn't move his hand, but continued to stroke her wrist, making the throbbing sensation spread out along every nerve ending. "Just be aware I can be as equally determined."

He was close enough that Angel could see the flecks

of silver in his blue eyes. He was close enough to kiss. All she had to do was lean in to feel him. Her skin tightened and heat threaded through her veins.

Angel dropped her gaze, letting it linger on his mouth. What happened when one kissed a vampire? Didn't their fangs get in the way? Every time he'd smiled, his teeth had been white and even, perfectly normal. "Do you have fangs?"

He chuckled. "Would you like to see exactly what I've got?" His keen gaze gave her the distinct feeling of being mentally undressed. Angel shivered in response, but nodded, curiosity beating out fear.

It didn't take all that much to release his fangs. Just being around Angelica was arousing enough to make his gums throb. Her elevated heart rate and pounding pulse were only more of a tease. The fact was he'd been holding them back for the better part of the evening for fear of scaring her.

Cullen released his fangs. They slide down easily, with the familiar audible *flick,* the tips digging into his lower lip. An aching thirst started in the back of his throat.

Angelica gasped, her free hand covering her open mouth. She slowly dropped it back down to her side. Cullen moved his hand away from hers, unsure of her reaction. Was she afraid of him now? That would delay his plan.

"Do you mind if I touch them?"

Cullen found her curiosity, rather than outright repulsion, quite endearing. But it was dangerous, not just for her, but for them both. The temptation to feed was too great.

For a second, he hesitated. Fangs were incredibly sensitive. The sensation of her stroking them would be just as potent as if he'd unzipped his pants and let her touch his shaft. Considering how long it had been since he'd had any real connection to a woman beyond the physical, he wasn't sure he'd be able to contain his rising blood lust. "Probably better you don't. I haven't eaten in a while," he murmured.

"They're a lot bigger than I thought they'd be."

"It's all proportional, I assure you." Inwardly Cullen laughed. If things went as intended, he'd be showing her a lot more than just his fangs.

Angelica nibbled at her lip. "So, you really are a vampire, then?"

"Fangs and all."

She pulled a waxy green leaf from the nearby foliage and smoothed it between her fingers. "How'd you get to be one?"

Bitter bile welled up in the back of Cullen's throat, turning his thirst sour. He didn't want to talk about Marie, not now, and especially not with Angelica. He wanted to be able to place all his focus on her to ensure the seduction took. "In the usual ways, I suppose."

She frowned. "That's it?"

"That's all I can tell you at the moment."

"So, someone bit you."

A heavy silence fell between them, pulsating in the velvet depths of the night like a heart. He didn't answer. He couldn't. Not if he didn't want to give himself away.

"Have you ever turned anyone else into a vampire?"

Now, that was outright laughable. Cullen had never gotten the chance. First, he had no idea what ingredients Marie had used to concoct the potion that changed him. Second, after forty years on his own, he'd been elated to find that there actually were other vampires around, but he'd been ostracized by them. The local vampire clan could not plainly identify his maker within their ranks. He'd been left summarily alone to figure out what his powers were and how to use them. Turning others into vampires had been too low on his list of priorities for him to care. What he needed to do was survive and break the curse that held him in perpetual servitude to the locket. "No," he replied.

Angelica locked her gaze with his. "Then how do propose to do it if I decide I want immortality after all?"

"I thought we might discover that together," he said, a husky edge to his voice.

Her skin contracted into goose bumps, and Cullen had the ridiculous urge to smooth them out with his hands. He shouldn't have been so pleased with her reaction—but he was. While it meant he was a step closer to getting her to willingly hand over the locket and regain the life he'd once had, it also meant more than that.

As he stared into her warm brown eyes, a startling thought took root in the back of his mind. What if his original mission had changed? What if he really wanted to have purpose and meaning in his life again?

His heart twisted at the thought of her suffering a fate similar to his, all because of a locket that had to be given to him freely in order to break Marie's curse. Whatever she wished for would not turn out as she expected. That was all he could count on...unless the curse was broken.

The shushing rush of blood beneath Angelica's smooth skin called to him, spiking his hunger and his desire to feed. The pressure in his fangs and his hardening shaft were equal. She enticed him on many different levels.

He leaned in, letting the lush scent of her arouse him further, making the need to feed on her lips just as real, just as potent as the need to feast upon the hot, sweet offering beneath her flesh. Cullen held his impulses in check. He just wanted a kiss. That was all. Just a kiss.

The soft sound of her breath catching as he gently brushed his mouth against hers drove rational thoughts out of his mind. The kiss started out pure enough, but the sweet flavor of cinnamon and chocolate and something that was uniquely Angelica drove through his chest with a pointed need, sharper than any stake.

Even with Marie, while there had been carnal pleasures, there had never been this: the taste of desire born of admiration. Even while he knew he had no business listening in on her thoughts, Cullen could still hear them, loud and clear. She thought him someone special. Totally out of her league.

How very wrong she was on that score. She may have been born with the name Angelica, but truly in all ways, her shortened moniker fit her. She was to him an angel. Pure. Lovely. Ethereal.

It was not he who was beyond her touch, but completely the opposite. She was lush beauty. Vibrant. Alive.

Angel leaned into him, her full breasts and soft curves pressing into his chest, her arms twining about his neck like a determined kudzu vine. The kiss turned deeper, and with every fresh taste of her, he found his thirst grew more persistent.

* * *

Angel had never been kissed like this. Cullen did more than arouse her—he tore into her very fantasies, making the line between imagination and reality blur and fuse into one.

Every touch of his sure, firm hands on her kicked up her need another notch. The way he cupped her breasts and teased them, the way he pulled her onto his lap and hugged her close, made her feel provocative and beautiful. Unlike her make-out sessions with Alex, nothing about this made her feel as if she were trying too hard. It came easily, seamlessly, like breathing, but much more.

He traced kisses along the edge of her jaw and down along the length of her neck, the pressure of his mouth winding up the core of her tighter and tighter. His fangs scraped a path along the curve of her neck and shoulder, making her gasp. His hands slipping around the flair of her hip drew her closer to him, until he'd scooted her onto his lap where his obvious arousal pressed against her hip. Angel writhed, needing release. She was profoundly grateful they were alone, even if they were outdoors.

Cullen pulled back a fraction, fierce desire making his eyes look electric blue. "You know, I realize I was remiss in my tour," he said, need adding a hoarse, rough edge to the Irish lilt of his words. "I never did show you my bedroom."

Angel nipped lightly at his bottom lip, drawing her teeth along the edge of it. He kissed her hard, the power of it stealing away her breath.

Her head buzzed. But the second he broke the mind-blowing kiss, she took a much-needed sip of air. "Are you trying to seduce me, Cullen McCormack?" Even to her own ears, the raw need in her voice was clear.

His eyes gleamed, his grip on her bottom tightening. "Absolutely."

Chapter 7

It was insane. They'd only met hours before, but in that short time Angel felt closer, more connected, to Cullen than any man she'd ever met. He understood what made her tick, was funny and kind and yet, at the same time, a man used to getting precisely what he wanted.

And he'd made it plain he wanted her.

His hands curved around the small of her back and his lips pressed a kiss to her forehead. "Close your eyes," he whispered against her skin. And when she did, he kissed each closed eyelid, as well.

Angel cupped the back of his head in her hand, making sure he didn't go anywhere until she got another kiss on the lips. The instant his mouth met hers, there was a momentary swooping sensation, a downward plunge on a roller coaster. She gasped and trembled in his hold.

And then the sensation was gone. And so was the hard marble bench on which they'd sat.

She snapped her eyes open to find herself inside an enormous candlelit bedroom, sprawled in the center of a four-poster bed. Each heavy, intricately crafted dark wood pillar appeared to have been carved out of the trunk of its own tree. Swaths and folds of heavy burgundy damask, rich and opulent, created a partially open curtain around the bed. Cullen took her with him as they landed on the soft mattress, and she welcomed the weight of his body as he held her against the cool linen sheets.

"You really don't waste any time when you want something, do you?"

Eyes gleaming, he chuckled softly and pushed aside strands of hair from her cheek. The seductive smile that curved his lip made her want another kiss. "All I've ever done is waste time. Waiting for it to be right. Waiting to understand what it all meant. Waiting for you."

His fingers traced a path from the center of her palm, up her wrist and the sensitive bend of her elbow, to her shoulder and neck until his thumb traced the sweep of her bottom lip. Every cell in Angel's body shivered in unison.

"Since you've never been with a vampire before, there are things you should know." He kissed her deeply, his fangs lightly abrading her bottom lip even as his tongue slid seductively along hers.

Angel was panting, her body hitting a fevered pitch as he pressed his weight against her, and she felt his knee come up between her legs. "First, blood lust and physical desire are two halves of the same coin. I will not feed from you unless you permit it, but it brings a change in the experience for both of us."

She nodded mutely as he began to kiss a heated path

down her neck and between her breasts. "Second, the mortal body might be limited, but the mortal mind is not. And when you take a vampire for a lover, there's no reason to limit yourself. There may be only one me and one you, but there are infinite ways I can pleasure you."

Angel writhed, grasping handfuls of the velvet coverlet and linen sheets in her fists. "Anything else?" she panted, heart manic, senses reaching near overload.

He raised himself up on his elbow and gave her a heated look that stole her breath. "Yes. I'd like to watch you undress."

A sudden rush of insecurity hollowed out Angel's chest. It was one thing to kiss in the darkness of the garden, where he could feel but not see her. It was another to strip, knowing what it would expose. "I don't think—"

He pressed a finger to her lips. "You don't have to. Let your limitations go. You will do things with me that you've never done with anyone before. Just accept that and you'll enjoy it even more."

"You zapped us here from the garden. Why can't you just zap away my clothes, as well?" she persisted.

His hot gaze bored into hers. "Because I want to watch you being unwrapped, like a gift."

Angel nodded and he kissed her deeply again. He shifted his weight when he broke the kiss and pulled her to a sitting position. Faster than she could blink, he'd moved to a chair across the room by the door. She keenly felt the loss of his firm body next to hers.

"How'd you get over there?"

He shrugged. "We move faster than the mortal eye can track, but right now that's not important. What's more important is that I stay here and you stay there,

so I'm not tempted to help you. Take off the shoes and
sweater first."

That wasn't so bad. She'd still have her shirt, leggings, bra and panties on. Angel pulled off each of her
ankle boots, letting them fall with a *thump* to the floor,
then pulled off her socks. She grasped the edge of her
V-neck sweater at her waist and pulled it in a slow slide
up and over her head. The buttons on her shirt pulled
tight, nearly popping apart. If she'd had any clue she
was going to be doing a striptease tonight for the sexi-
est man she'd ever met, she would have dressed completely differently.

"It's not what you have on. It's how you take it off,"
he murmured.

Angel narrowed her eyes. "Are you reading my
mind?"

The corner of Cullen's mouth lifted in a way that
made her want to kiss him and never stop. "Now the
leggings."

Angel scooted to the edge of the bed, then stood and
turned her back to him. She reached beneath her shirt at
the hips and slowly pulled the leggings down, bending
at the waist as she slid them down her legs. The sensation of a warm, lingering touch that caressed her from
her ankles, up behind the sensitive part of her knee and
around the inner edge of her left thigh made her gasp.
She twisted around but saw that Cullen was still in the
chair across the room. She could have sworn he'd been
touching her.

He smiled, his fangs indenting the curve of his bottom lip. "The shirt," he said, the deep tone of desire
making his voice husky and betraying how this display affected him.

That knowledge made all the difference. A power-ful warmth blossomed in her belly, not just escalating desire, but the sense that she had power, that he truly found her arousing. "I don't think so."

Angel turned and hooked her fingers into the edges of her panties and slowly slid them down until they were around her ankles. His gaze went from hot to fire-alarm blaze. Angel smiled and, using her foot, flung them at him.

He didn't give any more orders, but she figured she could take it from here. She unhooked her bra, and after pulling the bra out of one sleeve like a magician removing a silk scarf from the wrist of his coat, she flung that at him, too.

Cullen moved to the edge of his chair, the candle-light revealing his jaw ticking as it worked. She moved to take off the locket, the metal warm just above her breasts.

"Leave the locket on." His words were hoarse.

She took her time unbuttoning her shirt. She started at the top. And when she reached halfway, she paused to glance up at him. His eyes had changed from vivid blue to crimson. For a second she was startled by it, but then the female instinct assured her this was him on the edge of his control. Angel couldn't resist the chance to tease him. "Shall I keep going?"

He nodded, but his fingers were gripping the wooden arms of the chair and Angel thought she saw little puffs of dust rise up from each fingertip. While she felt bold, that didn't mean she still wasn't somewhat self-conscious about her shape. She turned, pulling the shirt off her shoulders, and let it slowly slide down until it hit the crook of each arm. The cool air met her exposed skin down to the waist, and Angel shivered.

She felt his warm hands cup her breasts. His stubbled jaw abraded her skin as he rained kisses upon her neck and mouth, breasts and thighs, that left her stunned and speechless. How on earth was he doing it? He wasn't even physically touching her.

"My gods, you are beautiful." Cullen sounded both in awe and in pain.

She glanced at him over her shoulder. "You don't need to flatter me."

In a flash of movement, he was there beside her, his very real hands brushing the shirt from her arms and letting it flutter to the floor as he hugged her to him, pressing the back of her against the rock-solid front of him.

"You are a treasure. A gift. Flattery would be meaningless next to such glorious truth." He leaned in, tracing kisses up from her shoulder to the sensitive spot beneath her ear as his hands skimmed over her body. But it wasn't just his two hands she felt. It was more. Way more. Through her passion-induced haze, she could count six, maybe eight, and at least three mouths. Suddenly she felt the sensation of fingers skimming along her cleft and kneading her bottom that left her aching. Angel rocked against the sensation, desperate for release.

A fine golden shimmer like the bubbles in champagne fizzed through her body, making her absolutely giddy. For the first time in her life, Angel felt not just attractive, but beautiful, worshipped.

She turned in his arms and kissed him, putting every new emotion coursing through her into it, as if this were the first kiss, and the last kiss, of her life.

He scooped her easily into his arms as if she were no more than the weight of a doll. "What is your favorite flower?" he whispered as he nuzzled her hair and kissed her thoroughly.

"Honeysuckle," she replied, barely able to catch her breath. "Why?"

He lay her down on the coverlet, and out of thin air a shower of pale blossoms, in shades of peachy-pink to deep yellow, began to drift down over her, their heady, sweet fragrance filling the air. A bubble of laughter welled up in Angel's throat. "Are you sure I'm not dreaming?"

He quirked one brow upward. "If you were, would you want it to stop?"

Angel bit her lip and shook her head. "But if this were a dream, I do know that I wouldn't be the only one without any clothes on."

Cullen gave her a grin as sexy as hell, complete with fangs. "My lady's wish is my command."

The second she got a chance, she was going to test out his comment about fang sensitivity and see if they really were an erogenous zone for vampires.

In a swirl of dark particles, his clothing evaporated, leaving him gloriously naked. Every ridge and ripple of muscle gleamed in the glow of the candlelight. Angel's breath caught in her throat. Holy hell. He looked even better than she'd imagined. And she had one damn fine imagination. He was every fantasy she'd ever had rolled into one seriously hot guy.

* * *

Cullen was almost at the end of his rope. The only thing keeping him sane was the fact that he could mentally make love to her even as he physically bided his time, waiting until she was ready.

He didn't want there to be any hesitation. No worry or fear or doubt about how truly beautiful she was to him. With her soft, silky pale porcelain skin and full, feminine curves, she was the picture of the perfect aristocratic woman from when he'd been young.

When he took her, he wanted it to be the singularly most powerful moment of her life, leaving her feeling as if she was the one calling the shots. Because she was, in more ways than she could possibly know.

Bracing the weight of his body with his hands, he positioned himself above her and indulged himself in the kisses that made his fangs and his shaft ache so damn hard he thought he might implode. Mortals were such fragile things, and Angel was far more tempting than he'd anticipated. The locket's golden glow just above the creamy expanse of her breasts reminded him he had other obligations, but he shoved those aside. Right now all that mattered was her.

The sweet confection of willing woman, hot with need and steeped in fragrant honeysuckle, filled his senses. Her kisses were wanton, lovely, totally uninhibited. But when she stroked one of his fangs with her tongue, he lost it and let the pleasurable torture continue until she broke away to take a breath.

Her eyes were luminous and her skin flushed, taunting him with the sweet blood simmering in her veins. He watched the artery at her throat jump beneath the creamy expanse of her skin. "Angel, will you let me taste you?"

Her bee-stung mouth, rosy and swollen from their kisses, curved into a come-hither look that stripped him of any remaining good sense. "Yes," she moaned.

She tilted her head to the side, exposing her neck. As she arched up against him, her skin felt slick with perspiration and feverish to the touch.

Cullen was lost. In one movement he plunged into her and began drinking from her vein, as well. The rich sweetness, like a floral honey, seeped into his mouth, the life force of it vibrant and alive just like its maker.

The soft, needy noises Angel made belied the fierce grip she had on him, her nails scoring his skin. She met him, taking from him even as he took from her. Somehow, in the midst of madness and pleasure that made him blind with the force of it, something soft and subtle crept in.

And as he held her in his arms, her cheek on his chest, the tangle of her hair against his face, Cullen realized he'd never felt at peace like this before. She shifted position, curling her soft body about him, and the smooth metal of the locket burned a path across his skin.

The locket. The key to a future where they could both be free—where they could both be together, if that was what she wanted. He hated to leave the moment, but he knew the clock on his chance to change their future was still ticking.

"Angel," he said softly. She stirred. Cullen let his fingers skim through her tousled hair. "Angel, it's time to go."

"No," she mumbled, snuggling closer.

Cullen kissed the top of her head. "I don't want to go, either, but we have no choice. You still have your wish to make before the sun rises."

"I wish I could be with you," she mumbled, her words tainted with the soft singsong quality of sleep to them.

Cullen froze.

Her wish.

He could not undo it. Not once it was spoken.

And never had a wish turned out well. The locket saw to that. He held her close and kissed her hair, knowing it was only a matter of time until fate tore her away from him.

Chapter 8

Darkness still claimed the streets of New Harmony. Angel clung to him for a moment, the heat of her body making the honeysuckle fragrance of her much more acute in the cold air.

She tipped her radiant face up at him and smiled in a way that twisted the bitter barb of truth even deeper into him.

"So, now what?" she asked, her voice light and easy.

"Now we wait for your wish to come true."

"My wish?"

"You wished we could be together."

Her eyes narrowed. "Why does it sound like you don't think that'll be a good thing?"

Cullen rubbed his hands on her arms, the red wool of her coat soft beneath his fingers. "What did your mother tell you about the locket?"

Angel fidgeted. "She said that a man would come asking for it and offering me a gift. If I wanted to keep the gift, I had to hold on to the locket. I can only assume she meant you."

Cullen nodded slowly. "What she didn't tell you is that no wish the locket has granted has ever turned out as expected. I wanted immortality, but immortality is an empty shadow of life when you are all alone."

A sad look of empathy flitted across her features. "I never wanted to be alone. I don't see how the locket could make my situation much worse than it is."

Cullen winced. "Trust me. You haven't seen two hundred years' worth of its manipulations."

She gripped the lapels of his coat with her slender hands. "So, my wish about us—it's doomed to failure?"

If he could have asked for the locket outright, he would have, but the conditions Marie had placed on the curse made it impossible.

If you tell her de truth, you try to take the locket, it will cut you down. You will come back, and each time der be a little less of you.

He'd only been foolish enough to try it once. He'd blacked out the minute the words had left his mouth, and when he came to, he'd aged ten years.

He hadn't tried that unfortunate path again. And he certainly wouldn't risk it with Angel. "I may be a vampire, but I can't tell the future. I only know what I've seen. The locket is cursed and I've tried everything to break that curse."

"How do we break it?"

Cullen looked away from her, pain radiating through his chest. He wanted to tell her, God above, did he want to, but he couldn't. "I can't tell you. It's something you have to figure out for yourself."

Angel sighed heavily. "It's just a locket. It can't possibly be this critical to anything." She dug in her purse and pulled out her ring of keys, then flipped through them, searching for the key to unlock the front door of her shop. Daylight was coming. Cullen could feel it in his bones. But there was nothing to be done about it.

Despite everything he'd shown her, everything that had passed between them, Angel had yet to offer him the locket. He was growing less certain that she ever would.

There was passion between them, certainly, but obviously not love. If there had been, then Marie's curse would have been broken. Cullen had to face it: his best efforts weren't good enough. Angel had made her wish, and unless she offered him the locket as well, it would come true with horrible consequences.

A cough sounded nearby, and Cullen gazed at the man hunched into his jacket strolling up the street, his breath a mist in the cold, early-morning air. His gut clenched in warning.

The click of the gun being cocked ricocheted through Cullen's keen hearing. For a moment he considered just ripping the bastard's throat out, but the last thing he needed to do was risk his fragile relationship with Angel by showing her what a monster like himself could truly do. Having her look at him with horror and disgust would be a hell of its own.

He settled for whipping around to face the man and stepping in front of Angel to protect her from whatever the assailant intended. If he got shot, it was no big deal, but if Angel were shot—it could cost him everything.

"What do you want?"

The barrel of the gun glinted in the streetlights. The man's dark eyes sized up Cullen and Angel in mere seconds. He hadn't shaved in several days and his jaw ticked as he clenched his teeth. "Give me your money."

Angel gasped when she saw the gun and clung to Cullen. Cullen hoped the gunman just wanted the cash, and pulling his wallet from his pocket, he took the stack of thousand-dollar bills he'd been prepared to give Angel. "Here. Three hundred thousand dollars. Get lost."

The man grabbed the cash, his eyes fever-bright. The stench of rotten vegetation typical of desperation and the saccharine stink of drugs saturated the air around the man. He waggled the cocked gun at Angel. "Her, too." As she dug in her purse for her wallet, her coat gaped open, revealing the golden locket nestled against the warm skin at the base of her neck.

He saw the thief staring at it. Cullen's gut contracted. *No. Anything but that.*

"Jewelry, too," the thief added with a jerk of his chin.

"You don't want that," Cullen urged, trying to throw a glamour on the man, but he didn't respond.

Angel's numb fingers fiddled with the latch. The chain slowly filled her palm. Cullen could tell she was trying to be brave, but her eyes were too bright, brimming with unshed tears, and the musty scent of sorrow swirled around her.

"You don't have to do this," Cullen growled.

"It's a locket. It's not worth my life. Besides, you said yourself, it's cursed." The heavy sadness cloaking her tone told him that it pained her to let it go. Fire erupted inside of him. He could kill the man. Easily. Swiftly. His fangs ached so badly it made his eyeballs throb.

"You don't understand, Angelica. You need that locket." *I need that locket. We need that locket.* He watched their last chance at being free of the curse fade away as the thief stuffed the wallet and watch in his coat pocket and snatched the locket from her hand before disappearing around the next corner.

Cullen stepped in the direction of the thief. Angel put her hand on his arm, holding him back, her fingers digging in.

"Let it go," she said softly.

It took everything within him to do it. She truly didn't know how much she asked of him, but Cullen gave in to her regardless. He turned and gazed into her face. "Don't you want it back?"

"Of course I do. It was the last thing my mother gave me, but it isn't worth risking our lives."

If she only knew how worthless their lives would now become without the locket, she'd see things completely differently. Cullen held her small hands between his. "I'm not risking death. Let me go and get it back for you. Please."

"Did you see that man's eyes, Cullen, I mean really look at them? He was desperate, not vacant or hard."

"A thief is a thief. I say we track him down anyway. He can keep the money as long as we get your locket back." Cullen looked desperate. For the life of her she couldn't understand why the locket, which had been *her* family heirloom, could mean so much to him.

"Wait a second. It means something to you, doesn't it? That's why the test. That's why the outrageous offer to buy it. Why do you want that locket so badly? I'm not letting you go after it until you tell me the truth."

Cullen growled and turned, pacing the length of the sidewalk. "Why can't you just believe me?"

"I need more than that. You owe me more than that."

He raked his fingers through his hair, making his polished appearance suddenly more chaotic. "Do you remember the bad relationship I said changed me?"

"Yes."

"She did more than change me into a vampire. She stole part of my immortal soul. She bound it into that locket. If I don't help you get it back, I may never—"

"Never what?"

"Never have a chance to be free."

"Free?" Her brow puckered. "Free? Are you telling me this entire thing was just a setup to get that locket back?"

Cullen grimaced. "At first—"

"At first? And what now? Am I still just someone you can dupe into getting what you want? Is that all I am to you?" Deep in her chest her heart splintered. She'd been used by men before, but this was different. Far different. It hurt worse, because some small part of her had begun to love him.

He grabbed her about the upper arm, his blue eyes blazing flame. "No." His fingers tenderly traced through the hair at her temple. "But I don't know what else to do. Everything I am is tied to that locket. And if he sells it or gives it away to another, the curse continues. And I lose you. Plain and simple. I have to go where the locket takes me."

The ache in her chest eased. "You really are like a trapped genie of the lamp, aren't you?"

He nodded, his expression morose. "The price of pissing off a voodoo priestess."

"Why didn't you just take it from me, before you let me fall in love with you?"

"You love me?"

She nodded. "I know it's crazy. But I also know I've never felt like this before." She didn't want to stand in his way, yet the thought of letting him go pierced cold and hard through her chest. Angel rubbed at the soreness just over her heart. All along her common sense had told her it wouldn't last, that there had to be a reason someone like Cullen was interested in her. And now she knew: the locket—just like her mother had said.

He'd sincerely thought about glamouring her and taking the locket. Hardly the stuff of heroes. But when the thief had intervened, his brain hadn't thought past the immediate moment. Protecting Angel had been all that mattered.

She'd been the one to see more in the thief. The desperation and need in the man's eyes. Perhaps that was why she saw the glimmer of a heroic man in him yet. She saw more in him than even he could see in himself.

Cullen tightened his hold on her, afraid that she might slip out of his arms and disappear as quickly as she'd come into his life.

"I can't take it from you. It's part of the curse. It can only be freely given, and once a wish is made, I'm bound to that wish for the lifetime of the owner."

"All this time, you've been trying to get it back to get your soul back, haven't you?"

He nodded. "When you said Belle Eau was lonely, that was an understatement. Immortality long ago lost its luster. Having no one to talk to who shares your passions, no one who cares for you as you do for them is a monotonous existence—a half life, really."

Angel spread her hands along his broad chest, the warmth of her touch seeping into his very bones. She loved him. It was unfathomable.

"Then let's get it back." Determination edged her words in steel.

Cullen sniffed at the cold air. There. A slight whiff of desperation tainted with pain and worry. The thief. He slipped his hand around Angel's and gave it a squeeze.

"Come on, I know where he is."

They walked quickly through the predawn streets of New Harmony. Angel had to practically jog to keep up with his long, quick strides. Her pace grew slower and slower, and Cullen found himself reducing his pace to make it easier for her. But time was running out. Dawn was already changing the dark of night to a lighter blue on the horizon.

By the time the sun rose above the mountain ridge, the magic of the locket would cease, bound up again until it reached its new owner's hands.

He couldn't take that chance. Not when he had more to lose now than he ever had. Before it had only been the last remnant of his immortal soul at stake. Now it was his heart.

Marie's deviousness all of a sudden became so much clearer. Losing what he loved would be far more torture than the loss of his soul. And she'd wanted him to know that feeling.

At that moment Cullen decided he could do anything, be anything to see Angel happy, and if part of that included being with her, so much the better.

They reached the parking lot to the side of a small convenience store on the edge of town. Angel was out of breath and bent double to catch it.

"Are you all right?"

She waved him off. "Go. Get. Him," she wheezed.

But before either of them could move a step, the thief came around the corner of the convenience store, two thin plastic sacks in one hand and a package of diapers under the opposite arm. Not at all what Cullen had expected.

His eyes widened. "You!" He pulled the gun from his waistband and pointed it at them.

"We don't mean you any harm. All we want is the locket back," Cullen said, but clearly the man was too shocked to hear him.

"You don't understand. I'm sorry I robbed you, but I've got no choice. I needed food for my baby, and the locket is going to be a Christmas gift for my wife. I'm not going to jail again. I can't." He held the gun at them, the tip of it shaking.

"You have a choice. We all have a choice. Now, give me the gun."

He took a step toward the man and the thief panicked. His eyes narrowing and his fingers squeezed. *BANG!*

Cullen watched in horrified fascination as he tracked the bullet speeding toward Angel, able to see it with his vampire vision, but powerless to stop it.

"Angel!" He stepped in front of her, taking the hit of the bullet, but it passed through the flesh of his side. She bucked behind him, falling backward, a bright red rose blossoming on her chest, saturating her shirt and the air with the scent of her blood.

Time stilled to impossible, unbearable slowness. Cullen had gotten used to the fact that vampires could move faster, so the lingering moment seemed even more painfully drawn out to him. He heard the skitter of footsteps as the thief ran and the clatter of the gun on the pavement, but all his concentration was locked firmly on Angel as her pulse slowed, filling his ears with the *ka-thunk, ka-thunk, ka-thunk* of her heart. Her skin grew waxen and shiny with perspiration.

There was only one thing he could do.

He crouched down beside her, drawing her into his lap. "Angel, stay with me."

Her frightened eyes bore into his, but when she tried to speak, she coughed, bright red blood staining her lips. She trembled as her body went into shock.

"I'm dying, aren't I?"

As much as it pained him, Cullen answered truthfully. "Yes. But I may be able to help you. Do you still want to be a vampire?"

She nodded. Cullen grabbed her hand and squeezed. "Then just relax. This will be over soon."

She'd already lost so much blood there was no need to nearly drain her. He bent and kissed her neck. Her pulse was thin and thready. He'd never created a vampire before and he hoped like hell he was doing it right. With a flick his fangs descended and he used them to slice across his wrist, letting the thin black ichor that flowed through his veins dribble into her mouth.

Angel coughed against the flow, but drank. Suddenly her eyes bulged and she grew stiff against him.

"Let it pass. The body is fighting to survive."

She grabbed hold of his coat. "Cullen. Save me."

The last few beats of her heart slowed until all he

heard was the faint *ka-thunk, kaa-thunk, kaaaa-thunk,* then stillness.

Slivers of golden light streaked across the sky as dawn broke. She lay still, so impossibly still that Cullen wondered if he'd somehow screwed things up.

"Angel? Angel, can you hear me?"

Angel heard him. She could feel the wool of his coat abrading her cheek, but she was immobile, frozen in her own body, unable to move or speak. Inside her head she screamed in frustration, and Cullen twitched.

Angel, can you hear me? his voice echoed in her head.

Cullen? Cullen! I'm here. I can't breathe! Why can't I move? Why are you talking to me in my head?

Just relax. Give the ichor time to work. You don't need to breathe. You'll be able to move soon enough.

He held her tenderly in his arms as they waited. The sound of sirens came wailing, coming nearer. Someone must have called the police when they heard the gunshot.

Angel winced and found she could blink her eyes.

"Welcome back, beautiful."

It took all the effort she had to turn her head and gaze up at him and smile. Cullen helped her sit up as an ambulance pulled into the parking lot. A flutter of panic lodged in her stomach. They were sure to notice the bloodstained shirt, the hole in her chest and the fact that she had no pulse. *Cullen, what are we going to do?*

Don't worry. I've got this.

She watched as Cullen turned and greeted the paramedics and police officer. He spoke in slow, even tones, and their eyes grew glassy and unfocused. "She has merely gotten grazed by the bullet. It was a random shot."

Angel bit her bottom lip, hoping that whatever he was doing would work. There was enough blood and the placement of the bullet wound right over her chest would easily enough prove everything he'd said was a lie. The paramedics briefly looked her over and seemed perfectly satisfied it was a flesh wound. The police officer took Cullen's statement, and soon enough they were left alone once more.

Cullen wrapped his arm around her waist and pulled her close.

"How on earth did you do that?"

He smiled. "I threw a glamour over them. It's a handy trick I'll have to teach you. Particularly useful when you're in negotiations over a piece you think should sell for more than the buyer is offering. It's one of many new skills I'll teach you."

"But they had to see the huge hole in my chest," she said as she unbuttoned her blouse and pulled back the shirt. Her skin was still smeared with drying blood, but only a small, white scar remained where the bullet had skewered through her. She sucked in a startled breath and stared at him. "It's gone!"

"Being a vampire has its perks."

She frowned slightly. "You said you could call things to you, materialize them."

For a second Cullen hesitated. "Yes."

"How?"

Was she truly ready? "Why?"

"I want to try something." The fierce determination in her eyes convinced him she'd try it whether he explained it or not.

He grasped her hand and cupped it palm upward in his. "First you need to think of the thing you want, picture not just the image of it in your mind, but the essence of it. How it feels or smells, the weight, temperature and texture of it. Let that sensation of the thing start like a heat in your belly and then fill you up."

Angel closed her eyes and concentrated on the locket. The smooth warmth of it. The way it felt against her skin. Until a slow, mellow warmth built in her core then radiated outward, like sunbeams, until her hand grew hot and she could nearly feel the locket in her hand.

"Heaven above. You've done it!"

Angel snapped open her eyes to find the locket safe and sound in her palm.

"I've tried that a thousand times, and the locket would never appear for me."

Angel smiled. "Maybe because you belonged to it, but it didn't belong to you." She slowly let the length of chain slide through her fingers as she let the locket fall and coil into his palm. "But now I give it to you. As a gift and a thank-you for saving my life. You're free now. You can do whatever you want."

The locket shimmered for a moment, a greenish glowing cloud covering both his hand and the necklace. Then, with a burst of light, both the glowing vapor and the locket disappeared.

Angel gasped. "What happened?"

All Cullen could do was smile. He brushed the backs of his fingertips of his other hand across her cheek in a whisper-soft caress that reminded Angel of butterfly wings.

"I believe that means we're free. Both of us."

"So, where will you go?"

"I don't wish to go anywhere without you. You are what I want." He drew close, brushing a light kiss across her forehead. "Now." The next brushed her lips. "Forever." Then he pulled back and smiled. "Always."

Angel wrapped her arms around his waist as she looked into the fathomless blue of his eyes and felt his next kiss all the way down to her toes. The warmth of knowing he loved her just as her, just as she was, wiped away all doubt. Whatever curse had held the locket, and them, the gift of love had set them free.

* * * * *

BRIGHT STAR

Linda Thomas-Sundstrom

To my family, those here and those gone, who always believed I had a story to tell.

Chapter 1

The earthy scent of a pine forest made the December night seem lush. For an immortal with his senses open full throttle, Dylan McCay found the fragrant Christmas tree lot nothing less than a sensory wonderland.

But there was no time to revel in the glories of nature. He had a job to do, and as he waited among the trees silently observing his target, he was surprised by what he found. The woman whose research of the heavens had come too close to the secrets the special beings of his world didn't want exposed wasn't the kind of troublemaker he had gotten used to.

Savannah Clark, PhD, astronomer, up-and-coming researcher into the age of stars, was female and younger than he would have imagined. She was fragile in appearance, almost too ethereal to be such a bother.

Yet her willowy frame housed an incredible intelligence, aided by a dogged persistence that was going to make her famous any day now. And because she was sharper than most of the others in her field, her research had sent up warning flags that had drawn him here from a great distance.

Hello, Savannah.

Tonight, she wore a crimson garment, its color both popular and indicative of the season mortals celebrated in December. Red was a color used to clothe a mythical Santa Claus but also had in its vibration the essence of violence. Red, crimson and scarlet attracted bulls in the Spanish arenas and also lured thirsty creatures out of urban hollows to drink blood from the necks of the innocent.

Savannah Clark was beautiful. She had an oval face and luminous skin. Her fair hair, cut to shoulder length and silky, radiated a golden vitality that stirred in him memories of the sun.

Despite those charms, she had to be stopped from furthering her research. He had to stop her. She was the singular objective for leaving his hundred-year, self-imposed seclusion behind. He just hadn't anticipated how being among so many mortals, after having been distanced from them, would affect him, or that seeing this woman in person might give him pause. He had expected someone older, with an appearance to match. Savannah Clark was light in spirit and fresh-faced.

Who could have predicted that her pert, compelling features would be dominated by large blue eyes and that her movements would be elegant, almost dancelike, when she gracefully raised an arm or turned her head?

Moreover, he was amused by a time that saw women, everywhere he looked, wearing pants. Savannah Clark's pants fit her like a scandalous second skin, showing off every lean angle and feminine curve.

These were details he should not have been noticing in an adversary he had been sent to censure. It was a shame, he thought now, that this fair-haired researcher whose progress on what had become known as the Christmas Star had roused the unwanted attention of his brethren.

I've come for you, Savannah Clark.

Dylan closed his lips over the points of his sharpened incisors that had extended with the first sight of this woman. His attraction had been immediate, as had his sudden curiosity about the sparkling lights and glittering chaos of the season the people around her celebrated. But he couldn't afford to regret what he had to do. His mission was imperative to the well-being of all people in the long run.

If Savannah actually found what she'd set out to find in her system of tracing stars back to their origins, publicizing her findings might end the world as most humans knew it. If mortals found out there were creatures other than themselves populating the earth, panic might ensue.

Given the importance of his task, it was interesting how thoughts of his agenda dimmed somewhat when Savannah Clark suddenly smiled at nothing he could see. That radiant, innocent smile caused the blood in his veins to swell in restless waves.

Her jubilant expression was like an open invitation for someone used to seclusion, and a kind of spiritual food he hadn't realized he hungered for.

Dylan continued to stare.

A few whispered words and a subtle meeting of our

eyes will put an end to this visit and send me back to where I belong. If I move closer to you now, it will be over in seconds, Savannah.

His shoulder blades twitched in anticipation over the time he was taking to accomplish this objective. His goal was to get in, take care of this problem and get out, unnoticed.

But he was…hesitating.

The last time he'd had a similar task, he'd met a crusty celestial heretic named Galileo who had caused all sorts of trouble. How hard could dealing with a young astronomer like Savannah Clark be, no matter how much he respected her accomplishments or appreciated her looks?

What is it about you that stops me from doing my task, I wonder?

He felt close to her intellectually. In following her writings, he had gleaned the way her mind worked. Her more obvious physical attributes would easily cause any male's imagination to spring into overdrive.

No matter what other titles he carried, he was male enough to imagine the warm, flawless skin beneath that red sweater. Beings like himself craved warmth and company above most other things.

Allowing himself another moment of leeway, Dylan pictured Savannah Clark's lush nakedness spread out beneath him on a bed of silk, with her hair fanned out around her like a sun-kissed corona. That image, seared into his mind, caused a flutter inside his chest that made his fangs ache.

Yet personal feelings didn't matter. He was supposed to be miles beyond things like that. All he had to do was take that first step toward Savanna. The rest would be easy. He'd done this before.

But he didn't take that step.

After traveling all this way, and after existing apart from the world of mortals, he suddenly wanted to trespass in their world, a world in which he no longer belonged, for a while longer.

With that extra time, he might find out what had sparked Savannah's interest in the Christmas Star, so that he could watch for that same warning flare of inspiration in others in the future. He might observe how mortals had evolved in their dealings with what were now called *holidays*.

The lights, sights and sounds surrounding him were comforting in a strange way. Everyone here, in this small, roped-off section of a parking lot filled with trees, seemed…happy.

What he felt as he watched Savannah Clark move among the trappings of the season was a rush of pure pleasure. And both heaven and hell knew how long he had been removed from sensations like that, in fact from all feeling, out of necessity.

He wanted to keep looking at her. Surely it was as important for him to understand her research as it was to suppress it?

She turned her head. Several strands of golden hair swung to curtain part of her face. Dylan leaned forward, wanting to catch hold of those golden strands with a need so strong it was accompanied by a sharp, unexpected stab of pain.

He could not touch her. No agenda stretched that far. He wasn't like her, and she most certainly was nothing like him.

But her turn had caused her sweater to open at the collar, revealing a triangle of ivory skin stretched across delicate bones. Above those bones lay an artistic lacing of fine lavender veins.

Dylan's body began to throb, as if he was at war with himself. Waves of pleasure beat at him mercilessly, when Savannah Clark had no right to affect him in any way. The spark inside her that signaled her life force was a difference too vast to be breached. The loss of his spark was just a memory.

Before realizing that he had moved, Dylan took a step toward her.

"Perhaps you," he said as he continued to watch Savannah, flashing his fangs briefly, "hold the key to this mysterious lapse in behavior."

In fact, he was almost sure that she did.

And what self-respecting being of any kind didn't like the challenge of a good mystery to solve, now and then?

Moving to the opposite side of the seven-foot Douglas fir that she had chosen to take home, Savannah gave the handsome stranger in the next aisle a covert sideways glance.

Though she liked what she saw, she knew it wasn't advisable to talk to, or stare at, strangers. Even if this guy had the "it" factor in spades.

He had a towering presence, broad shoulders and dark brown hair reaching to the chin of a face that seemed unusually pale in the moonlight, even for December. The whiteness of his skin stood out in the night like a star would among the dark heavens. And

once she made that kind of analogy—star, heavens—
Savannah was entranced.

"Of course," she muttered, "looks can be deceiving."

Still, she was willing to bet that someone so delicious would be good in bed, though fantasies like that were futile. She wouldn't have known what to say if he walked right up and spoke to her. Astronomers were geeks. Most of her time was spent alone, with a computer and a world-famous telescope.

All she knew about were stars. All she really cared about were stars. *So, you,* she wanted to tell the guy who had given her heart a jump start from a distance, *are a nonissue, and nothing for me to lose sleep over.*

In afterthought, she added, *Although I actually did wish upon a star tonight for a partner, companion, lover and mate, only hopeless romantics and idiots believe that a star can listen, let alone help that wish along.*

Wrapping both hands around the trunk of her tree, Savannah smiled wistfully at it. "It's just you and me, tree."

"Can I help with that?" someone behind her asked.

She turned toward whoever had made the offer. "Sure. Thanks. Help would be appreciated."

Blinking, her eyes came level with the top button of a dark coat. Without having to look up, her body issued a warning alert. *Can't be him. Not that guy.* She hadn't even seen him move.

It was that guy, though, not only two heads taller than she was, but oozing an overt masculinity that triggered an unusual rumbling sensation deep inside her.

"This tree is quite a bit taller than you are," he said in a voice that was deep, husky and sexy as hell. "I've been wondering how you were going to move it."

Being unused to people invading her personal space, Savannah found his closeness, after all those renegade wishes, unusually intimate. Stepping back, feeling a flush rise up her neck, she said, "It is rather large, isn't it? Still, if my ceiling was any higher than eight feet, I'd opt for something from the next row over."

Her heart was thumping monstrously.

"There are hundreds of trees here. How did you choose this one out of so many?" he asked politely.

"It spoke to me."

She glanced up to see if he smiled, and continued, "I guess it just comes down to personal taste. I like my trees fresh and fluffy. Some people prefer a leaner, more modern, less branchy aesthetic."

She sounded too much like a scientist. "On a more metaphysical note, maybe there is only one tree meant for me here, and I somehow magically found it. That explanation would be more in keeping with the spirit of the season, I'm thinking."

"So," he said, nodding slowly, "could it be said that a holiday tree from a place like this one should match a person's personality in some way, in order to be a perfect fit?"

"Are you saying I'm fluffy?"

"I'm merely trying to understand your interest in this particular tree and what made you smile when you found it."

He had been watching her, too. The realization caused the heat of a rising flush to reach her cheeks.

"It's a pretty tree," Savannah said. "I liked it. Simple as that, if you don't believe in trees actually speaking to people."

"Well, I like it, too," he agreed. "This was a good choice. I suppose admitting that says something about me?"

"Fluffy," Savannah said. "Totally. Sorry to be the one to deliver that news."

He grinned. When he leaned forward, Savannah allowed herself to imagine for one odd, highly electrifying moment that he was going to kiss her, unwarranted and out of the blue. But that turned out to be pure delusion on her part. The man beside her merely pressed a stray strand of her hair back from her face with his gloved hand, in a gesture as personal as any kiss would have been.

Struggling to speak, not sure how to respond, she said, "I can find another Christmas tree. If you'd like to keep this one, it's yours."

The object of her illicit desire was silent for a moment. Maybe he wasn't used to generosity and unselfishness in the season of giving, but the offer made her feel good. She'd give him the tree and that would be that, in spite of the warm current saturating the air between them.

"I wouldn't think of taking your tree," he finally said. "Thank you for the offer, though. It's kind of you to want to share the tree that spoke to you."

"Well, two kindnesses in one Christmas tree lot has to be some sort of record," she remarked. "I'm thinking win-win, right? Maybe score some points with the jolly old elf himself?"

Pulling her sweater tightly around her, Savannah watched the man's lips again lift in response to her elf remark. They were full lips, nice lips, though almost as colorless as his face.

She chanced a better look at him. He was, after all, the epitome of the tall, dark-haired and handsome cliché. Who could blame her for having delusions of grandeur?

The chiseled cheekbones were a true gift. His long, tapered nose gave him an aquiline air that didn't detract from the rugged, masculine thing he had going on. This guy was all man, for sure. Maybe too much so, since his eyes, which might have been light blue, were trained on her intently.

"Shall we go?" she suggested, wanting to avoid the directness of that gaze. "I really would appreciate the help if you're willing to drag this tree to the car for me. My hands are frozen."

A new tactile sensation followed her remark. He had placed something in her right hand. Gloves. *His* gloves. The leather emitted an aromatic scent of animal hide that in a contest might have won out over the coveted fragrance of pine. She'd been so wrapped up in checking out his features, she hadn't been aware of his hands.

"Helping you will be a pleasure," he said. "Win-win, I believe, was how you put it?"

Taking hold of the tree with both hands, he lifted the fir as effortlessly as though it were table-size…making her terribly aware of the layer of muscles that had to lie beneath his coat.

Savannah trailed after the handsome stranger. She didn't dare to check out more specifics. Already, she felt the rise in her pulse rate, a warning that she was out of small talk already and that decent goodbyes, in light of the gift of the gloves and his help with the tree, would be a chore.

Not to mention the variety of ridiculous bedroom images playing on a continuous loop in her mind.

But he didn't speak to her again. He placed the tree in the back of her SUV and turned to her only after the tree had been safely stored, standing close enough that she felt his exhaled breath ruffle the fringe of bangs covering her forehead.

After that, he tilted her head back with a finger under her chin and gazed into her eyes as if he had the ability to see down into her soul. And maybe he could see down there, because his lips feathered over hers with a touch that was barely there, yet wickedly seductive.

The lightning in that touch of his mouth to hers careened through Savannah with a force that rocked her stance. She opened her eyes to see that a pained frown creased the man's forehead and that for a few brief seconds, his incredibly chiseled face exposed an expression of unmasked, raw physical need that caused her heart to stumble over several necessary beats.

Somehow, her lips moved. "Merry Christmas," she said, for lack of anything more clever to say. "I hope you find the right one for yourself."

She offered him the gloves she hadn't used. Instead of taking them, he took her hand in his. He closed his fingers over hers, his thumb resting on the pulse that throbbed in her wrist. Savannah fielded a sudden urge to melt into his arms. She could have sworn he was waiting for her to do that very thing.

"I have no doubt that I'll find the right one," he said after a moment of silence had passed. "No doubt whatsoever."

In the deeper silence following his statement, he failed to ask for her phone number or request a date.

After several erratic, thunderous seconds, Savannah reluctantly withdrew her hand and turned. She got into the car, started the engine and backed the car out of the parking space with her eyes glued to the rearview mirror.

In that mirror, her eyes met his.

Her heart gave one solid kick after another that rocked her all the way to her toes. Moisture gathered at her temples and between her breasts. In uncharted depths, she felt as if this guy was calling to her in some way—even though his lips didn't move.

It took several rapid breaths to regain her equilibrium. The thing that stopped her from going back to him brazenly with her phone number in hand was the mixed bag of signals he had offered: a touch of lips that wasn't really a kiss; a few seconds of hand-holding; the gift of some really nice gloves.

"It's possible you're a Christmas angel, sent to remind people of the season of giving," she proposed. Besides helping with the tree, he'd made her feel special, if only for a few precious minutes. She should be happy with her little Christmas miracle and accept it for what it was.

Now that guy would find his own tree—a worthy, friendly, cheerful holiday endeavor...while she would indulge in some hot, erotic dreams.

Shaking off the ludicrous belief that if she turned around she'd find him waiting where she had left him and that he'd be waiting for her, Savannah sighed.

He hadn't asked for anything further from her, so she had no right to have expected anything more from the odd encounter. Yet, damn it, if the guy wasn't some kind of beautiful pervert, she had just possibly eclipsed the

chance of a lifetime because of that one awful word…
stranger.

She didn't actually hear him whisper, "Soon, Savannah, it will all be over."

That was preposterous and couldn't be right, because regretfully, it was over already.

Chapter 2

Dylan's mouth felt dry as he watched Savannah Clark drive away. His throat had begun to burn. There was an unusual tightness in his jaw from withholding his innate power.

He shouldn't have touched her. That was a mistake.

The strength and sparkle he saw in her was what had kept him riveted, that was all. He'd been human once and hadn't thought about those times until now. She had made him remember.

After he had taken his final breath as a mortal, he'd been saved by the light and grace of an angel. The reward for his service to her cause, in the fight against darkness, was that he retained his soul. But regardless of what Savannah Clark had stirred in him, his job was to take away some of what had drawn him to her. He had to erase a few details from her mind, leaving parts of her mind blank.

He had to diminish her.

His whispers would make her forget about that Christmas Star and its secret celestial twin that no one was ever meant to find—a simultaneous event masked by the brilliance of a star that had guided wise men to a manger.

Finding that other event might expose the dwelling place of his brethren to the Fallen, the disgruntled ones cast out of the heavenly realm that also craved light but were doomed to exist without it.

The fear was that if Savannah answered the riddle of the star she sought, she might find the other.

It didn't matter that she had single-handedly brought back to him the pain of recalling his own former humanness or that there was pure joy in repeating her name. Feelings had no place in an immortal's life. Desire for a beautiful human soul was out of the question. The fact was that if Savannah were to complete her research on that star, she would find him in the details. Him and others like him.

Dylan grew restless as her taillights receded. He had missed the opportunity to take care of this problem. He had been distracted.

Finally, with an immortal's incredible speed, he started after Savannah Clark, determined to put selfish needs aside and fulfill his duty.

The drive to the small cottage her parents had left her took ten minutes. Savannah sat for longer than that in the driveway, staring at the quaint one-story house and the tiny front yard dotted with solar-lit plastic snowflakes.

"Home, sweet home."

She pulled the tree out of the car with a good, hard tug. "You'll like it here," she said, dragging the fir toward the front door, panting by the time she had reached it.

She scrambled to get the key in the lock and shoved the door open. The tree left skid marks of dew and pine needles on the foyer's wood floor as she wrestled it inside.

"Only six more paces to go, and you will find your place of honor," she promised, straightening for a breath and to brush away a tickle at the base of her neck that might have been a draft seeping through the front window's panes.

Catching sight of her reflection in the glass, she laughed. Pine needles stuck to her hair and her sweater. She was an unruly mess, and she'd dared to imagine that a gorgeous hunk of stranger had been attracted to that?

Movement drew her attention. She craned her neck.

Looking beyond her reflection, she sobered quickly, certain there had been another face out there; one that shouldn't have been here at all, on the sidewalk in front of her home.

Tingling sensations engulfed her arms, tripping the leftover rumble still rolling around inside her. She'd know that face anywhere.

Dropping the tree, she turned. Though she might have been tongue-tied in terms of small talk, she had never been a weakling when push came to shove. A weakling wouldn't have been allowed to get ahead in the male-dominated profession she'd chosen.

Instead of hiding or calling the cops, she went to the front door and flung it open. She stepped outside.

"What's going on?" she asked the man standing

there, immediately confirming his identity by the way her heart continued to pound. "What do you want?"

"I know I shouldn't be here," the man from the tree lot said.

"So, what? You followed me? You do realize what that looks like?"

"I do know," he said. "I'm sorry."

"You're admitting to being a stalker, then?"

"Not exactly, though I doubt if I can convince you of it in this day and age. Things aren't as simple as they used to be, are they? In these times, people have to be wary."

Savannah didn't see a car behind him at the curb. She still felt the illicit brush of his lips across hers. "Why are you here?"

"I wanted more time with you."

"Maybe you could have mentioned that before."

She would have jumped at the chance if he had brought this up earlier and in public.

"I have a tree in the middle of my living room and work to do. So, look, I appreciate your help with the tree, but this is my home, and I don't know you."

"I can help with the tree, if you'll let me. I'll tell you about myself and why I'm here."

Savannah shook her head. "I don't think so. There are rules about this sort of thing for a reason."

She hated those rules now. This guy was an exotic dream come true.

"What can I do to convince you?" he asked.

"Give me your cell number. I'll call you tomorrow."

"I have no phone."

He hadn't raised his voice or advanced. His body was highlighted by the faintly garish light of the glowing snowflakes beside him. His handsome face was calm, his expression questioning.

"Do you live around here?" Savannah asked, smart enough to be aware of the fact that danger might have found her. At the same time, she couldn't help but think that her wish for company, and this company in particular, had been heard by somebody.

What if his presence was some kind of sign?

"I live abroad," he said in the sexy, lightly accented voice that intensified her inner longing tenfold.

Savannah used the doorjamb to steady herself. "What's the use of getting to know each other if you don't live here?"

"We have things in common that I'd like to speak to you about."

"And you just happened to stop off at a Christmas tree lot?"

"I'll confess to having followed you there."

This was a shocking discovery. She winced. "Really? I wonder what those things we have in common might be."

"Stars," he said.

Savannah wasn't sure she had heard him correctly and truly hadn't been expecting his reply.

"One event in particular," he clarified. "The so-called Christmas Star."

He appeared suddenly at the bottom of the steps, materializing there while Savannah had glanced up at the sky. She hadn't seen or heard him cross the lawn.

"You knew who I was at the tree lot," she said.

"Yes. Savannah Clark, of the Duncan Observatory."

"I'm sorry to hear that. I thought…" She let that one

go. The guy hadn't been attracted to her. He had some sort of business agenda.

That hurt a little.

"Are you an astronomer or astrophysicist?" Her voice had slipped an octave.

"Neither. Though I do know what you're after and have read your published research on the Christmas Star."

"What am I after?"

"You want to find out what that event really was and affix a date to it, as well as its precise location. You've been driven to find these things and are closing in on the answer. Am I right?"

She nodded. "Everyone familiar with my research knows that."

"I might be able to help you."

"In what way?"

"I know something about that event."

For a moment, Savannah forgot what was going on, as well as the dangerous aspects of this meeting. Quite possibly, this guy might be a colleague, which would make her attraction to him acceptable, if unrequited.

"Prove that you know something. Tell me about my research on that star."

He glanced up at the sky in the same way she had a minute before. "Your last paper proposed that the Christmas Star might not be a star at all, but a supernova."

"Do you even know what the word means?" Savannah asked.

"A supernova is a stellar explosion that often can outshine an entire galaxy."

Being ungodly handsome *and* knowledgeable made

for a heady combination. If that brief kiss in the parking lot had started something, this just sealed the deal.

Though the night was chilly, she felt feverish and the back of her neck was damp. Given the fact that her research was to be fiercely guarded until publication and she was really attracted to this guy, should she honor his request for some time and talk? Could he be trusted? And could she trust herself around him? She looked for a way to justify this meeting, deciding that he could be a reporter, a theologian or a priest with concerns that she might mess with the legends and beliefs affixed to that star.

Glancing to his throat to see if she spotted a white clerical collar, Savannah instead found a lightly raised line of scar tissue that encircled his neck. At first glance, the white band had the appearance of a tattoo. Tattoos were popular. She had one in the shape of a star on her right ankle.

Not a priest.

"Then again," he said, bringing her attention back to his face, "since you already know everything, of what use is anything further I might have to share with you? Is that what you're thinking?"

"That's not it at all," Savannah countered, wanting to prolong this meeting because heaven help her, in spite of the doubts, she desired company tonight. She felt lonely and alone, and it was almost Christmas, a time for joy, sharing, and the companionship of family and friends—both of which she sadly lacked.

"I'd like to share some conversation with you tonight," the man across from her said, his tone a vibration that ran seductively along the length of her spine.

He went on. "It's possible that I might know things

you don't know about the heavens. I'm willing to trade confidences with you, if you'll also talk about something I've been wondering about."

"What might that be?"

"Your enjoyment of this holiday is what I'd like to know about."

Truly, she hadn't been ready for that. And she had no right to be disappointed that what he wanted didn't involve her body and a large, soft mattress.

"How can you not know about Christmas?" she asked.

"I know of it, of course. I'd just like to understand what it means to you. What finding that star means to you. But it's cold out here, and you're trembling, chilled to the bone. Can we go inside if I promise to help with the tree and whatever else you might need help with as penance for disturbing you? If you're worried, you can keep a phone in your hand, with a finger on the dial."

"Do you have a name?" Savannah asked.

"Dylan. McCay."

"Do I need to be afraid of you, Dylan?" Her question was absurd, because what kind of homicidal maniac— if that's what he turned out to be—would answer that question truthfully?

"I won't harm you. I'm no threat to you physically," he replied. "You can check me for weapons if you like."

It wasn't the weapons Savannah was worried about. It was the rest of him, the glorious whole of Dylan McCay, along with the unexpected bonus of his knowledge of her research.

"Come back tomorrow," she made herself say, knowing that if he turned his back, she'd recant.

"Tonight is all the time I can afford. I have to be somewhere by daybreak."

"Like a vampire?"

He took seconds to reply. "Yes, like that. I've taken far too much time here already."

Savannah smiled. "I'm flattered."

He smiled, too, as though her expression was contagious. That smile gave him a boyish air and made him more approachable, more believable somehow. The earnestness of his expression also seemed to snap into place some kind of conspiratorial bond that made it all right to break a few rules.

If this guy was a stalker, he was also a damn good actor who had studied his part. Stars, supernovas and help with a tree?

She wanted more than anything to spend time with Dylan McCay. That truly would be a wish come true.

She could invite him inside, take a chance, if precautions were taken, and she just happened to know how to take them. She'd turn on the computers and tape recorders she'd placed in nearly every room to record any spontaneous ideas she had. She would use them to record this meeting with Dylan McCay.

The visual part of the feed would go to the observatory data banks. If anything happened to her, someone there would find the record, use face-recognition programming and chase this guy down. Geeks knew all these tricks.

It was chancy, but a chance she had to take. Sheer providence might have sent this guy to her on yet another lonely December night. Plus, he'd get her tree ready for trimming…if he didn't try to murder her first.

Win-win? Trusting in the goodness of others? These

things were Clark family goals. Who was she to break with tradition?

"Can you wait here for a minute, please?" she asked. When he inclined his head, she left him on her front steps and went inside to prepare the way for who knew what…hoping he would turn out to be the angelic creature she'd imagined him, rather than a devil in beautiful disguise.

When she had finished, she opened the door and stepped aside for him to pass. He hesitated for a moment before she invited him in.

Tall, enigmatic Dylan McCay stepped into the foyer and the smell of cold nights, wool coats and another unidentifiable scent that suggested he'd bathed in an aphrodisiac combined to form a heavenly fragrance.

Savannah met his intense blue gaze. Heat flooded her body, pushing the night's chill into the past. The masculine power he gave off curled around her like little fingers of flame.

This was a man with a business agenda?

It was hard for her not to react or respond to this kind of attraction. Conversation alone wasn't going to suffice, and she hoped her willpower would be strong— at least for the get-to-know-him part of this meeting.

She hadn't been wrong about the attraction—or the fact that he felt it as much as she did.

With her hand gripping the doorknob and her heart racing, Savannah said, "Make yourself at home."

Although her guest didn't move, his next smile was a thing of real beauty.

Chapter 3

It took all of Dylan's willpower to keep from lowering his mouth to the soft crook of Savannah Clark's neck. Her body was giving off a luxurious kind of sexual heat that made her fragrance sultry. Savannah Clark was like a piece of candy offered up to a starving soul.

"What's that delightful smell?" Dylan hoped that a question might lessen the extraordinary heat of the moment.

"Cinnamon candles and my friend over there." She pointed to the tree, the turn of her head exposing more pale skin that lured him with the smooth grace of the forbidden. He had to tear his attention away from that enticing bareness. Though he had fangs, his kind didn't thirst. Yet tonight, so close to Savannah, his fangs seemed to have a mind of their own.

The discernible tick of Savannah's pulse filled the

hallway with its echo, each beat marking the passage of time with a reminder of how little of it he had to share with her. Dylan raised his hands to trap that pulse beneath his fingers, and stopped himself. Just one look, now, into her eyes, and he'd avoid confronting the rest of this mysterious dilemma of justification, lust and restraint.

Do it.

She stood inches away.

All he had to do was whisper his instructions for her to forget about that star.

He felt her hands on his shoulders and had to hide his surprise. When she said "Take off your coat" in a breathy voice, he was slightly taken aback.

The warmth of her hands seeped through his clothes, penetrating his skin layer by layer, first with a hint of heat, then real fire. At the same time, her invitation seemed filled with the expectation of comfort and companionship, rather than danger and withheld secrets. He had never been offered such an innocent invitation to share space, certainly never from a target.

This was strange and troubling. The way his skin danced beneath her touch, as if anticipating more touches to come, was as much a discomfort as it was a pleasure.

He searched Savannah's face for hints of apprehension over having him so close and found none. He smelled no fear on her. Savannah didn't know what kind of being stood beside her and what he had come here to do. Her eyes were incredibly bright.

He was keenly aware of every detail of her movement, as if it were somehow suspended from time. He saw each golden lash that lined Savannah's blue eyes and the delicate flush of pink tinting her cheeks. She was biting her lip, and he wanted to do that for her. His fangs weren't the only parts of him that ached.

Heaven forgive me, I need more from you than your research, Savannah. You make me want to be a man, with feelings I thought I had lost.

This was a shocking discovery. If he were a man, instead of what he was, things would be simple. He'd take her in his arms and to bed. He'd give her pleasure and take some back, then be there when she woke in the morning, able to soak in every nuance of her wide-eyed, golden existence. If mortal, he might have stayed here with her forever.

These were painful ideas. Immortals couldn't afford to think or look back. Still, his heart had begun to beat with Savannah's heart's rapid rhythm, as if it were his own. That beat had the power to seduce in a way that nothing else could.

Dylan tore his gaze away. He would do his duty, but he had to understand this sudden problem with his resolve first. He needed some mental distance from Savannah in order to get his bearings.

He glanced at the colorful braided rugs covering the wood floors, and the soft furniture along the walls that were dotted with pictures in silver metal frames. The lamps near the front window cast a soft light.

The sideways slide of Savannah's hands from his shoulders to his chest brought him back to the situation at hand.

She slipped her palms under the edges of his coat and pushed the coat to the side, her fingertips lightly rubbing against the silk shirt he wore underneath. Withholding a sound, Dylan worked to keep his body motionless—even though the physical sensations rushing at him were overwhelming.

Savannah had no idea what her touch was doing. Removing his coat meant he'd play the game out for a while longer and see a little bit more of what this woman had to offer.

He let her have the coat, though the imprint of her fingertips lingered after she turned to hang the garment on a peg near the door. When she turned back, she said in that same breathy voice, "Maybe you can get that tree out of the way while I get the cookies?"

Dylan made no move to disconnect from her extraordinary circle of heat. Again, he was wavering.

"Are you hungry?" she asked, tilting her head back to look up at him. "The cookies are in the kitchen. I baked them yesterday."

Dylan thought about asking what a cookie might be and how it fit into her holiday sphere of influence, but that would have revealed too much about his long seclusion from her world.

"Cookies sound delightful." He was careful to hide the fangs that were a reminder of the thin line he had almost walked before seeing the light.

"Great." She smiled again, better at disguising her feelings. Her tone was steadier now, though her body language told him a different story. She was a ball of nerves. Every strand of her golden hair quivered ever so slightly.

Savannah Clark was as drawn to him as he was to her, and this posed a real challenge.

"If you'll drag that tree to the stand, I'll be right back," she said, breaking free of the spell binding them together by heading toward another open doorway, giving him a great view of the back side of her commendable anatomy.

"Santas or stars?" she asked over her shoulder. "I made both."

He stared at her, completely at a loss.

"Stars, then," she said. "That seems appropriate."

Leaving behind a fragrant stream of scented pheromone particles as strong and vibrant as the tail of a comet, Savannah Clark disappeared into the adjoining room. For the second time in an hour, she had left him standing in her wake.

He was surrounded by her world, and it was filled with enough color, dazzle and scent to render the world he would go back to a colorless, loveless, lifeless place by comparison. Slipping back into the shadows seemed impossible now that he stepped out of them. Yet Dylan knew he was a visitor here.

He didn't belong in Savannah's home.

May the angels forgive him, he thought. The worst thing possible had happened. He had become a sucker for his prey.

Savannah pressed her back to the kitchen wall. Her breath came in great rasps that made her chest rise and fall as if she had been running. These reactions were due to the man in her foyer and the belief that she might have wished him there after all.

She leaned around the doorjamb, watched him finally head for the tree. He glanced around, his attention landing on the Christmas tree stand in the corner.

With the same smooth, effortless grace she had witnessed in the tree lot, he lifted the fir, carried it to the stand and set the tree upright. After studying the tree stand, he crouched on one knee to tighten the screws that would hold the tree in place. Back on his feet, he viewed his work with a critical eye.

Dylan McCay had to be the finest specimen of manhood she had ever seen. His black silk shirt billowed slightly above the waist of his pants when he moved and clung becomingly to his shoulders. His legs were long and lean. His dark hair swung sensually against the back of his neck when he turned his head. The inexplicable mystery of why these things affected her so strongly kept her nerves humming like the old wall heater.

Satisfied that he was okay for the time being, Savannah placed a few frosted sugar-cookie stars on a plate, poured milk into two crystal glasses and closed the refrigerator door with a bump of one hip. Before heading back to her guest, she glanced at the recording system on the counter. Because the visuals sent to the observatory would capture everything she did tonight as well as everything he did, she prayed that she wouldn't make a fool of herself.

"Perfect," she said to Dylan brightly, stepping into the living room and setting the plate of cookies down on a table parked in front of her quilt-covered sofa. "Your penance is complete."

Her guest looked at the plate and raised an eyebrow.

"Old family recipe," she said. "Cookies make the house smell like Christmas and taste like sugar-coated sin. Clarks have made these same cookies for generations. I even leave some of them out for Santa, sure I'll score more points."

Dylan didn't reach for a cookie or pick up a glass. It was possible that his family didn't have traditions. He might not believe in the Christmas fuss at all. He hadn't, she reminded herself, been in that lot to buy a tree.

Of course, his less-than-enthusiastic reaction to her baking skills could also mean that he wasn't sure if astronomers could handle themselves in a kitchen.

"I eat Santa's share of cookies myself on Christmas Eve, you know, and just pretend there's a giant elf in a red suit coming down the chimney to get at them," she said. "Sometimes it just makes me feel good to temporarily believe that I'm a child again and that my family is still here."

"That's Christmas for you?" he asked. "An elf and some cookies?"

"Not entirely. It's what I like to remember about the things surrounding the Christmas holidays and about my family who aren't with me now. I like to keep track of all the things we shared to celebrate the season, from when I was a kid on up. Don't you?"

Dylan shook his head. "My family didn't hold to such things. It's a pity, though, after being here and seeing this."

He walked to the window and looked out at the night. "What happened to your family, Savannah?"

"They died."

He half turned back. "I'm sorry."

"So am I. But you wanted to know about my Christmases, I believe."

"Yes." He looked to the corner. "How about the tree?"

"Trees in the house are all about nature and spirit, things that everyone should be reminded of this time of year, no matter what they believe," she said. "Plus, like the cookies, they flat-out smell great. No other time of the year indulges the senses like Christmas."

"What will you do with the tree now that it's here?"

"Decorate it with lights and the ridiculously shiny things my family made through the years. I probably have strings of popcorn that are ten years old."

"All this brings you closer to your family?"

"Every bit of it."

Savannah took a cookie from the plate and held it without taking a bite. "I've answered a couple of your questions, so how about answering some questions about you?"

His blue eyes found hers with a directness so personal in intensity it brought another blush to her face. Savannah dropped her attention to the black silk shirt that rippled across his chest like poured liquid, and again felt that hint of a warm current filling the space separating them.

"You came here to find me, you said, and to talk about my work, but I think you might owe me more of an explanation." Her voice sounded weaker than she would have liked.

Dylan's face sobered.

"I came to see if you believe that star was a supernova. And if not, what you think it was," he said after a pause.

"Are you asking for insider trading, maybe hoping to beat me at my game, Dylan?"

"I'm no scientist," he said.

"Yet you know about my research."

"I'm interested in what you've concluded and if you've pinpointed when the phenomenon actually occurred."

Savannah sat down on the sofa and tucked both legs beneath her. "I believe you also mentioned that you knew something about the star and used that magical statement as your ticket into this party."

He nodded. "So I did."

Savannah waved a hand. "I'm listening."

"Can I ask one more question first?"

"I'm pretty sure that might be cheating or reneging on the deal."

"There's something I have to know before I say anything on the subject."

"Oh, all right."

"Are you interested in the religious side of the story of that star, Savannah?"

She shook her head. "I'm only interested in finding it. I'm a scientist, not a theologian. I'm not out to prove or disprove anything having to do with anyone's beliefs."

"You don't want to see if the biblical stories are correct, or incorrect, as the case may be? That isn't what drives you?"

"Heavens, no. Tracing star histories is what I do, and I picked that one because this time of year holds such good memories of my family."

She took a small bite of the frosted star but found swallowing tough with her dark-haired guest watching her. Although they were six feet apart, he felt closer. She had a feeling that talking kept them from being in each other's arms but that even that barrier was thinning.

"Do those things concern you? Is that why you want to find out if I can prove anything about that star? I know this kind of research isn't popular with some people, especially if the event turns out to be something different than they've imagined. I've been careful with my ideas so far because of that, but eventually I will publish what I find."

Even though Dylan McCay smiled, the smile didn't quite reach his eyes. He was troubled. Some new emotion in those blue eyes darkened them and made her think of sadness and loss. She recognized the haunted cast in his blue gaze. She'd had her share of loss.

She wanted to see him smile in the way he had smiled in her yard, open and earnest, relaxed. She wanted him to sit down next to her and tell her exactly what he had in mind.

Why had he wanted to know about her tree and what it meant to her when he'd come here to talk about the star?

"Does that answer your question sufficiently?" she asked.

"Yes. Thank you. I appreciate your candidness."

"Then the next question will be to ask you, point-blank, what my research means to you and why you've come to see me."

He seemed to carefully weigh his answer.

"The timing of the appearance of the star you seek means something to me and to my…people," he said.

"People?"

"Those I live among and work with."

"Does it mean something to you, Dylan, personally?"

"What if I told you it meant life or death to many kinds of beings?"

"I'd say you were way too serious about a celestial event that happened a very long time ago and the part I have in researching it."

Her gorgeous guest again faced her fully, his tall

frame blocking out the night outside the window. The ball of longing inside Savannah grew. She fixed her attention on the scar on Dylan's neck, not wanting to look at his eyes. Was he trying to talk about an event that was tied to that raised white mark?

"Whose life and death?" she asked, realizing that her question had taken the conversation into a more personal arena.

She watched his hand go to his neck.

"Have you found that star?" he countered.

She had to answer because he was looking at her so eagerly and as if her answer mattered to him more than she could guess.

"Not as of yesterday," she confessed.

She had been right. Her answer mattered. Dylan looked so relieved to hear this news his stance lost some of its formality. His shoulders loosened. His features softened in a transformation that was visually stunning.

This version of him took her breath away.

Savannah dropped the cookie and bent over to retrieve it. When she sat up, he stood before her with his hand outstretched.

The gesture had to be a statement for something she hadn't quite grasped. Or maybe he just wanted to touch her as badly as she wanted to touch him. Nevertheless, self-preservation sat high on her list, as did maintaining her dignity. He hadn't answered any of her questions to her satisfaction and therefore hadn't earned earnest answers in return. He owed her more than this.

Instead of touching him, she placed her cookie on his upturned palm and crossed her arms. "How could an old supernova mean life or death to anyone, if that's what it was?"

She tilted her head back to look up at him, ignoring the crush of emotion she felt each time she viewed his face.

He was eyeing the star-shaped cookie when he said in a velvet-toned voice that was like an itinerant stroke of his fingers between her thighs, "It wouldn't mean anything in and of itself, but whatever that star phenomenon was might have hidden something else that does."

He set the cookie on the plate. His eyes came level with hers. "That doesn't matter now, not if you haven't found anything of importance."

His relief was evident in that remark.

"I like you, Savannah. I'll admit that coming to your home was to explore the reason for feeling like this so quickly. You seemed so happy with your tree that I wanted to share in that happiness. I was envious of it."

He made a gesture that took in the room, though his gaze remained on her. "I knew you were truly special when I saw that. I believe it even more strongly now that I've seen your home."

His confession made her heart race faster, beat harder, for no real reason at all.

"You're glad that I haven't fingered that star?" she asked.

"Yes."

"Why?"

"Because it means that there's a chance I might get to see you again."

He wanted to see her again.

Savannah's stomach tightened with an excitement she hadn't fully appreciated until that moment. Her feelings were validated and reciprocated. He'd made excuses to come here, when seeing her again had been the ultimate goal.

So, what did a person do when faced with an honest-to-God miracle?

"You've made the extra time I've spent here worth every second," he added. "After meeting you in the trees, I thought that you also liked me. Was I wrong?"

"Possibly not, but you still haven't contributed to the conversation about that star much, at least not in a way that makes sense."

She noticed how Dylan had turned his attention to the plate and the cookies on it in a manner suggesting that he was contemplating objects completely foreign to him. A tickle of something that felt like the arrival of a hazy premonition made Savannah reach for her throat.

He continued reluctantly. "Some speculation is that the Christmas light show was a comet, but you haven't landed on that conclusion."

"Oh, I've looked at it," Savannah said. "Because a comet killed my parents, I've saved that theory for last."

Dylan brought his face close to hers. His expression showed concern. "Can you tell me what happened to your parents?"

"As amateur astronomers, they had been following a comet sighting when their car crashed in the desert. Searching the heavens was part of my life early on. It's why I became an astronomer. I wanted to know everything about what they were searching for. I wanted to find what had eluded them and make them proud of me, whether or not they were here to see it."

Her guest shut his eyes briefly, as if what she'd told him resonated with him in some way. He said with the authority of someone possessing absolute knowledge of the subject, "That celestial event you're looking for wasn't a comet or a supernova, Savannah. It was a star waking up for a purpose. A brilliant, sparkling star brightened by a master artist's heavenly hand."

After a pause, he went on. "It was the flare of a special symbol for a special time that you and a lot of others celebrate to this day."

His expression softened. "If you believe that a tree spoke to you in a parking lot, maybe you can trust what I'm saying about the mysteries of the universe."

A weighty silence filled the room. Savannah didn't try to break it.

"Perhaps I've said too much." Dylan McCay beamed his bright, slightly haunted blue eyes her way.

"Yes, well, I'm sure I'll get to all theories sooner or later," Savannah said with effort. Dylan's sexual vibe was starting to outweigh the need to chat about stars and research. The tension between them appeared to be clouding her mind.

She pointed to the plate on the table in front of her. "And by the way, that treat isn't poison, I swear. It's just a bit of dough and colored frosting."

Dylan's grin returned, if somewhat dimmer this time. "Your home is as warm spirited and inviting as you are, Savannah. It's been a long time since any of those things mattered to me, and tonight I find them irresistible. Tonight, I find it difficult to concentrate on anything other than you."

He moved around the coffee table, reached for her and pulled her to her feet with a gentle snap of his arms.

"You want to keep traditions going in order to keep your family's spirit alive. I find this not only commendable but heartwarming." His voice was magnificently gritty. "I will tell you this, I wish I'd had a family like yours. You are very lucky."

Her chest met with the hardness of his body. The luxurious fabric of his shirt, smooth against her cheek and saturated with his masculine scent, was a further seduction.

Savannah thought about protesting this break in the rules, but this was part of the fantasy that she had subconsciously willed into existence. She had longed for him to hold her, and somehow he'd known.

His hands stroked the length of her arms with a tender precision that was new and erotic. Each inch he traveled created swells of reaction that were startling in intensity.

Moving to her spine, his fingers wafted over the tight weave of her sweater and over each vertebra beneath it in a downward line so intimate she stifled a gasp of surprise.

Answers to other questions that should have come up, such as who did he think he was and what did he think he was doing, didn't matter at the moment. Being in his arms felt good and right. However false the notion might have been, she suddenly felt wanted, needed, safe. And she didn't feel so alone.

Neither of them seemed to be breathing. Savannah waited in suspense for what would happen next, aware of each move he made until his hands had reached the base of her spine.

He didn't stop there or hesitate. His palms flowed over her curves. He cupped his hands around the trembling flesh of her backside and tightened his hold. They were groin to groin in the most personal of positions, and his interest was obvious. He was hard and waiting.

She did not utter one word of protest against this. All of her senses rushed to where his hips pressed to hers. Every last nerve ending tingled and burned, reveling in their closeness. She was going to have the rest of that dream after all. If her research never brought a complete answer, it had at least brought her this.

Dylan's hands moved again. His fingertips brushed over her lips in an earnest exploration, tracing their shape with an agonizing precision. Dampness continued to gather at the nape of Savannah's neck, at her temples and between her thighs. An unusual flicker wavered inside her before finally erupting into a brilliant, scorching flame.

She shut her eyes. Had to. She couldn't risk looking at Dylan, fearing not only what she might see in his eyes but what he might see in hers. She was in accord with this kind of closeness, so long overdue. The stars had sent Dylan to her as an answer to her loneliness. He actually was her Christmas surprise.

"Trees, popcorn strings and cookies," he whispered, his fingers dragging slowly along the line of her jaw. "What about these things brings your family closer, I wonder? I have to know, Savannah, why you love those things."

"They are things composed of light, Dylan. I'm in need of light and happiness. Everyone is."

"Yes. That's it." His voice was filled with an emotion Savannah couldn't fathom that deepened it further. "It's always the light."

When she met his gaze, the feeling of being lost in a winter whiteout came, dissolving the room behind them. Walls disappeared, as did the floor and the ceiling. Wrapped in Dylan's arms, she felt as if she were suspended in the air.

A shudder ripped through Savannah that she felt also tear through him. Their bodies swayed together, in unison, as if they were already mingled and one.

The whiteness broke apart when he spoke.

"I hadn't planned on taking such liberties." His quiet tone stirred the air between them. "I'll go now, if you wish it."

She couldn't open her lips; couldn't contemplate him leaving, but finally said, "Yes, go. Go now."

She didn't mean it. She meant nothing of the sort. Sadness crossed Dylan's features, accompanied by an expression that she took for the pain of regret. He didn't want to leave her. Possibly he felt as she did and, outside of the attraction to her, longed for support and joy and warmth on a chilly December night.

When he dropped his hands and stepped back, she fell, feeling the floorboards strike her feet. She almost shouted to protest the sensory interruption of losing Dylan's special ability to elevate her above the most mundane things.

Inclining his head so that his dark hair spilled across his cheeks, Dylan turned from her.

Savannah's body raged against the separation. Her mind cried out with a violent soundlessness. Being with him was all that mattered. Within the circle of his arms, things had felt so right. Her instincts were seldom wrong, and they now suggested that she and Dylan truly might have been meant to find each other. Two lost and lonely souls had been made to meet up, brought together by a similar purpose. *Those damn stars.*

"Wait," she said. "Who are you, really?"

"Someone who cares more than he should" was his solemn reply. "Someone who wasn't prepared for your brilliance and its effect on a needy soul."

Magic words. Passionate syllables. The correct ones.

"Stay, Dylan," Savannah said. "Please stay."

Sadness hung on his features like lurking shadows that Savannah wanted to chase away. She hurried on. "I want to know everything about you, and if that isn't possible, then one night with you will have to do."

"Savannah…"

"I don't fear this," she said. "I don't fear you."

She witnessed the change in his expression that tele-graphed his longing for that reply. He wasn't able to hide his feelings from her and hadn't really been able to from the start.

"Kiss me," she said. "Just one kiss and I'll know if this is right and if what I'm feeling is the truth."

"What are you feeling?"

"The need to surrender fully to what the stars have provided."

He didn't wear a smile when he stepped closer, or question her strange remark. He didn't pull her to him again. He angled his mouth toward hers, complying with her request.

The shakes that rolled through her were like the whips of a lash and threatened to rival the explosions of a star's extraordinary birth. Adrenaline shot through Savannah unchecked, forcing her heart into overdrive. She couldn't catch her breath.

When Dylan's mouth rested on hers, it was a ten-tative gesture. He didn't ravage her mouth or take ad-vantage of her self-proclaimed helplessness. His lips merely touched hers, as if testing the limits of his own willpower.

His breath was cool. His lips were tender. The kiss was but a taste of the things she wanted from him. There was nothing gentle or chaste about her unspoken needs. Those needs raged like the flames of a wind-driven wildfire, reaching out to him, needing to engulf him.

Withdrawing his mouth, and with his eyes never leaving hers, Dylan took her hand in his. He laced his fingers through her fingers, in the manner of a binding promise. There could not have been a sexier or more meaningful meeting of flesh. His fingers and the soft pressure of his lips had said it all.

There were no longer two people in the room, but two spirits heading toward a union. The linking of their hands and mouths was a pledge and the opening act of another chance that had to be taken.

When Dylan backed up a step, Savannah gasped. But he didn't leave or wait for any further request from her. Instead he lifted her into his arms. Their faces were close, though not touching. Her breathing sounded harsh in the quiet of the room. Dylan seemed to be holding his.

He moved, walking confidently, carrying her as if she were a prize. Through the hallway he took her, and into the bedroom beyond it, where he paused beside her bed, its surface dimly lit by the lights from the street outside.

Savannah glanced down at that bed only once, aware that Dylan awaited her final decision. The fact that this was her decision gave even more rightness and meaning to the moment. He'd leave if she asked him to. All she had to do was speak those brutal words.

"I have no intention of saying them," she whispered.

Having crossed that line, the next one was easy. Savannah made the first move. She gave her full permission for what would happen next by bringing her lips up to his, by parting them and sighing into his mouth.

Ignoring the faint, persistent ting of the house's alarm bell going off in the distance, she waited impatiently for Dylan to shed his reserve and for tenderness to become a thing of the past.

Chapter 4

Dylan accepted Savannah's mouth, closing his mind to the fact that acting on his desires was not only wrong but forbidden.

Savannah was alive, human and fragile. He had to take care to hold himself back, especially when it had been decades since he had allowed himself any degree of physical pleasure, and when his needs were overflowing and plentiful.

He just couldn't make those warnings stick.

His mouth covered Savannah's hungrily, greedily, forcefully, fearing she'd retract her invitation if given the chance. He swept her mouth with his tongue, forgetting about his fangs, and demanded that she react in kind. The fiery fierceness of his kiss left her breathless and limp in his arms.

Yet she rallied as his demands escalated. The rise of

her sexual energy that he'd earlier witnessed as a corona of radiant fire stunned him with its intensity. Her arms encircled his neck. She held him close. Her tongue met his in a wicked dance of give-and-take.

The coolness he harbored dissipated, and he grew steadily warmer as Savannah's flames transferred to him via her lips and her sweet, sweet heat. Releasing her would have been out of the question. Turning back didn't enter his mind.

He didn't want to set her on the bed. In his arms was where she belonged. In this bedroom with her was where he belonged. For now, he could be what both of them wanted him to be.

To hell with the rest.

His hunger began to rage. His fangs narrowly avoided splitting her lip, but she didn't seem to have felt their presence. In her mouth he found evidence of her own hunger, and the background beat of her thundering pulse. He took all of this in, absorbing every bit, exploring every corner of her glorious mouth until he could stand no more waiting.

She curled up when he laid her on the bed, as if missing him for those few seconds. Leaning over her, with his hands on the pillow, he growled once, deep in his throat, before bringing her back to her feet.

The sweater came off, over her head. Savannah shook her hair back into place; it swung across her naked shoulders in silky strands of pure, priceless gold.

Standing before him, inches away, she lowered her arms. Her eyes were wide and her pupils dilated. Possibly she was in shock for allowing things to get this far, just as he was.

A filmy bit of white lace covered her breasts, tied

to her shoulders with thin satin ribbons. The lace tore with the briefest tug of his hands. The ribbons easily gave way, revealing small, firm, rounded breasts, their tips as pink as Savannah's mouth and raised into delicate, swollen buds that felt hard against his palms. Those buds would be succulent, he knew, but that kind of sweetness would throw him over the edge. In his chest and his groin a new fury to possess her had become insistent.

Savannah's bare torso was slender and taut. Her waist was tiny. He could have counted each ridge of her ribs. Every new discovery only prolonged getting to the core of her heat, a place he desperately wanted to find and lose himself in.

Savannah uttered a sound of need that by itself could have brought him to a peak. She wasn't ambitious or greedy. That was the thought that filtered in as his body hardened. She was merely inquisitive, alone and hungering for closeness. She sought retribution for her family's death by chasing down celestial events similar to the one that had killed them. She was an exemplary human being.

Maybe some of that goodness would rub off.

He reveled in this closeness to her and all that she stood for. He had no idea how he had gotten this far without taking her already, without driving his cock into her creamy inferno and drinking the cries of pleasure from her lips. Time refused to stand still while he briefly contemplated these things.

Savannah pressed her half-naked body to his, driving her breasts against him. Dylan tore his shirt off and tossed it to the floor. He wrapped his arms around his beautiful Savannah. Blissful in the sensations of their naked chests meeting, he let out a groan of delightful despair.

This was not enough. Not by far.

He took her mouth with the fierceness of a madman, forcing her head back with his hands in her hair. Her passion, tantalizing, delicious, flowed through him like the rising waters of a raging stream. The electricity in this kiss buzzed and stung his world-weary senses.

Then she was on the bed, and he was removing her shoes and her pants.

She said nothing, did nothing to stop him. Her lips were parted, reddened and waiting for more.

When his own shoes and pants joined hers on the floor, Dylan moved up beside her. Perched on his hands, he allowed her ragged, fevered breath to warm his face.

She reached for him, gripping first his shoulders and then allowing her hands to glide to his neck. She touched his scar with her palms, and the old wound blazed with a startling, searing pain that radiated in every direction.

Shocked by this, swearing silently, Dylan lowered himself onto her body. Her breasts would have to wait. Her mouth could wait. She had touched his scar, made it live, and now his needs were too great.

With one hand, he parted her long, sleek legs, searching her softness for the entry he needed to put his pain to rest. Finding what he needed, and that Savannah was damp, expectant and willing, was almost too much to bear.

She was ready for what would happen next between them, and he had very nearly bypassed any remaining thread of self-control. He had only this one night. *They* had only this night.

She had used the word *vampire* in jest, without realizing how close she had come to being right about that.
He was taking from her now, not with his teeth but with
his body's desire to soak up every bit of her. He had
every intention of giving back.

Meaning to wait, to listen for what she might say now
that the most intimate of acts was to begin, he breathed
her in. He calmed her with a gentle touch to her face as
his chest rose and fell as rapidly as hers did, and with
the sound of her heartbeat in his ears.

Would she stop him now? Turn away? Come to her
senses?

*You have no idea what I am, Savannah, and what
I can do.*

He said aloud in a hoarse tone, "You have no idea
what this means to me."

Her face was hot. Her thighs, beneath his, were hot-
ter. Savannah's lips trembled, not with fear but with
expectation. The sight of her blue eyes closing was his
encouragement to go on.

"So be it, my love."

He dipped into her slowly at first, easing his cock
inside, planning to prolong the pleasure. She caught her
breath and held it. He couldn't hold out.

Drawing his hips back, keeping close watch on
Savannah's face, he thrust slowly but steadily into her.
Her body offered up a spasm of acceptance that sent
Dylan's senses spiraling. Her mouth opened in a silent
cry. She was looking at him now, meeting his gaze as
if seeking information that his body couldn't tell her.

Withdrawing quickly, Dylan lowered his mouth to
hers and felt her body loosen. He let his hips go in

a plunge that went deep, filling her, demanding a response.

Her hips began to move, rising to meet his, straining against him as she took him in. She closed herself around him as he buried himself inside her, stroking his erection with her perfect, blistering tightness. Her mouth opened for him in a kiss that was beyond belief.

Control a thing of the past, Dylan began to move with a rhythm that matched hers, withdrawing and entering her pliant slickness repeatedly, over and over, each thrust deeper than the one before. He desired to reach the core of Savannah Clark, knowing that even if he did, he'd want more, and that he was doomed by the very act he craved.

The duet and force of their bodies merging rendered everything else, every thought and feeling, meaningless. The bed shuddered beneath this taking, and the headboard groaned.

Dylan knew the exact second that the crescendo in the woman beneath him began to hurl toward the surface. Wanting to meet it, he entered her one more time with a shove fueled by lust, greed, love or whatever they had going on between them.

With his body screaming in need and tempo, and Savannah's sudden, gathered motionlessness, he didn't do the thing his nature demanded of him. He didn't claim her or possess her. He shut his eyes and gave himself up to her. Himself and all that he was.

Yours, Savannah. All for you, he thought as he climaxed.

The void inside Dylan lit up with a fiery glow that made him shout...and his voice, sounding unfamiliar and changed, merged with Savannah's startled cry of ecstasy.

* * *

Dylan noticed that Savannah's breathing had finally slowed.

She lay in his arms, spent, lost in a peaceful, dreamless sleep that he encouraged with the calm, careful movements of his hands on her body.

Giving her these moments of peace was a necessity. Though he wanted to face her and confess everything, he couldn't. His mind warned him that he had already given too much away.

He had, in fact, given her his soul.

These last few seconds with her were needed, but watching her sleep made him more restless. His heart, usually silent, had liked sharing her beats. He was sharing them still, heard them continuing in a long, lingering echo that spoke of life and of living.

"You are a beautiful enigma, with your silken hair and the face of an angel, a face I will never be able to forget, Savannah."

She was perfect, yes, except that she was mortal.

This woman had brought him back to the remembrance of his life before immortality, the textures, sights, sounds and delights. Her gift of acceptance tonight had created a fissure in the senses an immortal needed to close off in order to survive.

Emotions long lost had been found.

His heart beat for her. His soul cried out for her.

Dylan looked at her now with not only lust but what felt curiously like love. Love that could never be returned. Her bruised mouth and the blue spots already starting to appear on her arms and thighs from the fierceness of their lovemaking would bring her to her senses. And he would be gone.

As an immortal, he should have had immunity from this new kind of pain, but he'd been caught off guard. It almost seemed as though some larger force had caused this slip in character by bringing them together. He had to think so. Serendipity? Fate? Not chance. It couldn't have been chance, because this seemed like so much more to him.

"Sleep, my dearest Savannah," he crooned as she nestled deeper into the crook of his arm. "It will all be over soon enough. There will be no pain, I promise."

He dreaded the moment that was coming, knowing it had to arrive. The sun was rising. Needles of fire nipped at his bare skin. He had to get out, get going.

Carefully, Dylan slipped his arm from under her. He sat up, trying not to look at what lay beside him, but quickly turned back. With her scent stamped into him, and the taste of her on his lips, he again leaned close.

With gentle fingers, he moved a strand of what felt like finely spun gold away from her ear and began to whisper the words she would never consciously hear; words that stung his soul and left it exposed and hurting.

"Forget…"

Chapter 5

Savannah opened her eyes. A surge of adrenaline made her sit up with the blanket clutched tight.

"What the..."

She was in bed and completely naked. Evening light threw shadows through the half-open blinds, meaning that she'd slept the day away.

Clutching the blanket tighter, she glanced around the room, seeing no sign of her bed partner, horrified that she couldn't remember his name. Finding no lingering warmth on the bed next to her let her know that he'd been gone for some time.

Closing her eyes didn't help anything, but she shut them anyway and muttered, "Everyone has one-night stands."

Waking to no sign of that one-night stand, though, was a very sad thing.

She moved an arm and winced. Moving a leg, she groaned. The night had been better than good, if stiffness was a sign. She still felt soft inside.

Sliding to the edge of the mattress, she looked to the hallway door with something vague nagging at her consciousness. She could almost envision the guy there. His name sat on the tip of her tongue, though she couldn't quite get to it.

A ringing sound made her cuff at her left ear. She sat up straighter. The sound wasn't in her head; it came from the other room. It was a bell insistently tinkling.

The alarm.

Pushing to her feet, struggling to remember what had happened before the sexual antics that had led her to take a stranger to her bed, Savannah found some details imbedded in her brain but was missing others. A velvet voice had whispered to her. She had made love with a hard, cool body, and now every limb, and also her ego, felt bruised.

That was nothing, though, when compared to the pain that streaked across her forehead when she tried to think about what her lover had looked like and what they had talked about.

Had they been discussing stars?

That bell...

They must have set off the alarm on the monitoring system.

Dragging herself to the living room, finding no sign of her guest there, or of anything being disturbed, Savannah eyed the tree in its stand.

Yes, that was right. She had bought a tree from a place on the edge of town, following her usual December routine. "Nothing out of the ordinary."

After killing the bell, she ventured into the kitchen and stared at the red light blinking on the recorder. She'd had the foresight to record everything. This was either very good or very bad, depending on what had occurred.

The little blinking light on the monitor source caught her attention, and her heart gave a leap.

She staggered to the counter and stared. What might have amounted to a night of porn, in pictures, had been sent to the observatory. For some reason, she'd left that monitor switch on.

"Damn." Getting to the observatory before anyone else saw those tapes was paramount, crucial. She didn't have to think twice about that.

But first, she had to fill in a few blanks. She rewound the tape and laid her hands on the counter to brace herself. Voices came on from conversation in the living room. *Dylan.* That was his name. Dylan McCay. She'd said his name several times in a breathy tone. Obviously, she had liked this guy.

The fast-forwarded tape went too far. About to rewind, she heard a deep, rich voice whispering in a way that brought chills and an almost desperate, immediate desire to repeat the night's escapades. That voice struck her deep in her bones. It was like a velvet cloth being dragged across bare skin.

Her body recognized that voice.

But what she heard didn't just sound like crazy sex talk; it sounded like a threat.

"I have come to censure your research," he said softly. "I've come to stop it, Savannah. You must forget about that star."

Listening to this now made her light-headed. A moment came when she thought she might faint. What star was he talking about? What did she need to forget?

She had to hear more.

"It's an objective that rules my existence," he said. "That Christmas Star and what it hid."

She stopped the tape with fear growing. Stopping her research was his life's objective? What would make him say that? She had wanted him, and he had admitted to having sinister purpose in coming here?

"You must forget," he whispered on that recording. "Forget it all, for now, my lovely Savannah. My love."

The seductive voice caused a crack in her reasoning. More memories began to punch through the fog of forgetfulness. Details flooded in. Savannah sank to the floor, recalling the man in the Christmas tree lot with the beautiful smile that been here, in her home and in her bed, because of an unforgettable attraction.

And he'd had an agenda after all?

"You son of a…" she shouted, feeling vulnerable, frustrated and angry.

With a sharp bite to her swollen lip, she looked at the recorder. Listening to the rest of the tape was imperative, but it was even more important for her to get to the observatory. Hearing the voice on that tape had brought everything back.

When the recording ended, Savannah looked to the window to see that the sun had set.

Somebody at the observatory might have already viewed the pictures that went along with these recordings.

Though swearing wasn't her forte, Savannah made a damn good attempt at it as she got to her feet.

* * *

After squealing into the parking space and hitting the curb with both front tires, Savannah leaped from the car. The hallway was dark when she entered the observatory, but she didn't need lights. She sprinted through two more sets of doors, and the floor of the dome rose above her, sprinkled with circular rows of tiny lamps that lit up when she hit a switch.

The expansive room housing the telescope was kept cold to protect the lens. After the previous night's antics, Savannah relished the chill.

Circumventing the stairs to the scope, Savannah hustled to her portion of desk space and tossed her things onto the metal cabinet beside it. By the looks of things, her recordings hadn't been noticed. The red lights of the recorders were like taillights in the dimness. The monitor attached to it was dark.

"Thank you, last night's non-nosy science guy!"

Savannah turned on a halogen lamp and dropped into a chair.

"Monitor on." Her fingers moved over the buttons and dials. "Feed geared to its starting point."

Counting to ten, wanting to scream ahead of time to get that over with, she pressed the monitor switch and sat back.

The camera showed the kitchen first, on the top right corner of the screen. No one had been in there after she'd set it to record, so the kitchen was empty of life.

Next up was the living room. The camera hadn't yet caught her glorious, devious guest.

Then the screen went fuzzy with static and a series of wavy black lines. Frustrated, Savannah turned the dials. The bedroom appeared. She held her breath.

Her voice on the recording was winded. "Stay, Dylan," she heard herself say. "Please stay. I don't fear this. I don't fear you."

Dylan McCay responded in that same deep voice from the recorded tape, but Savannah stared at the screen for several seconds before realizing what was wrong. Confused, she pressed her face closer. She started to shake, trembling so hard, she could barely sit upright.

Her image was there, in her dimly lit bedroom, on that monitor. But her guest's image wasn't. It was as if Dylan McCay was the invisible man.

Rewinding, she started over and found the same thing. She knew that she hadn't dreamed Dylan, because she heard his voice.

She hit the rewind button harder this time, with both hands.

"It doesn't matter how many times you look at it," a familiar voice said from behind her. "I won't be there."

Chapter 6

Savannah shot to her feet and turned to confront a reality that no longer made sense and quite possibly hadn't from the start. Dylan McCay stood there in front of her, though it should have been impossible for him to get into a secured building. He stood there looking as solid as anyone could be, and yet he had not appeared on that screen.

"We don't photograph or reflect," he said calmly. "The theory goes that after we lose our mortal selves, our spark goes with it, taking away our reflection. Since we're no longer the beings we were before death, some outward, physical relationship to those parts of us is gone."

Savannah's mouth went dry. "I see you," she said.

"You can see us in person if we choose to show ourselves," Dylan said.

"Us?"

"Myself and the others like me."

She blinked slowly. "What do you mean when you say 'after we lose our mortal selves'?"

"I was mortal once, Savannah. Now I'm something else."

"A ghost? Because that's the only way you wouldn't show up on this monitor."

He shook his head. "Not a ghost."

"Then how did you get in here? Whatever method you used, please use it again to get out. I have enough problems at the moment. I think that I…"

He stepped closer to her. "You touched me, Savannah. We…" The remark went unfinished. He started again. "Surely you know that I'm flesh and bone. You'd be certain of it. I'm just not like you."

"You're trespassing." Her charge was weak.

"I came here to explain about last night. We didn't settle the issue of the reason for my visit, and I owe you that."

"I thought we settled things pretty nicely," she said.

"I meant what I said about liking you, Savannah, and wanting to be with you. That came as a surprise and wasn't supposed to be part of the deal."

The remark hung between them, floating like a cloud.

"Deal?" she said.

"An agenda brought me to you, though it's not what made me stay. After meeting you, I found that I couldn't do what I'd been sent to do. Nor could I leave. I couldn't leave you."

Savannah struggled to take this in. "What do you want from me, Dylan? If that's your name."

"It is my name, and I shared it with you when I haven't done so with anyone else. I trusted you with my appearance, my voice and a warning about why I had come. I didn't take all that from you when I left. Not permanently. I've remained at great peril to my cause."

She turned her head to look at the image of her bedroom, frozen on the monitor. "What do you think you are, if the term *ghost* doesn't apply?"

"Immortal."

Savannah felt the blood drain from her face and wondered if he was a madman. When Dylan took another step closer to her, she backed up until her thighs were pressed to the desk.

"That's ridiculous," she insisted.

His hands came up in a gesture of placation, the same hands that had pleasured her earlier. "I would have thought so once, too. But I remember my death and being reawakened to the light. I bear the mark of having passed through death and wear it like a collar. So, tell me, Savannah, do you have another explanation for why I'm not on that screen?"

"Glitch. Has to be a…glitch."

He smiled sadly, and her stomach wrenched in reaction. She had liked that smile. Heaven forgive her, she liked it now. Was Dylan McCay merely the embodiment of her need and desires? Not real at all?

"I am the offspring of an angel," he said soberly. "I'm a product of light meeting with mortal flesh and heaven meeting with the earth. I'm a soldier in the fight with darkness, and a foe of the Fallen. And yet it took a woman like you to put the spark of humanity back inside me and to remind me of the kindness and generosity some mortals possess, as well as how far removed from those things I've become."

Savannah shook her head violently. "I can't listen to this. Can't believe this." Nevertheless, a feeling of rightness suggested he had told the truth.

"I'll go back to the shadows," the man who had captured her with a smile, and who had been intimately inside her, said. "I won't take one bit of your light from you, my dearest Savannah, without your permission. I merely made it harder for you to remember why I had come so that I'd have time to think about what to do."

He raised his hands, then dropped them to his sides. "You will be safe only if you stop searching for that star. I would not see you hurt, or my brethren. This is the dilemma I face."

Savannah tried to soothe her shakes by placing her hands behind her. There was nothing she could do to hide the way her voice shook. "I don't even know what that means. What light could you have taken from me, if you had chosen to?"

He tapped his head with two of the long, lean fingers that had traced her lips so agonizingly well. "I was sent here to remove the necessity of continuing with this particular research from your mind and memory."

"You can do that?"

"Yes."

"And instead you settled for my body?"

"Instead, I found happiness and joy, perhaps for the first time in my long existence. I found trees and sugar-covered dough and the concept of a magical Santa Claus who can close the gap between good thoughts and dark thoughts, and between the living and their departed loved ones."

He took another step. "These things are magical, special, and so are you. You're angry and hurt that I left you on your own. I don't blame you. I had to leave so that I could think this through."

Perhaps seeing the direction of her next question on her face, he said, "I'm no vampire, Savannah. I thirst for light and knowledge. I was born in the light of love but had forgotten about love as an ideal to strive for. I've misplaced the beauty of how love makes us feel."

His dark hair glistened in the fallout from the tiny dome lights, and Savannah remembered how soft it had felt on her face and when it had brushed her naked shoulder. Did being unearthly beautiful mean that he was unearthly? Was it his Otherness that had captured her from the start?

Dylan McCay actually looked like an angel.

That hidden light behind his blue eyes was shining now. Her recognition of it left her feeling even more confused.

"I discovered how much being with you meant to me, knowing I couldn't have more time," Dylan said.

Savannah winced. She felt dizzy. Her knees felt weak and as though they wouldn't hold her up for much longer. In spite of that, her will remained strong.

On some level she had known and accepted that one night was all they might have together. She had been willing to settle for that, or so she thought. She was a grown woman. She was supposed to be able to deal with rejection. But in his presence, with his explanations confirming that he had wanted more time with her, without being able to face his feelings, her anger fizzled.

"I've been left before by people I cared about," she said. "It hurts."

Waking in her bedroom to find Dylan gone had brought back the pain and sorrow of her parents' deaths.

"You made me feel special. I sampled something extraordinary," she said. "And then you disappeared."

Was that what bothered her the most, or the potential evidence of Dylan's madness?

"I divulged secrets that have been safely guarded for centuries," he said. "You alone know what those secrets are."

"Hidden celestial events? The fact that an immortal came to my home to check on my research? Who would believe that if I were to shout it out loud? I'd be the nut of the scientific world."

She quieted slightly. "My research has saved my sanity, Dylan. It has taken the place of friends, lovers and family."

"And I would give anything to have it not mean so much to my people and yours. But it does."

"So, you want to take the research from me now, the way you had meant to last night?"

"There are plenty of other stars, Savannah. If you forget about that one, I'll know you're all right, even if I can't see it with my own eyes, even if I can't be here with you to fill the empty space in your soul."

He was serious, his gaze almost beseeching.

Damn if she wasn't starting to believe him.

The way the shadows hugged his face…

The graceful turn of his head…

"If you're going to take it from me, then tell me what it is about that star that makes knowing about it so dangerous," she demanded.

"The star you've been searching for isn't meant to be found, Savannah. Miracles aren't to be explained. Believe that star existed and that it also, all this time later, brought us together. Can't that be enough?"

His voice had grown hesitant. He wasn't immune to the strain of the moment, Savannah realized. The sexual tension between them hadn't lessened any, with all the craziness surrounding this meeting. Dylan could very well be certifiable, and she still desired him. She longed to have his hands and mouth all over her, which proved, once and for all, that hearts worked independently of superior reasoning skills.

He spoke again. "In this case, the search for that star has caused two lonely souls to meet, while stumbling upon the possibility of love. That is what kept me from doing my job and also kept me from leaving."

"Love?" Savannah repeated, glancing up.

"I love you, Savannah," he said. "I love you with every fiber of my immortal being, which means that when I love, I love forever."

"You just met me. We…"

"I have loved you for years," he said, reciting those words with a passion that all women wanted to experience in their lifetime.

With her heart booming, Savannah met his eyes.

Dylan feared the way Savannah's body swayed.

His powers didn't exempt him from this confrontation or make it any easier. Though he had been determined to see this through, he just stood there, waiting for Savannah to come to her senses.

If he'd been that vampire, he would have bitten her right then, passing some of his angelic light into her bloodstream. That light would extend her life, allowing them years together, decades. Longer.

It was a terrible thought, born of the passion he felt for Savannah and fueled by a need for her that he couldn't escape.

"I can't remain with you, protecting you. I can't take you with me, when I want one or the other of those things so very badly."

He had been desperate to view her reaction when confronted with who and what he really was. He now desired to give her a choice as to what the next move was to be.

When viewed with insight, giving her a choice seemed selfish. If he had taken the star from her completely, as had been his plan, Savannah wouldn't have been hurting at all. She wouldn't be confused. She'd have remembered nothing about him or how the star reminded her of her family. Now she faced it all.

At the moment, she had nowhere to go, having backed into the wall of knobs and lights behind her. The interesting thing was that though she looked at him with wide, questioning eyes, there was no real fear in her even now.

"Are you lying about everything?" she finally asked in a soft, insistent voice.

"An angel offered me the choice of dying in the dark or living in the light, Savannah. Given that kind of choice, I wonder what you would choose."

Dylan waved at the giant lens of the telescope above their heads. "No one is supposed to know the truth of some things for a reason. Why else do meanings elude us?"

A frown creased Savannah's forehead. Her hand fluttered there, as if that area ached.

"Why would an angel offer anything or concern itself with things happening here?" she pressed.

"The angels came to create a wall against the dark."

"That star had darkness in it or beneath it?"

"It has no darkness, but it masked another event that saw the creation of my kind. That celestial event masked the spark of the angel coming to ground. The Fallen ones would like to know about this, about those of us tied to that angel and where we reside. Your research might provide that for them."

She didn't speak to that. Dylan held out his hand. On it was a small golden vial. "This is the gift I offer to you. A compromise of sorts."

"What is it?" She was right to be wary.

"A mixture of the two special essences of frankincense and myrrh. It is more precious than gold, and a blessing to those who taste it."

She glanced at the vial.

"Because of my feelings for you, I'm offering you a choice," Dylan said. "It is to agree to let the star go, allowing you to remember this meeting and all that I've said, or to drink from the vial in my hand and forget everything. Which, I wonder, would suit you better, and which option would prove to be painful?"

The woman across from him paled.

"My purpose wasn't to cause you pain, Savannah, but to protect you and others from finding out about what exists on the fringes of your world. You can see the need for this, surely?"

"Yes," she replied weakly. "If it were true."

When he saw her slump down, her frantic energy finally depleted, Dylan closed the distance. He gathered her into his arms, a breach of the etiquette of giving Savannah choices that didn't include him getting close.

His smile had no mirth in it and merely served to expose his fangs. Savannah's head was back. She was staring at this mouth.

"In knowing what I am, would you have others see this and worse?" he asked.

She didn't answer.

"The potion in this vial contains the power to restore and rejuvenate. Mixed in equal parts from plants blessed by angels, the concoction has other properties, as well," he explained.

"Poison?" she said through her swollen lips.

"No, my dear Savannah, my love. What it does is repel the shadows. One drop of it on your tongue and the light of the angels seeps into your soul for good and forever. No darkness can touch the person who drinks from that bottle. None of the Fallen can have you." He spoke the final words regretfully. "But neither can I."

Although she was as white as paper, her features set to an expression that resembled stubborn resolve. Dylan mustered his courage to tell her the rest.

"If you sip from this bottle, none on earth with Other blood in them, whether that blood be dark or light, will have the power to override the mixture's magic. You will be untouchable to all immortals, and I…" His voice cracked with emotion. "I will lose you forever."

She averted her eyes from his, as though she fought for control of her feelings. Dylan wanted to comfort her, kiss away her troubles, see her happy again. He knew now that he'd been dead inside for a long time and that the woman in his arms had made him live.

"You have awakened me to the grand prize coveted

by all mortals and perhaps Others as well, Savannah. Love. Giving it and being loved in return." He barely got that out and had to go on. "If you taste this potion, you will be free."

Savannah moved in his grip. Freeing her hands, she took the vial and held it up between them. "If I drink it now, we'll be done with this nonsense?"

"Yes," Dylan replied, but his soul separated out the false threat behind her words. Savannah didn't want to be rid of him. She had heard the story he'd told, seen the fangs, and against all odds, for reasons beyond belief, she refused to let him go.

He felt her pull, as if she'd tugged on a string tied between them. He felt the flare of her heat. Savannah Clark truly was one of those rare individuals who, after offering her acceptance unconditionally, had a hard time taking it back. She had found something in him that she thought she could love and wouldn't have taken him to her bed if she hadn't.

Savannah Clark was like no being he had ever come across on this earth. Surely the heavens knew this and would someday reward her for it?

"If I believed you, I'd wonder why you don't drink the stuff in that bottle and why beings filled with the light of the angels don't seem happy," she said, her voice slightly stronger.

"I believe that souls only stretch so far and that it's too late for me. I was sent to you for a purpose. I'm standing here now because I respect you, I trust you, and because I love you for everything that you are."

"And in loving me, you'd lose either way, whether I drink this or don't," she pointed out.

He nodded. "You will be free of me either way."

Her eyes met his, again seeking something there.

Dylan pulled the stopper and held the bottle to her lips.

"No," she said. "I'm not ready to forget. I felt a connection. I feel it now."

A defiant glint sparkled in her eyes. "You didn't do what you were supposed to do. You came back to make sure I'm all right. Now you're saying you love me. So, I'm to let that go?"

"Your light is so very tempting, and I am weak against the sheer force of it. You, of all people, know what it's like to crave that light."

"I do know," she said, trembling now, with her heart drumming inside her chest.

Going to her was automatic. Pressing her against the wall of panels, with his body plastered to hers and his face close to hers, was a necessity.

"You will leave me if I promise to forget that star," she said, "and I will remember everything?"

"Everything."

"Then I'd like a kiss," she said breathlessly, bravely. "Just to know the truth and what I'm supposed to do."

Listening to her was absurd and another distraction of the kind that had gotten him into this mess. Dylan felt every shudder than ran through her and every breath she labored to take. He had to steel himself to keep from doing as she asked.

Obsession might have been a good description of his feelings at that moment. That and the pure, radiant joy of holding her.

He was bursting with the aliveness of the feelings running through him. He felt elated about the possibility of one more minute with this woman in his arms.

It would be his last time spent with her, but his spirits soared. He felt happy.

For only a few precious seconds.

Could he imagine going back to a world without her in it? Without the colorful customs she loved that proclaimed peace on earth and goodwill toward men?

He would accept that outcome if Savannah was safe.

"There has to be a third option," she insisted. "You must tell me what that is."

"There are no more options," he said, but if he was to lose everything, he had one more wish, and that was to fulfill her request.

He kissed her hard. He caressed Savannah's mouth with his, maneuvered her lips into acceptance of this one last slip from grace, engrossed by her raging inner fires.

Savannah's tightness began to unfurl. Her lips became pliant and needy. With only one uttered gasp, she kissed him as though her life depended on it.

Contrary to the way this should have gone, and with everything hanging in the balance, Savannah Clark was as hungry as he was and just as determined to make this moment count. In a night that defied reasoning, whatever they had shared—the smile, the confessions, the meeting of their eyes—had sealed their fate.

She was volcanic in his arms, and strained toward him as if desiring to be absorbed and as if she'd have all of him. The moment was as frightening as it was powerful, because no matter what she chose to do, she'd be imagining herself the only one to suffer a change.

That wasn't the truth.

What he hadn't already given up Dylan would willingly give up now, for this kiss, for her body against his, for her belief in him and his purpose. If losses were tallied, he'd have lost the most.

Take this pain from me, he said to the sky above them and to the stars Savanna loved as he went on kissing her.

Take the rest of my life. Do with me what you will, but let me have this one last thing.

Savannah's body bent beneath the pressure of his. Her pulse throbbed through him, inside him, beat after beat, striking his neck, his chest, his groin, manifesting as an extreme sexual longing.

He could have kissed her like this forever. He could have taken this further, consumed by greed, knowing all the while that wouldn't be enough.

But time was fleeting.

She began to tear at his clothes, making soft sounds in her throat. Without thinking, Dylan's hands tore at hers. Half-naked, they paused to look at each other, openmouthed, panting with the effort of restraint.

"It's you," she said, shaking, serious. "I choose you. I suppose I've waited for you as long as I've waited for that star. You might be a dream. I might soon wake up. You can't take these feelings from me with some magic liquid."

The chaos began as their eyes again met. Though Savannah shivered in the cold room, she reached for her zipper.

Pulling away from his grip, she fought for a breath and turned, racing to the stairs, starting up, climbing toward the dome wearing nothing but her pants and her shoes.

Her hair glowed like a helmet of burnished gold. Like a halo. The image drove Dylan nearer to madness.

Part of the way up, she turned to look at him, waiting, moving her fingers down the front of her pants. "You will be out there somewhere, thinking about me? Always thinking about me, Dylan?"

Dylan heard the zipper's threads opening. His eyes met hers. "Yes," he said. And then he ran to meet her, taking the steep metal stairs two at a time.

A blast of cold air reached him as he neared the platform where she stood, the air hissing as it met with the fires still heating the air between him and the woman he loved. Above those sounds, Dylan heard the metallic grinding of the dome opening above their heads.

He met Savannah with a questioning glance. She was luminous, naked and alert.

"Everyone has secrets," she said, pointing to the telescope, which had begun to turn. "We haven't gotten to mine."

Her quaking fingers were at his belt, then his buttons, moving with precision. All of Dylan's thoughts dissipated, other than the one new goal he held above all others. Love her. Show her how much he loved her. Let her know that somewhere in the wide world, he truly would be there, in the distance, calling her name.

They were on the steps, on their knees, then on the cold platform floor. There were no walls here and only a single, rounded railing, icy to the touch.

Dylan arched over Savannah. It wasn't the chill of the metal that made her cry out; it was the look in his eyes as he angled his thigh between her legs and lowered himself to her. She observed every move with her big eyes open, savoring the details of their final meeting.

Dylan had promised himself that if this dream were to be replayed, and if given the opportunity to meet her like this again, he'd take all the time this merging needed. He broke that promise.

Unable to resist her golden allure, or the invitation in her eyes, he pushed the hard evidence of his love for her inside Savannah, first slowly, then with a fierce, full thrust. He slid his hands beneath her, lifting her hips upward and into him, wanting to speak to her, finding that words were beyond him.

He'd have cried out if that were possible. Savannah uttered no further sound. Whatever had made her do this, and take him in like this, kept her gaze riveted to his face.

Her legs closed around his waist, allowing him full access to the place he sought, giving him permission to enter. Only then did she speak. "Merry Christmas, Dylan," she said.

Those whispered words whipped him into a frenzy. He moved his hips and dipped in and out of Savannah's mesmerizing lushness, finding new depths, new feelings and a raw excitement in those discoveries. With every glide, every push, he wished to have more of her, and more of this, from this night forward and forever. And it was too late.

Savannah, his own earthly angel, would be taken from him.

Her insides vibrated, sending out rounds of shock waves as his cock plunged ever deeper. The earthquakes inside her grew steadily stronger before she whispered again in singsong phrases, "'Star light, star bright, grant the wish I wish tonight.'"

And suddenly, her hot, wet rocking motions ceased. The storm inside Savannah had reached its full potential, and Dylan faced it with her. God, yes, he met it, head-on.

Burying himself inside her, reaching the heart of her taut, flaming body, Dylan again found the spot that had, the night before, sealed their souls together.

With his eyes wide open, he met the storm of their bodies merging, melting, soaring beyond anything he had ever known, and he opened himself, accepting the sensations, willing them on.

Pressed tightly into Savannah, he cried out, his cries joining with hers as the pleasure burst forth.

Savannah clamped tightly to him, until finally, breathless from the force of what they had shared, their bodies shuddered to stillness.

It took a long time for Dylan to focus. Slowly, he realized that the space where they lay was lit by an intense, blinding light that captured them, still joined, as if someone had focused a spotlight on the platform.

Around them, above them, the air snapped with streaks of wayward electricity as if a true storm gathered, though the black sky, seen through the open dome, was clear and punctured by stars.

Uneasy, Dylan rocked back onto his knees, pulling Savannah up with him. She raised her face to the sky.

"Secrets?" Dylan repeated the word she had used earlier.

"Wishes," she said. "If wishes are heard tonight, here beneath the stars, maybe you can stay."

Dylan wanted to protest. He thought to ask what she meant by this and what the light was that had captured them. He didn't ask either of those things.

A tingling sensation made him swipe at his neck. His hand came away with moisture on his fingers, an oddity for a being that didn't sweat. The air seemed incredibly cold, when he should have been well-adjusted to the chill.

His scar ached with a warning that he might have trespassed too long and that his time was up. Fear came to him.

Not yet. I can't go yet.

When he rested his hands above his collarbones, he found little left of the ridge of old tissue from the wound that had sealed his fate. No pain threatened when he fingered his throat.

Strange.

Anxiously shielding his eyes with one hand, he looked at the opening in the dome, concerned about what this extraordinary beam of light meant. He got to his feet, with Savannah beside him.

Together, they stood on the iron platform, bathed in the glow of that light, their bodies still shaking from what had come before. Savannah moved first. "Supernova, right over our heads?" she said.

Dylan's mouth felt dry. When he licked his lips, there came no prick of fangs. He staggered and caught himself. Savannah pressed her body close, gazing up at him with determination in her eyes.

"Wish," she said. "Do it now, Dylan. Quickly. Wish to stay with me. Say it out loud."

"I want to stay," he said. "God, yes, I want to stay."

His fingers again sought his neck. The scar was gone. He touched his mouth. The fangs truly had disappeared. He felt different—heavier, weightier and a little off balance. His knees stung from kneeling on the iron grate.

Something else nagged. Inside his chest, his heart was beating rapidly, irregularly and on its own. His breath was coming in loud rasps. Not Savannah's breath, his.

This couldn't be true or right. He had to be dreaming. Possibly he was still inside Savannah, riding the crest of a glorious climax.

No. That wasn't it. Savannah was beside him. Her hands were on his chest. He felt the smooth texture of her skin against his. Her scent was in his lungs.

"More," she said. "Wish again. It has to work. It brought me...you."

He did as she asked, using the phrases she was chanting.

"'Star light, star bright...'"

*What if...*he thought.

What if miracles did happen and someone actually had heard this plea?

What if their lovemaking, beneath the stars Savannah loved, proved to be some sort of magical key for bridging the gap between his world and hers?

Maybe this sudden strangeness, and the light above them, meant the return of the angel who had come to earth so long ago and that she would now honor his only request.

Again, he glanced up at the sky, unsure, desperate to know what was happening to him. Savannah's open, trusting expression pulled him back. She was chanting that song as if she'd make it work with the force of the effort she was putting in. She was here with him, beside him, urging him to believe in her special way because she wanted to believe it so badly.

Dylan allowed himself to believe in that wish with every fiber of his being, and that out there somewhere, Savannah's star had shone for them, on them, bringing them together, making him whole and offering him a second chance at life. At living.

"I need to move the lens," Savannah said excitedly. "I need to move it now." She lifted her mouth to his. "Stay with me, Dylan. Don't go. There's so much I need to know."

He had to move, had to speak. He didn't know why, or how, but in the area of his beating heart, he felt his soul conform to a new shape. That shape matched Savannah's.

He was feeling human. *Mortal.*

Hell, he remembered the feeling.

Searching Savannah's face urgently, he saw hope resting there. If this was true, and miracles did happen, the woman beside him didn't even know the extent of her power that helped to make this transformation possible.

"Go," he said to his lover, his earthly angel, his sensationally naked mate that he promised, on the spot, to treasure to the end of his days if he'd been granted the right to stay.

"I'm here," he said, then started the poem over. "'Star light...' God '...star bright...grant the wish...'"

If he was mortal, Savannah would never be alone again. He would be there to love her. Maybe she wouldn't need that damn star. If allowed to do this, change, be transformed, he would continue to fight the dark as best he could. His lips moved with this silent, solemn vow.

A warm hand rested on his arm. The wonderful fragrance of cinnamon drifted in the air when Savannah moved.

"Go find it," he repeated. He was smiling ridiculously and wondering if his face could withstand this new and jubilant expression.

He felt the brief but wondrous touch of her fingers on his face in a way he hadn't before.

She was smiling, too, as if she understood what he hadn't fully been able to grasp. "Come with me," she said. "We can look at the stars together. We can find other stars together."

He caught Savannah as she turned. He faced her as a man, with a man's urgent need to possess.

"Merry Christmas, my love," he said to her, because that phrase seemed to nestle at the heart of all of this. It seemed to stress the glory and the joy of what he was feeling.

Savannah Clark continued to smile. Instead of chasing that star, supernova or whatever strange, timely celestial phenomenon had occurred above them, she threw herself into his arms.

As their bare skin met, the sheer force and breadth of their wishes and the magic of holidays, along with one special woman's acceptance of what had transpired here tonight, made them sink to the floor, entangled in each other's arms, forgetting everything else.

* * * * *

HARLEQUIN NOCTURNE

NEW YORK TIMES BESTSELLING AUTHOR

HEATHER GRAHAM

THE KEEPERS L.A.: A NOVELLA

THE GATEKEEPER

THE GATEKEEPER

Heather Graham

Right when L.A. was on the verge of exploding with underworld activity, the Gryffald cousins were called upon to take their places as keepers of the peace between humans and otherworldly races. Hollywood, they were about to discover, could truly be murder....

Discover The Keepers: L.A.: a dark and epic new paranormal quartet, led by *New York Times* bestselling author Heather Graham, debuting in January 2013.

Turn the page now to sink your teeth into *The Gatekeeper*, the sensual and gripping prequel story.

Chapter 1

The City News and Herald
Las Vegas

Are Zombies Roaming the
Streets of Las Vegas?

The scene on historic, neon-lit Fremont Street was an unprecedented bloodbath last night as a crowd of several thousand went into a panic, killing and trampling one another as they scrambled to survive a "zombie apocalypse." The frenzy began when the body of Marston Greenwood, thirty-eight, of Portland, Oregon, was discovered in the midst of an Old West display beneath a blazing green neon *Z*. The man appeared to have been partially consumed by some sort of animal, which sent the crowd into a frenzy just as, ironically, the cast of the new *Zombieville* revue appeared on the street for a promotional stunt—with tragically unfortunate timing. While eyewitness accounts vary, one survivor, Sam Nichols of Nunnelly, Tennessee, claims, "Some guy who walked like a mummy and had a serious skin rash stumbled toward a woman just as she discovered the body. She screamed, and the man next to her—I think he was a Texan, 'cuz he was fast on the draw—tried to protect her and shot the zombie or actor or whatever the hell he was. Then people were screaming, running like crazy. There was a giant hairy creature roaring down the road, and I couldn't tell the showgirls from the hookers or the actors. Music was blaring from somewhere, but you could still hear everyone screaming. Looked to me like zombies or werewolves or vampires or God only knows what were ripping through the streets, tearing into everyone."

Despite Nichols's claims and other similar reports, police and state and federal authorities have characterized the tragic incident as a case of mass hysteria in reaction to the combination of an unfortunate death and the ill-timed promotional performance by the *Zombieville* cast. The agencies have joined forces for the continuing investigation into the tragedy. Pending notification of family, the names of the dead are being withheld.

While the area is currently closed, Mayor Herman Langston is assuring the local population and tourists alike that the situation is now under complete control. "Vegas is open for business. Police are out in force, and while we're all shocked and saddened by the horrific events of last evening, we will not be shut down by this tragedy that has been visited upon our exceptional city. The local hotels and casinos are offering free rooms and entertainment, so if you already have plans to visit us, don't change a thing. And if you don't already have plans, then this is the time to make them."

Saxon Kirby stood in the morgue staring at the body of lynching victim Joe Moore. Art Krill, the medical examiner, was carefully removing the rope used to hang the man. He spoke in his dry monotone so the microphone clipped to his chest could record his findings.

"The deceased, identified as Joe Moore, thirty-one, resident of Las Vegas, Nevada, actor by trade, appears to have been in excellent health before his death. X-rays show that the deceased's neck was not broken and that he died…"

Saxon didn't actually need to be there. There was nothing for him to do but stand around and watch. But he was a cop, a detective, and his presence was expected. He was pretty sure that no one needed a medical degree to figure out that the poor guy was dead and that he had died slowly, ripping desperately at the rope around his neck as he kicked and fought before finally losing the fight. The smell in the room was rank, but then, hanging wasn't an easy way to die. The body gave in and the bowels emptied. There was no dignity in death. He'd met Joe Moore a few times. He'd been a decent guy and a half-decent actor who'd finally gotten his big break with a role in *Zombieville*.

Yeah, his big break.

Saxon looked out at the stainless-steel gurneys filling the room. The statistics were horrifying: nineteen dead and forty-nine in local hospitals, some in critical condition.

He turned and exited the autopsy room, his strides lengthening as he left the morgue. Outside in the bright Las Vegas sunlight, he headed for his car.

"Detective!"

He stopped and turned.

Captain Clark Bower was there. It was unusual to see him at the morgue. Then again, this entire situation was unusual.

Bower was nearing retirement. He was a good captain, but at the moment he just wanted to finish out his last three months in office.

"Captain," Saxon said.

"You're leaving already? I thought—"

"Captain, what am I going to learn here that we don't already know? Joe Moore was hanged. Eleven died of gunshot wounds, and the others were stabbed or trampled. I was here earlier for the autopsy of the man who was…cannibalized—and that mattered."

Bower gritted his teeth, looking up at the sky as if asking the heavens how this could have happened now. "The mayor is down our throats, Saxon. The police chief—"

"The mayor wants to be reelected. This town runs on tourism, so naturally he wants an explanation for everything that happened, and he wants it fast and all wrapped up in ribbons. It's not like we can blame it all on some crazy with a gun permit. Every man out there—assuming we find every man—who shot his piece will claim self-defense. I don't need to hang around the morgue, Captain. I need to find whoever killed Greenwood and dumped his body on Fremont so something could chew his face off."

Captain Bower nodded. His jowls weighed his face down heavily. Bower had been in charge of units that had solved some of the most vicious murders in the city, but right now he looked as if he were a cast member in *Zombieville* himself. He was a big man, but it suddenly looked as if his skin was hanging off his bones.

"Yes—find who murdered the man. Or who found his gnawed body and threw it into the street. Get to the core of this and—Lord help us all, Saxon—do it fast. I'd say you could start with—"

"I know where to start, Captain. I have connections on the street. I know what I'm doing," Saxon told him quietly.

Bower nodded. "Then do it."

Saxon turned and continued to his car.

But he wasn't really heading out to see a snitch.

At the Wolf and Crown, one of the newest and most elegant casinos to grace the Strip, he pulled up to the valet stand and tossed his keys to one of the attendants, Billy Shield, a kid he knew pretty well.

Billy grinned as he caught them. "I'll have it ready the second you want it," he called. Billy knew that even though Saxon was a cop, he tipped.

Saxon headed past the flashing slot machines. He was barely aware of the din that filled the casino as he strode across the elegant marble floor toward the elevators, and he ignored one of the executive guard dogs who saw him, frowned worriedly and hurried in his wake.

The elevator door closed after him just as the suit rushed up.

Saxon knew the code to reach the level devoted to the private office of Monty Reilly, owner and CEO of the Wolf and Crown.

The elevator opened on Monty's floor.

And there was Monty.

He was still in his bathrobe. A silver coffee service sat on his desk. There was an urn of coffee on it with a large bottle of bourbon next to it. To his credit, Monty wasn't sitting there petting one of his scores of buxom fortune-hunting beauties. He was pacing. He'd dragged his fingers through his dark hair a dozen times and looked like hell.

"Saxon! I knew you'd be coming, but you got to believe me, this wasn't done by one of mine. I'm telling you—"

"Sit down, Monty."

Monty, who had the smooth look of James Bond—at least when his hair was combed—sat immediately and stared at Saxon. "It wasn't one of mine," he repeated.

Saxon walked over to the desk and leaned on it, staring back at Monty. "It all started with the discovery of a corpse, Monty. A corpse that had been eaten. Gnawed. Devoured."

He'd seen that body, and he knew a werewolf's marks when he saw them.

Monty swallowed hard. "Come on, Saxon. You know that a body doesn't last long in the desert without something eating it. A coyote, a—"

"A werewolf, Monty. And you're the Keeper of the

Vegas werewolves. Your charges have been getting out of control for a long time. And I know you have a pretty good idea which one of them did this. I'll bet you cash money that a werewolf was responsible for the disappearance of that craps dealer two months ago and for that pretty blonde singer who left work and never returned. And I know damn well that a wolf was responsible for those bones we found out in the desert last month. What the hell is going on, Monty?"

Monty looked away.

"Who is it, Monty?" Saxon sat on the corner of the desk, crossing his arms over his chest. "That new hotshot from Toronto who gave me grief when I kicked him out of the Wolf's Den? What's his name? Jimmy Taylor? Or how about the billionaire pulling your strings—old Carl Bailey? He's been talking all over town about going back to the old ways. And God knows, he has both the power and the money to get rid of any witnesses. Then there's the new girl I've been hearing about, fresh in town, Candy Laughton. She's been working the elite clientele—'entertaining' them. Stripping, maybe more. God alone knows what really happens when she gives a guy a private lap dance."

Monty swallowed. "Come on, Saxon. You don't know that a werewolf is to blame. That guy from Toronto is just a jumped-up punk with a big mouth and too much money. Old Carl Bailey is all talk. And Candy… She's just another wannabe, even if she's an especially pretty one. Saxon, I'm telling you the truth—I don't know who did this. I mean, you don't even really know that it was a werewolf."

"We both know the truth, Monty. And when the first

disappearance happened, you should have been right on it. Damn it, Monty, it's your job, your calling."

Monty rose. He was going to lose all his hair, Saxon thought, if he kept running his fingers through it so hard. The Keeper shook his head. "I thought everything was going well. I mean…what control do I really have? They're the biggest players in the city, some of them. You know that. They're powerful…. They're—hell, Saxon, stop looking at me like that! There really aren't any rules…no justice system for us to rely on. I can't haul anyone into court. I—"

"Monty, Keepers maintain control."

"That's not fair, Saxon. Sure, we're supposed to control the other races. But what power do we really have? It's not like everyone signed off on a bill of rights. Once it wasn't a big deal. The populations in the New World were small—hell, the worldwide population was still small—and it was possible to discreetly handle situations. But there's no recourse for me now, nowhere to go—and no real laws."

"You should find a way to handle it," Saxon said. "But since you can't, I will."

"This is everyone's fault—not mine!" Monty insisted.

Saxon felt tension riddling his body. He wanted to land a punch on Monty's clean-shaven jaw; he wanted to shake him out of his comfortable suck-up position at the casino. Monty was a figurehead. He wasn't running the werewolves—they were running him.

But one thing Monty had said was true: there was no overall governing body for the Keepers to rely on when they were dealing with their charges; there were no real laws. Life and society had changed over the years. For well over a century now, the Keepers had been keeping control all over the world—preventing the mass extinction of human beings by keeping the werewolves, the vampires, the shifters and all the other paranormal races in check. But Monty was right. They were living in a world where populations had exploded. If a Keeper in one city was weak, hell, just move there and behave as irresponsibly—as violently—as you wanted.

Saxon cursed the fact that there was no judicial system for Keepers and their charges.

There should be.

Except he didn't even know who to talk to about forming one.

And for the moment he couldn't worry about it. He had to find the werewolf chewing his way through Las Vegas.

Hell.

Did he start with the kid, the billionaire or the stripper?

Chapter 2

The Rock Candy Club occupied the penthouse level of Candy Country, one of the few casinos that hadn't been built using Carl Bailey's money or ended up with Carl Bailey owning a huge percentage of the shares, whether by name or through one of his many business ventures.

Carl had wanted in; Saxon knew that. But one of the major investors was Reginald Holland, a vampire who held sway in New York City. None of Carl's goons were going to get to Reginald in his cement castle in the Big Apple, and Reginald could not be bought. Saxon had never met him, but he hadn't heard about any vampires causing problems in New York, so presumably Reginald was working hard at living the American dream—controlling his appetite for blood with domestic animals, the small forest creatures that inhabited Central Park or, most likely, blood banks.

Saxon smiled, pleased that Carl Bailey hadn't managed to take ownership of the entire city.

The Rock Candy Club was reached via private elevator.

The women who worked there weren't listed in advertisements—nor, he suspected, on any IRS forms—as either prostitutes or strippers, though both professions were legal in the city.

The Rock Candy Club hired entertainers.

To be fair, the women were reputed to be quite entertaining.

There was a guard outside the elevator. It wasn't so much that you needed ID to reach the upper floors, but you did need an impeccable credit rating to reach the penthouse level.

Saxon produced the exclusive platinum card that he carried for precisely such an occasion. Sometimes in Vegas it was necessary to play the part.

The guard let him by, but there was another "host"— not as tall as Saxon but massive and broad like a steel-hulled ship—ready to greet him in the elevator.

Werewolf, definitely.

Big, hairy, broad-faced werewolf.

"Welcome, sir," he addressed Saxon politely. He wore his suit well, though he did seem to chafe a bit in the tailored shirt, high collar and tie.

"Elven?" the guard asked politely.

Saxon merely nodded.

The man cleared his throat. "Begging your pardon, sir. I didn't mean to pry. We don't see too many of your kind here, on account of…"

His voice trailed off as Saxon pointedly ignored him.

Elven were invariably tall and generally blessed with

exceptional looks. That was why so many of them had successful acting careers out in Hollywood; not only did they tend to be tall, blond and good-looking, they were usually also blessed with a considerable amount of charm.

Both sexes were also revered as lovers, endowed with stamina and, in the males, sexual equipment to match their well-toned physiques.

"Actually," the guard said, "we don't see many of your kind in Vegas at all."

"I'm sure that's true," Saxon agreed.

"And certainly not…here. You know what I mean. Here. Looking to spend money on…entertainment."

Saxon wasn't feeling the patience for a pissing contest. On the other hand, he didn't want to start off on the wrong foot before he'd even made it into the club.

He grinned at the guard. "I've heard great things about this place."

The guard smiled back at that. "It's spectacular." He lowered his voice as an indication of confidentiality. "Ask for Candy."

"I hear she's new," Saxon said. "And exceptional."

"She may or may not agree to see you," the guard told him. "She's selective."

Luckily Saxon didn't have to continue the conversation any longer. The elevator had reached the penthouse.

The door opened.

At the end of a hallway stood a beautifully constructed glass enclosure, the customary pole at the center. The pole was wrapped in a shimmering sheath of fabric that matched the temptingly designed outfit worn by the dancer on display.

She was incredible. Lithe, her every movement was

seductively smooth as she danced to a tune he knew well and barely heard.

She wasn't half-naked, like the typical Vegas entertainer, or even provocatively dressed. Clad from head to toe, her exceptional allure came from the figure within, which was tall and lean and wickedly curved. *Limber* didn't begin to describe the exotic way she could twist and turn. She moved around the pole with the animalistic grace of a cat.

Saxon was dimly aware as the guard behind him said, "Enjoy yourself, sir," and the elevator door closed. He continued down the short hall that led to the foyer—and the glass-enclosed dancer. The place was elegantly and tastefully furnished in antiques; paintings graced the walls. None of them were sexually explicit. One was of a medieval damsel clad in delicate, draping white, bending down to draw water from a shimmering stream. Another was of a knight in shining armor, a fair lady gently carried in his arms. The rest were similar in subject matter and tastefulness.

Saxon barely noted them or the decor. His attention was fully caught by the dancer.

Her hair was dark—not black, but a sable color with streaks of auburn running through it. Her face was delicately, aesthetically sculpted, yet her lips were almost supernaturally full.

Her eyes, when she deigned to notice him, were an intriguing mix of green and gold, as sharp and beautiful as diamonds, glittering like the fabric that covered her.

And when they met his, they filled with disdain.

Once she caught his eyes, she didn't look away. She stared at him and continued dancing as if he were no more than a fly buzzing nearby.

"Mr. Kirby?" someone murmured in a silken voice.

He turned. A blonde with the perkiest—and undoubtedly heavily silicone-enhanced—breasts he had ever seen was coming toward him. She was clad in something that resembled a stewardess uniform from the earliest days of commercial flight.

"Welcome," she said. "They told me you were on your way up. Please, if you'll join me in the antechamber, we'll discuss what brings you to us, what fantasy you would like fulfilled and what kind of entertainment will satisfy your heart's desire."

Antechamber? Interesting word for a business office.

He smiled. "Of course."

He was loath to leave the entry. He could almost feel the hot gold-and-emerald gaze of the woman behind the glass.

Not to mention her contempt.

He forced himself not to look back, though it was difficult.

But he followed the buxom blonde. She led him into an elegant office. Her desk—which still held the obligatory computer and phone—was carved ebony with handsome ivory insets. Her office chair was upholstered in a deep burnished crimson, like the massive chairs that sat across from it. Marble statuary graced the edges of the room, and a plate-glass window looked out over the sunbaked brilliance of the Vegas Strip.

"So…" she said, sitting down and folding her long-fingered, exquisitely manicured hands, and smiled. "What is your wildest dream, sir? How may we entertain you? Do you dream of angels or demons? Or perhaps something in between—a dance of innocents and vixens together? Is your dream girl slim or curved or…?" She lifted her hands, the fabric of her suit jacket stretching across her breasts. "We seek to entertain, sir. Our performers are among the most talented in the country. But we cannot entertain you unless we know what it is you seek."

He leaned forward and met her eyes, then gave her a charming smile. "Candy," he said.

She paled slightly. "We have Asian beauties who can twist and turn in ways that you've never imagined. We have Russian acrobats who sail across a room as gracefully as the last great ships that rode the oceans' breezes. African women whose movements can rival the rhythm of any heart. Irish lasses who can dance their way into the bloodstream."

"Candy," he repeated.

His hostess sat back, perplexed. She pursed her perfect cherry-red lips.

"Candy—despite the name of our establishment— has not been with us long. She is a rare and exotic talent, so rare that her contract here allows her to choose when to entertain privately."

He nodded. "Candy."

The woman sighed.

He tapped his platinum card on the table as if in thought. "Perhaps you would see if the young woman might be willing to give me just a few minutes of her time."

"I…" The blonde clearly intended to protest.

He leaned closer to her and deepened his smile, seeking her eyes and staring into them. "Candy," he said again.

She rose without breaking eye contact. "I'll speak with her."

He nodded, watching her go. Once she was out of the room, he was on his feet. He quickly made his way around the desk to the computer and looked up Candy's employee file. She was listed only as Candy—no last name. Her hours were listed as "general entertainment," and, as the blonde had said, there was a notation by her name that read "Will choose individual clients."

He frowned as he heard the blonde returning, her heels clicking on the marble floor.

By the time she entered the room, he was back in his chair. He quickly stood, looking at her expectantly.

"Candy will see you," she said and turned. "This way, please."

He followed her down an elegantly paneled hallway until she stopped, opened a door and ushered him in.

Saxon stepped into the room, but he didn't see Candy. Nor did he notice when the door closed behind him.

A marble-floored entryway led to a large, richly carpeted room. Sunlight poured through French doors that led to a balcony and offered a view of the nearby fountains at the Bellagio and a stunning view of the entire Vegas Strip.

A huge Venetian-tiled whirlpool bath looked out toward the balcony. Heavy furniture in oak, mahogany and ebony filled the room, along with a massive bed whose hand-carved head- and footboard supported an elegant canopy.

He knew he was being observed.

He noticed an Oriental screen beside the whirlpool.

And as he watched, Candy emerged from behind the screen.

His breath caught in his throat when he recognized

the dancer who had seduced and entranced and hypnotized him from behind the glass.

She wasn't dressed as she had been before or as he would have expected of an "entertainer." She wore a plain white terry robe, her hair sleek and curling around her shoulders.

She was tall, perhaps five foot ten. Elegant in build, and supple, as he'd already seen when she'd danced.

She moved so fluidly that she seemed to float slowly across the room.

She wore no makeup. Her eyes, which seemed to gleam with a hypnotic beauty, were unadorned by shadow or mascara. Her lashes were rich and thick all on their own, her face pure perfection.

When she spoke, her voice was a husky alto that teased his senses. "So, you have come just for me, I hear?"

"Yes."

She smiled and came closer. "And what is it that you desire? A dance? Ah, but you've already seen me dance. Perhaps you're looking for something more intimate, more…personal?"

She stopped directly in front of him and slid her hand up his shirt. Then she placed both hands on his chest, the subtle pressure of her body pushing him toward the bed. The backs of his knees met the mattress, and he held steady for a moment.

"What are you offering?" he asked her.

It was difficult to maintain his composure in the face of her pure sensuality. She seemed to offer the wildest and most intimate and intriguingly carnal pleasures the mind could imagine.

And he was Elven.

Also a cop—trying to stop a murderer.

He let himself fall back onto the bed, wondering what her next move would be. In seconds she was straddled over him, and his wrists were imprisoned by her long fingers as she stared down at him.

"Elven," she said.

"Yes."

"And a cop," she added.

He smiled. Time to turn the tables. She wasn't prepared when he flipped her over and straddled her, pinning her wrists to the bed.

"Werewolf," he said, meeting her eyes. "Hunting your way up the Strip and through the desert."

Her eyes widened, and she stared back up at him. "What?"

"You heard me," he told her, but his gut told him that she had nothing to do with the rash of deaths.

He was fighting to keep his responses to her in check, but he could feel her beneath him with every fiber of his being.

"Elven cop, yes," he said. "And I intend to stop the death and insanity before more innocents die and their deaths bring our entire supernatural society crashing down."

She was still staring up at him, and her frown seemed real. "Get the hell off me," she told him. "Unless you... can't." Her suddenly seductive tone told him exactly what she was thinking.

"Don't flatter yourself. You invited me here, after all."

"Don't flatter yourself, Elven. I had to know what you were up to."

Those golden eyes studied him, reached into his soul.

Then they suddenly cleared and turned innocent—even vulnerable.

"Just what do you think I'm doing?" she asked, making no attempt to hide her annoyance.

"I have no doubt that you entertain your audience. I just worry about how many pieces your audience is in when you've finished your performance."

"Don't be a fool," she told him. "I'm here to stop what's happening. I'm not causing it."

He stared down at her. How the hell did you trust a woman who could torment a man to insanity with her eyes alone? "Why should I believe you?" he asked.

"Because of Angie," she said softly.

He waited for her to go on.

"Angie Sanderson." He could have sworn that tears glistened in her eyes. "She disappeared six weeks ago, right after Carl Bailey gave her a job singing at one of his casinos. She had the voice of a lark. If you're a cop, you must have seen the report."

He had.

And he had suspected that her disappearance was related to the case he was looking into—he'd said as much to Monty.

True, lots of beautiful, talented young women came to Las Vegas, and plenty of them ended up disappearing. Some simply gave up on their dreams and left. Some were consumed by the city, finding work but not the glittering careers they had come in search of. Some changed their names when they vanished into the city's seedy underbelly because they didn't want their families in Kansas or South Carolina or whatever wholesome place they came from finding out what they were really doing.

But Angie…

He could remember the "Missing" posters that had gone up all over town.

She was blonde and blue-eyed, young and innocent. She had done her shift one night, singing her little heart out—and been reported missing when she hadn't returned to work the following day. The casino cameras had lost her once she'd mingled with the throng of humanity on the street.

"What do you have to do with Angie Sanderson?" he asked. "It's not your job to find people. And if you really are innocent, then you need to get out of here—since it's dead obvious one of your kind is up to something very bad."

Candy looked at him with her golden eyes gleaming with tears.

"I don't believe 'my kind' have anything to do with this. As for what I have to do with Angie…she's my half sister. And I don't care if you're a cop, an Elven or an archangel come down to claim us all—I'm not leaving until I find her!"

Chapter 3

Saxon got up and moved away from Candy and that far-too-tempting bed.

He needed some distance. First the woman had been the embodiment of exotic beauty and erotic movement. Now she seemed like a little girl lost. It didn't matter which, really. When she looked at him, he felt as if he were being drawn deep into a netherworld where he could easily become lost forever—and he didn't dare take that chance. Especially not now, with a murderous werewolf on the loose.

"Your half sister?" he said, studying her. "Half... what?" He conjured the picture of the missing woman. Blonde, angelic.

Elven?

Candy shrugged, then sat up and ran her fingers through her hair. "Half sister. We share one parent."

"And?"

She took a breath, then said, "I'm a bit of an un-usual...being."

"Go on," he said firmly.

"Our mother was the sweetest, gentlest and most amazing woman you could ever meet. She met one of her own kind—an Elven—and they had Angela. Then Angie's father died."

Saxon felt his muscles tighten. Elven normally led very long lives. "Because your mother met your father?" he asked.

The look she gave him was so scathing that he felt as if he were melting in the pool of her contempt.

"Angie's dad died because he had it in his head that he should serve his country," she said quietly. "He was in the air force, and his plane went down in the water and he...died. I'm sure you understand."

Saxon nodded. Of all the underworld beings, the Elven had been the last to come to the New World. They didn't melt if they touched water, but they were crea-tures of the earth. Despite their strength and normally robust health, they couldn't survive long in or even over water. Because of that, they hadn't come to the New World en masse until flying became commonplace. A few adventurous and hardy souls had made it over via ocean liner, but the crossing had been difficult. Not ev-eryone who attempted it had succeeded, and the weak-ened survivors had been easy prey on arrival.

"And your mother married a...werewolf?" he asked.

"You really are a condescending SOB, aren't you?" she said sweetly.

"Don't be ridiculous. I'm not a prejudiced man," he denied quickly.

She shrugged. "You are—but perhaps it's not entirely your fault. You're Elven."

She said the word as if no explanation was needed, and she was probably right, he thought.

"So, yes," she went on, "my mother married a were-wolf, and I don't know a soul who doesn't like my father. He was the best father in the world to my sister. He doesn't know yet that she's disappeared. Neither does my mother."

"And they don't know that you're working here, either, do they?" Saxon demanded.

She exhaled. She was obviously trying to come up with a good explanation, but then she simply said, "No."

He shook his head while looking at her. "So, how are you going to explain to your father that you've been dancing in a strip club and pretending to be a prostitute?"

"That's the point, don't you see? My mother is an actress. Angie and I grew up in the theater. I've done nothing but act—act like something I'm not—since I got here."

"You've acted out wild romps with men?" he said incredulously.

"If you know so much—"

"I know you've agreed to see only a few private clients. But you're growing legendary—there's talk about you around town."

"Really? That's wonderful. I'm getting to where I need to be," she said, smiling.

He walked over to her and pulled her to her feet. "What's the matter with you? You're dealing with ruthless men—ruthless creatures who can rip you to shreds and scatter your bones across the desert. Have you actually slept with these monsters?"

"No!" she protested. "I told you—it's all an act. I'm trying to find out who killed Angela, and I think I know."

"What? Who?"

"I'm trying to get to know people who are close to Carl Bailey," she said. "Everyone's on guard, too intimidated by him, on his own turf. But people are less wary, more willing to talk, when they're away from work. Maybe Bailey himself will even show up here one of these days. I'm certain he's behind her death, if he didn't kill her himself. He has his eye on this place, and I think he'd do anything to get it. If Angie heard something about what he was up to, something he didn't want her to know, he wouldn't have thought twice about siccing some killer werewolf on her. As for my…sexual activity, I accept very few private clients. Luckily for me, my performance has earned me the right to choose who I do and don't see."

"This is dangerous. You're dangerous!"

"Good," she told him flatly.

"And how do you get rid of those clients without… delivering?" Saxon demanded. He reminded himself that he wasn't her father. He had no right to sound so angry. But…

She was dangerous, all right.

She shook her head and offered a dry grin. "I make them believe they were involved in an experience that was pure magic."

"And how do you do that?"

"It's in the eyes," she said softly.

"You have werewolf eyes, animal eyes," he said. His voice was harsh.

"Yes. And I could have made you leave here without suspecting a thing, thinking you'd been to heaven and back," she told him.

"I doubt that," he assured her. "I'm Elven, remember?"

"And I'm half Elven—and half wolf," she reminded him sweetly. "Should we test it out? Or perhaps you should leave now. And make sure you arrange an exceptional gratuity for me, will you?"

He walked over to her, jaw locked, frustration boiling inside him. "What's the matter with you? Your sister disappeared. Do you want to disappear, too?"

"I'm forewarned—and I do have that wolf thing going for me, after all."

"You can stop that. Some of my best friends are werewolves," he said.

She laughed. It was a nice sound. An honest sound. "Sorry, but that is so, so patronizing."

He flushed, then was annoyed with his own reaction. He was a cop, for God's sake. "It's not patronizing. It's just the truth," he said. "Listen—"

"I'm not going away. I'm free and over twenty-one. And here in Vegas, my activities—or whatever activities you suspect me of—are completely legal. You can continue on your quest—just leave me alone to follow mine."

She surprised him by smiling again. A real smile, not pretending to be a hard-core temptress or making fun of him.

"Let's start over, shall we?" She walked over to him, offering her hand. "My name is really Calleigh. Calleigh

McGowan. From San Francisco. I'm a Libra—usually very fair in all things. I love long walks in the forest, and I think there's nothing quite so beautiful as a full moon rising on a clear night. And you're…?"

He couldn't help it; his lips twitched. He gave her his hand. "Saxon Kirby. Detective by trade—and inclination. I have a deep-seated need to help the underdog, and I loathe watching the powerful take advantage of the weak." He paused, shaking his head. "What the hell am I doing standing here still talking to you?"

"Admitting that I'm not going away, that I may actually be—" she paused to laugh "—of some help. Face it, Carl Bailey is always surrounded by security, and he may have half your department in his pocket."

"All right, back up."

"I said *may*," she stressed.

"And Carl Bailey may not even be behind these deaths. It could be any one of a whole list of suspects, including the new hotshot in town—that Canadian wolf who's been throwing around so much money."

She could manage a truly impressive stubborn set to her chin. "I'm telling you, it's Carl Bailey. He runs the werewolves of Las Vegas. The Keeper here is…weak."

Weak. That was an understatement.

"It's not like that in San Francisco," she said. "There are laws in San Francisco, and everyone knows you obey them or you pay the price."

Saxon frowned. San Francisco had laws—why couldn't the rest of the world manage it?

No time to dwell on that now.

"I should call your father," he threatened.

She looked away nervously, and he realized he'd hit on the key to keeping her safe.

"You don't know who he is," she said, but she still wouldn't meet his eyes.

"I'll find him. I know he's in San Francisco," Saxon told her.

She shook her head. "Don't you dare! He doesn't know that Angie is missing. He doesn't know that I'm here. He and my mother—"

"Listen to what you're saying! Do you want them to lose two daughters?"

"Care to let me finish?" she asked him coolly.

"All right." He stood back, arms crossed over his chest.

"Not too long ago, my father got a request from a Keeper in London, via Larry Miller, our Keeper in San Francisco. They were having some trouble in Chelmsford—a banshee rampage. Anyway, they were seeking my father's advice." She was quiet for a minute. "My dad has a background in law enforcement and the judicial system. He's gone to work with the English on a central plan so they won't find themselves in this situation again, and my mother's over there with him. It's very secret. I don't even have a way to reach him. He calls every few days to check on me. He thinks Angie is so busy with a show that she's impossible to reach, so..."

"So, you've been lying to him," Saxon finished. "Your father is Theo McGowan, then? The former congressman?"

She didn't respond. She didn't need to.

He shook his head. "Great. Theo McGowan's daughter is in Vegas pretending to be a stripper, and he has no idea."

"You won't find him."

"Actually, I wasn't thinking about that. I was thinking how great it is that the San Francisco Keepers actually cooperate with their international counterparts. But that's not important right now. What's important is—"

"Finding Angie and stopping this killing spree," Calleigh said. "And that's just what I intend to do."

"Calleigh, listen, I'm a cop—"

"And I'm a big girl. You can't stop me. What you can do, if you want, is help me," she told him. "Meanwhile, your bill is getting higher and higher," she warned him. "You need to get out of here before you go bankrupt."

"Calleigh, I can't let you do this."

"It's not your call. Right now you need to go. We can talk later," she told him. "Trust me. If you don't give me away, I'm safe, at least for this afternoon, even if I can manage to lure Carl Bailey here. If—"

"Carl Bailey is old, Calleigh."

"And I'm young."

"My point is, he knows every trick in the book, and he hasn't got a moral fiber in his body. He'd just as soon kill you as look at you if you were in his way."

"Then I'll have to make sure he doesn't realize I'm in his way. How about I meet you tonight and we can make a plan to work together?" she said. "Please. Frankly, I don't want to be responsible for a good cop going bad to pay his bill for my services."

He hesitated. "You're not lying to me to get me out of here?"

"No. I swear. I'll do anything to find Angie, so if you're really going to search for her and not think of her as a showgirl gone bad—"

"Calleigh, Missing Persons has been on it—"

"And done nothing."

"All right. We'll talk tonight. But if you don't show, I will find you here, and I will find a way to arrest you."

"I'll meet you."

"Where?"

She scratched out an address he knew vaguely. It was one of the local equestrian facilities where the members of the show circuit trained their hundred-thousand-dollar mounts.

"This is where you're living?" he asked her incredulously.

She nodded. "The house belongs to a man—a human being—named Dirk. He's in love with Angie, and he's going insane with her gone."

"And he knows what you're doing and hasn't tried to stop you?"

"Seriously? Even if he wanted to—which he doesn't—can you imagine any human who could stop me? I need to find my sister."

Saxon knew that he would find Angela Sanderson, no matter what. She was Elven.

He looked at Candy—at the hope in her eyes.

He could only pray that, with everything else that had been going on, there was the ghost of a chance that he would find her alive.

Chapter 4

Saxon had several hours to kill until he was scheduled to meet up with Calleigh.

He headed back to his station house, sat down at his computer and pulled up the information on the cases that he was now convinced were linked.

Two months back: bones found in the desert. They might have been the result of an accidental death—and the surefire way the desert had of cleaning up the dead. A forensic examination of the bones had been inconclusive. There were no chips or marks on them to indicate that a bullet or a knife had been the cause of death. There were tooth marks on the bones, but while the ME considered them likely to be postmortem, Saxon had his own theories on that. The dead man had been about six feet tall, between forty and fifty years old—and somehow he had managed to die ten miles out in the sand, where vultures, coyotes, beetles and whatever else had pretty much taken care of all his soft tissue. His dental records had led nowhere. He'd been wearing a denim shirt and jeans, size nine boots and a buckle that advertised a Tennessee country-rock band.

He'd died minus a wallet or any other identification—or someone had intentionally removed them.

Saxon had attended the autopsy because the bones had indicated a possibility that the victim had been one of the Elven, who had strong, elongated bones.

But in the end the ME had determined that the skeleton had belonged to a man—just a man, and nothing more. A dumb man—traveling in the desert on foot with no wallet—but a man. Except that Saxon didn't think that little of humanity. And no mortal man could have gotten that far out in the desert on foot. It was too convenient to think he'd simply lain down in the sand to die, then was fortuitously consumed by the local wildlife. No, someone had taken him out there and left him to die, or killed him elsewhere and dumped him in the desert for the body to be eaten and the evidence destroyed.

Murder number one, he thought. At least that he knew of.

Then there had been the craps dealer. Rutger Heinz. He had come to Las Vegas because he'd been entranced by what he'd seen and read about the city while growing up in Bavaria. He'd arrived just five years earlier, attended the University of Nevada, then taken a job.

At Monty's casino. Which was mostly owned by Carl Bailey.

Security cameras recorded Rutger's exit the night he had gone missing. He could be seen getting into his car and driving away. And then, somewhere in the congested traffic of the Strip, he had disappeared. And he hadn't been seen again.

Not long afterward, Angela Sanderson had disappeared. Exquisite, beautiful, Elven. Young, talented, ready to take on the world. With everything to live for.

One thing he'd noticed on the casino security footage of both Rutger and Angela before they'd disappeared was that there had been a very high proportion of werewolves around. It was a tentative connection to the murders, but his gut told him it was real nonetheless, that werewolves were involved in the disappearances as well as the killings.

Then, yesterday, the half-chewed body of the Oregon tourist that had caused a disaster on Fremont Street.

Two officially dead—and his concern as a homicide detective.

Two missing and, he feared, most likely dead.

The dead man found right there on Fremont Street seemed to be a sign that the murderer wanted to be noticed. It was like a cry for recognition.

Why would a killer make such a point of calling attention to himself? One possibility: it could be a cry for help. Maybe he abhorred the killing but couldn't stop himself and was hoping the police would catch him. Or maybe he was showing off for someone.

Another possibility: the killer was so mentally deranged that he was certain he wouldn't be caught; as a narcissistic personality, he considered his own desires of uppermost importance and couldn't imagine that he could be caught.

Yet no matter what else was true of the killer's psyche, the validity of this was not in question in Saxon's mind:

the killer was a werewolf. A werewolf acting as pack leader, as alpha, and trying to convince the rest of the pack that it was time for the wolf pack to take their place as kings of the city.

Las Vegas was one of the pleasure capitals of the world, a neon-lit paradise where every vice known to man—and Others—could be indulged. Where money—and women—changed hands from minute to minute. A city where Carl Bailey was already the de facto king.

What more could the man want? Saxon wondered. Why would he kill—or, more likely, have someone else kill for him? He had money and hundreds of people working for him, worshipping his name. He had power, scores of mistresses, every conceivable comfort.

Maybe it wasn't Carl Bailey, Saxon reminded himself.

He shook his head.

No, Carl had to be involved. The new wolf from Toronto hadn't been here long enough to make the kinds of connections you needed to kill someone and dispose of the body.

Still, it wouldn't do to count the guy out. A smart detective considered all possibilities.

He rose. He supposed he could pay Carl a visit. But he wanted more evidence than what he had—which came down to pretty much nothing—when he actually accosted the man.

He wanted to arrest the bastard, just on general principles, but he had nothing to hold him on.

Besides, how much good would it do when he finally did have enough? How much sway did Carl Bailey have in the courts? Was there any hope the werewolf would actually wind up paying the ultimate penalty under the law?

There should have been another law. A universal law for the nonhuman races. The kind of law that the Keepers had surely used to rule over their creatures, once upon a very long time ago.

Saxon reminded himself that he was a cop. Even if he could prove beyond a shadow of a doubt that Carl Bailey was a murderer, the man was protected by his rights under the Constitution. Saxon couldn't just walk in with a silver bullet and shoot him down.

They desperately needed real laws for the Otherworld. With real consequences.

It was a waste of time to rue the fact that Monty Reilly was either as crooked as Carl Bailey or totally ineffectual. There were two lost people out there, alive or dead. One of them a woman who was, in a way, kin. He had to find them.

He put through a few calls and found out that the new wolf in town, Jimmy Taylor, was playing craps at one of Carl Bailey's casinos.

He decided he felt like gambling.

Jimmy Taylor was in his late twenties, tall, leanly muscled, and he had a thick lock of dark hair that fell over his forehead and the heavy-lidded bedroom eyes that women seemed to find attractive.

The guy could have made it in movies. He should have headed to Hollywood—the kingdom of stars—Saxon thought.

But he'd come here instead—to the kingdom of high stakes.

Carl Bailey's Galway Glen casino was, like all his

properties, expensively and expertly decorated. There were salutes to Ireland throughout. The Tralee Tavern, located above the casino floor with a view of the action, was done in shades of green, and the bartenders were all female and all wearing short green skirts. Carl liked women—the prettier the better, the bustier better still. It was pretty much a given that if a beautiful woman wanted a job—and was willing to kowtow to Carl Bailey—she was guaranteed a job at the casino.

Saxon knew that Carl hated him. He knew from the minute he entered the casino that the security cameras were on him and his presence would be announced to Carl, wherever in the city the man might be.

He didn't head straight to the gaming tables but decided on a drink first. He settled into a green upholstered chair at the Tralee and took a minute to appreciate the ornately carved wood of the bar itself, designed to look as if it had been cobbled together from logs in a forest. Eyes peered out from between artificial branches, as if mischievous leprechauns were watching out for those who'd come to imbibe. A realistically carved female figure, one of Ireland's famous selkies, looked down from above the bottles of expensive liquor shelved behind the bar.

His waitress was in her early twenties. She shimmered a bit when she moved, and he instantly thought, *Shape-shifter.*

"Good evening, Detective Kirby," she said. "Are you here to ask questions? Or are you…off duty?" she finished flirtatiously.

"I'm off duty. But I always like to ask questions," he told her. "I can start with how do you know my name?"

She flushed. "I guess you're not going to believe I've waited on you before and you introduced yourself?"

"No."

"Okay, so…the truth is, Mr. Bailey alerted the employees to keep an eye out for you to show up. He doesn't want to cause a stink by refusing you entrance. He does want you watched."

Saxon looked over at the selkie statue above the bar. He knew she had cameras in her shimmering eyes.

He waved.

"Why does he want me watched?" he asked innocently.

"He says you're on a vendetta—blaming the werewolves for everything that's been happening lately."

"Could be a shifter pretending to be a werewolf," he said with a shrug. "Or a person. It's not as if vicious serial killers can't be human."

"So, what will you have?" she asked, apparently deciding not to pursue the topic of his intentions.

"I think I'll stick with the theme. A good Irish beer, please."

She left to get his beer, and his eyes idly tracked her journey back to the bar. He noticed that there was a platform in front of the selkie statue, and as he watched, one of the servers climbed up and took her place on it. Traditional Irish music started playing, and she began to dance, her feet moving with skill and speed to rival the best performer back on Irish soil.

The waitress returned with his beer.

"She's good," he said, nodding toward the dancer.

"Yes—we don't get hired if we can't perform."

"What's your specialty?"

"I'm a vocalist," she said.

"This is where that singer used to work," Saxon said, keeping his tone casual.

"What singer?"

"The one who disappeared."

His waitress shrugged. "Girls come and go in Vegas. You get a better offer, you move on."

She started to turn away, but he grabbed her wrist to stop her. "This girl didn't get a better offer. She disappeared."

She tried to wrench herself away from him. Without blinking, he made a vise of his hand.

"Damn Elven," she muttered.

"You don't need to fear the Elven. You do need to fear your boss."

"Let go of me. They'll notice, and I'll get in trou—"

"Then smile and act like you're flirting with me."

She smiled, and he kept his eyes locked with hers so she didn't give the cameras a guilty look.

"Did you know her? Angela Sanderson?" he asked. She was obviously frightened, her eyes widening in shock, but she didn't say anything. "You did know her," he said.

She leaned close to him and laughed, as if he'd said something funny. "I replaced her," she said, swallowing. "They said she wasn't coming back. But that was before I knew…"

"Before you knew that she'd disappeared."

She looked even more terrified, if that was possible. "I have to go," she insisted, trying to pull away again.

This time he released her. When she was gone, he drank his beer, then headed for the craps tables.

He spotted Jimmy Taylor at one and took a spot at the other end. He bought in for several hundred, aware that Taylor was staring at him angrily. Jimmy ignored the other man and laid money down on the pass line.

A man at the middle of the table was rolling. "Lucky seven, lucky seven!"

The dice landed on four and three. The players applauded.

Jimmy Taylor continued to ignore Saxon as the run continued. The same man rolled an eight next, and more money landed on the table. He hit several more numbers and then an eight again. The table cheered. There was money everywhere.

But Taylor didn't seem happy. And when the roller came up with another seven, Taylor actually looked relieved, though sighs went up elsewhere around the table, along with some applause for the shooter, who'd made a lot of money for most of them.

Taylor went to cash in. Saxon held his ground, putting down his money while the next shooter started. On a whim, he played a nice sum on craps. The shooter hit an eleven, and Saxon realized he was coming out ahead, a nice plus for his investigation.

He watched as Jimmy collected his money and headed toward the bar. He waited through the next roll, then cashed in himself and headed back to the Tralee.

There was Jimmy Taylor, his hands rough on a young waitress's shoulders. Saxon was tempted to step in, but he reminded himself that he was playing for higher stakes. And he knew Jimmy wasn't going to hurt the girl anyway—not in public and not in one of Carl Bailey's establishments.

He followed when Jimmy left the bar. He thought at first that the guy was going to head upstairs, which could prove tricky. Carl's men would be on him like an infestation of lice if he tried to go up to the rooms.

But either Taylor didn't know he was being followed or he didn't care. Either way, he apparently had a destination in mind. Or maybe—Saxon warned himself—a plan.

Taylor headed out to the streets. Saxon followed him down the neon strip until he took a sudden turn into a back alley. Okay, so a plan it was.

It occurred to Saxon long before he entered the obvious trap that he would need some help, which was easy enough to arrange. It was good to be a cop. But first he wanted about two minutes alone with Jimmy Taylor. After that, it would be great to have some help. He hit the speed dial on his phone and gave the code for "Officer in Need of Assistance."

Then he took a deep breath and ducked into the alley, keeping close to the wall of the building on his right, one of the smaller casinos and most likely another of Carl Bailey's properties.

There was a doorway marked Employee Entrance about thirty feet in, and Taylor was heading right for it.

Saxon hurried past boxes and an overflowing Dumpster, and before Jimmy could put his hand on the doorknob, Saxon grabbed his shoulder and spun him around, forcing his thumb on a pressure point in the younger man's throat as he slammed him against the door.

"Where is she?" Saxon demanded.

The other man couldn't breathe, which made him desperate. He tried to make the change, no doubt intending to rip Saxon to shreds with his teeth and claws, but Saxon just increased the pressure on that vulnerable point. And if the other man couldn't breathe, he couldn't make the change.

Jimmy sagged, giving up, and Saxon eased up just a hair, then repeated, "Where is she?"

"I don't know what you're talking about, so kill me if you want to. But you'd better be quick. You're going to die soon enough yourself."

"Not likely. You've got good hearing, right? I can already hear the sirens."

"Great. I'll have you charged with police brutality," Taylor told him.

"Where's your evidence? There's not a mark on you. Now, you have thirty seconds before I put a shade more pressure on your neck and zap your nerves. You'll be a paralyzed pup the rest of your life."

At last Taylor looked scared. "If I talk to you, I'm dead anyway!" he said.

"Dead is probably better than the way I'm going to leave you," Saxon said. "For the third time, where is she?"

Taylor blinked. "You're talking about that girl, right? That singer? I told him to leave her alone."

Saxon tensed, accidentally increasing the pressure on Taylor's throat. The werewolf let out a sharp squeal and started talking again the minute he eased up.

"I didn't hurt her. I didn't do anything to her. I just drove her out there."

"Out where?"

"His lair in the desert," Taylor said. "Five miles out on Highway 15 there's a big stand of cacti. You can't miss it. His place... It's there, but it's underground. You—"

Saxon heard footsteps. He pressed Taylor's neck hard

to silence him. It had to be Carl Bailey's men, and considering the speed with which Taylor had given in, he might be someone worth keeping around.

He spun around and saw four thugs heading his way. Two dumb human guards with no clue, along with a vampire and a werewolf. He smiled.

"We can go at it, boys, but I think you hear the sirens. Now, here's the thing. This young pup of Bailey's doesn't give the police any respect. He took a swing at me. He's going to spend a night in jail, and then the little bastard will be arraigned and dumped back out on the streets. I think we should leave it at that."

"You know we have to report this incident to Mr. Bailey, Kirby," the vampire said, assuming the lead.

"I'm counting on it," Saxon said.

"You okay, Jimmy?" the werewolf asked. "We look after our own, so if you want help, just say the word."

Jimmy managed a nod. "Damn straight I want help. You need to bail me out. Fast!"

"You bet, Taylor. And don't worry none—Mr. Bailey looks after his own kind."

The four thugs turned and left seconds before two patrol cars, sirens screaming, drove into the alley.

"Take him in. Assaulting an officer," Saxon said, shoving Taylor toward the officers emerging from the second car. Then he bent to speak to Keeghan McMurtree, the driver of the first.

McMurtree was a leprechaun. A tall one. Despite his race's reputed ability with money, he wasn't lucky at gambling. He was a damn good cop, though, driven by his disgust at all the killing he'd seen back in the old country—among humans and Otherworld races alike.

"Anything going on I should know about?" Saxon asked.

McMurtree nodded. "Just a warning. Captain is in a state, anxious as all hell. That business yesterday with the dead guy getting eaten, you know."

"I know," Saxon said. "I've got a few things to follow up that might put him in a better mood."

McMurtree nodded. "Take care, buddy."

"Will do. Thanks," Saxon said.

McMurtree drove away, and Saxon stood there for a long moment, considering the state of his investigation.

So…it wasn't the stripper and it wasn't the tough new wolf in town—who wasn't so tough, anyway. And he'd never thought it was a shifter in wolf's clothing, much less some human nutcase. Given everything he knew about the man and everything he'd learned today from Calleigh and Taylor, there was only one person—one werewolf—it could be.

Carl Bailey.

But that bastard was too clever by half. No way was he doing his own dirty work. Nope, Carl was definitely not working alone.

Saxon glanced at his watch. It was time to head out to ranch country.

He would keep his meeting with Calleigh brief, just long enough to tell her that he had what looked like a decent lead, and if she stayed home and played it safe, he had a chance of finding her sister.

But when he got to the address she had given him, Calleigh wasn't there.

He knocked, and the door was opened by an awkward young man with a baby face and the look of a dreamer in his eyes.

It had to be Dirk, human owner of the house.

"You the cop?" Dirk asked anxiously. When Saxon nodded, the other man rushed on. "Calleigh's been telling me about you. She said you sounded as if you really care. You have to help. I don't know what to do. Like now. I don't get it."

"What don't you get?" Saxon demanded. He grasped the younger man's shoulder, steadying him, looking into his eyes, demanding silently that he get a grip.

"I don't know what happened. She was here, right here. I was just out back, feeding the horses, and I heard her say someone was coming. I thought she was talking about you, but when I came back in she—"

"Dirk, where's Calleigh?" Saxon interrupted.

"That's what I'm trying to tell you! She's gone, and I don't know where!"

Chapter 5

Gone? Calleigh was gone? Saxon could barely wrap his mind around it. Was this revenge because he'd arrested Jimmy Taylor? Or had Calleigh's amateur investigation made her too noticeable—and too dangerous—in the eyes of Carl Bailey?

And did any of that matter in light of the possibility that she might have fought back against her kidnappers and gotten hurt, or been dragged away half-dead?

"How long ago?"

"Ten minutes."

"Did you hear a car? Were the horses acting up?"

"Um, yeah." Dirk stared at him blankly. "Yeah, sure, the horses were going crazy."

Saxon turned and hurried back toward his car. Dirk ran after him. "Hey, what do you want me to do? Should I call more cops?"

Saxon swung around. "Don't do anything or call anyone. Get back in the house and stay there."

Saxon waited long enough to make sure Dirk did as instructed, then got in his car and drove away. He didn't go far, though: just down the road. Then he parked, got out and headed back toward Dirk's place, making sure to stay out of sight as he carefully approached the house.

He heard one whinny from out back, but that was it. Horses had a tendency to like Elven.

They were fearful around werewolves.

And Dirk had been dating an Elven, so he knew about the other races, which meant not only that he could have known what the horses' behavior meant, but that he had known it. So, he'd neglected to offer the key piece of information: the horses had been acting up....

Saxon slipped close to the rear of the house, where French doors leading out to the back had been left slightly ajar.

He moved in closer, listening. He could hear Dirk talking to someone on the phone.

"Yes, I know for sure he headed out. He left five minutes ago, at least. If Jimmy told him what he was supposed to, he'll be heading straight out to the lair—alone. He even told me not to call any other cops."

Dirk never heard Saxon enter, never heard him move. All he felt was the cold steel of Saxon's semiautomatic as he pressed the muzzle next to his ear.

"Ask him about your reward," Saxon whispered.

He was afraid that Dirk was going to fall down, his terror was so great.

"Man up and ask, or you'll be eating bullets for your last supper," Saxon warned.

"Hey, um, when do I get what you promised?" Dirk

managed. His voice wasn't entirely steady, but it would pass muster.

Saxon heard the angry words coming from the other end. "You'll get your payment soon enough. You gave us the one girl. We'll give you the other."

Saxon heard the click as the other man hung up. He frowned just as Dirk finally collapsed, falling down as if he were a marionette whose strings had been cut.

Tears sprang into the younger man's eyes. "I'm sorry, I'm so sorry. It's just that…I had to give him Calleigh. He swore that Angela was still alive and that he'd give her back if…if I gave him Calleigh."

Saxon felt his fury draining away; this kid was a mess. He wasn't a criminal—he was simply cowardly. No, not even cowardly. He was just pathetically in love and utterly useless.

He dragged Dirk back to his feet. "Listen up. I'm going to go get both of them back. You're an idiot if you thought your girlfriend would be returned. Bailey considers them a threat, but he's a man with an eye for a pretty woman, and that means he's going to use them both up and spit them out when he's tired of them. They'll end up as more bones in the desert if I can't save them. I can't take you with me—you'll just be someone else I need to protect—but if you pick up a phone and call anyone, you'll be signing their death warrants and your own. Do you understand?"

Dirk nodded, sobbing. "You have to understand… I love her!"

This mess of a human being was in love with an Elven, and apparently she loved him back. Sad. Truly sad.

"Who were you talking to?" Saxon asked.

Dirk was sniveling. Saxon had to nudge him to get an answer.

"Monty. Monty Reilly."

"Reilly is in on this?" Saxon demanded.

"He, um, he says that Bailey is going to rule Las Vegas and all of the desert. That there's no point trying to stop him. He said Angela and I could get out before... before the killing started if I just gave him Calleigh."

Dirk was full-on sobbing again when Saxon bent down beside him. "I need a horse. I don't want to take my car, because they'll be waiting for me."

"The mare...Mistress Mellora... She's like a speed demon, and she's used to the desert. She's a Thoroughbred-Arab cross," Dirk managed.

Saxon didn't wait to hear more. Time was of the essence.

He slipped out back and quickly found a bridle and a stall with a placard that read Mistress Mellora. In less than a minute he was on his way.

The desert could be unforgiving, but Saxon had come to know it well, because it was such an organic part of the place he had bizarrely chosen as home. And as he rode the fleet-footed mare across the rough terrain, he thought about how to use it to his advantage.

Carl Bailey had no doubt built his lair underground so he could carry out his crimes—and practice whatever depraved behaviors turned him on—undetected. It was also no doubt where he was preparing for the werewolf attack that would end with his takeover of Las Vegas.

But no wolf's lair would have just one entry, because then it would be too easily turned into a trap. The question was, where would the back door be? And how would it be camouflaged against the desert floor and sparse vegetation?

It would have to be hidden by either a field of scrub brush or a group of cacti.

Finally he found what he was seeking. It was actually hidden by both scrub brush and cacti, and shadowed by a small dune for good measure, but footprints—both human and wolf—in the sand gave away its location.

After dismounting, he stroked the horse and thanked her in a whisper for the ride; then he gave her a slap on the rump that sent her running for home.

He crept low among the cacti until, just as he'd expected, he found a wooden hatch flush with the ground and hidden under the brush.

They might not be expecting him to come in the back way, but even so, he would be an idiot not to expect an armed guard immediately inside.

Silently, he worked the latch, grateful for the darkness that was swiftly falling over the desert. He glanced up before entering. Bad luck. The full moon was rising.

He quickly lifted the door and slid through, stopping at the top of a flight of stairs leading down into the lair. As he'd expected, there were guards on duty: two of Carl's chowhounds. Luckily they weren't taking their work seriously. They were standing together, rifles slung over their shoulders, extolling the virtues of the Cuban cigars Bailey had procured for them.

Saxon marveled at the fact that they were so involved in their conversation that they didn't see the sliver of moonlight that slipped in with him—or him. They didn't hear him, and they didn't smell him. Maybe Carl had convinced his crew that brute strength alone made them superior, but these brutes were capable merely of chewing up the unwary.

Whatever the reason for it, their lackadaisical attitude worked for Saxon.

He was able to step right up to the two of them as if intrigued by their conversation and equally enchanted by their Cuban cigars.

"Nice," he said.

When they looked up, he cracked their skulls together.

They fell without a whimper.

He was hindered by the fact that he had no idea where he was going or just how extensive this underground lair was, but he was also determined to succeed.

He moved quietly through the hallway, listening, barely breathing. He heard music—the kind of music that belonged in an epic fantasy film, accompanying a phalanx of armed horsemen as they galloped out to do righteous battle.

He turned a corner, following the music, then paused. He could see a group of about twenty wolves in human form inside a room, the same room where the music was playing.

And among the werewolves gathered there he saw his quarry: old Carl Bailey.

Old he might be, but Carl Bailey was anything but decrepit. He'd been around for centuries. Werewolves weren't immortal, but they aged very slowly.

Carl looked like a distinguished gentleman of sixty plus. His hair was silver-gray. His posture was still straight. He had his share of wrinkles, but they sat well on his sharp-boned face, adding character rather than age.

He was gesturing animatedly, speaking over the music—stirring up the passions of a roomful of his fellow werewolves.

"It is time! It is time to rise up and become all that we can be! The rules—the laws we have forced ourselves to obey—are not for such magnificent creatures as our kind. We are strong. We are predators. The laws of men are not for us. I am your rule. I am your law. And my law says that we are meant to live and conquer as the greatest force on earth!"

His words were met by a roar of approval.

"Show yourselves in your true nature!"

As Carl shouted, the men and women in the room let out a second roar—a roar that became a howl.

Saxon watched as Carl's followers began to change.

Most of the werewolves that he knew personally— friends, fellow cops—managed the change in as sleek and beautiful a manner as could be imagined.

This was not sleek or beautiful. This was something so low and brutal and ugly that he found himself staring transfixed, despite his repulsion. Clothes were ripped off. Teeth gnashed as they nipped at one another, trying to show dominance. Some changed fully, others were arrested in some blasphemous form, half human and half beast.

Only Carl Bailey had yet to change.

He pointed to four of the wolves in front. "You! The Elven cop is on the way. Go out into the night. Take him by surprise. Tear his limbs from his body and gnaw his bones. Rip off his face."

As they turned to obey, Saxon flattened himself against the wall. They were so eager to do their master's bidding that they raced right by him.

He followed swiftly. He hated this—hated killing. But he had no choice.

As soon as the wolves had rounded the corner, Saxon drew the knife he kept at his calf and made a leap for the one in the rear, who went down without a sound. The next wolf died just as easily.

The third made a sound low in his throat as he died, causing the fourth to turn. He bayed and came at Saxon, preparing to leap.

Saxon pulled out his repeater and brought him down with one silver bullet. In the close confines of the tunnel, the report sounded like thunder.

Saxon turned and braced himself against the onslaught he was certain would follow. When nothing happened, he moved silently back toward the meeting room and realized that the roar coming from within, combined with the music, was so loud now that they hadn't heard a thing. He pressed himself against the wall again and listened.

"My friends!" Carl announced. "Tonight I have the ultimate appetizer for the feast that will be our reestablishment of the old order. Tonight you will dine on the most delicate flesh."

Saxon tensed against the wall, readying himself for whatever was coming next.

From across the way, a door opened and a woman was shoved into view. She was dressed in white, as blonde as a ray of sun and appeared to shimmer even in the dark fortress of the wolves. She stood tall, staring defiantly at the werewolves slavering at her.

That had to be Angela.

Saxon saw that her wrists were bound with stout ropes.

One of the half-turned creatures moved toward her.

Before Saxon could intervene, a second woman was pushed up next to her. She, too, was bound at the wrists.

Calleigh!

She stood as tall and proud as her sister, a Rose Red to Angela's shimmering Snow White.

And when the first monster half laughed and half howled as it moved closer, she had plenty to say.

"Look at you! You're pathetic. Are you foolish sheep when you should be wolves?" she demanded. "Follow this man and he will lead you straight to death! Do you think the vampires will stand idly by and let you destroy the precarious existence they've established in the world of men? That the Elven will let you rule viciously and unchallenged? Touch me," she vowed, "and so help me, you will pay a bitter price."

The monsters hesitated, but the bloodlust still gleamed in their eyes.

Then Carl Bailey roared out in fury, "Why are you listening to her? She's weak, a half blood, willing to say anything to save her worthless skin. Show her the true power of her own kind—a power she has eschewed! Show her what she should have known, what she should have been!"

He strode over to the two women and stood beside Calleigh. "She is tainted, of course, by the Elven blood she carries. She has sullied our line. But she has the wolf in her still. Watch her squirm and howl in helpless agony as you rip apart her sister—the Elven! And then let her, too, know what it means to suffer fury and death."

Saxon prepared to move, but the instant Carl reached

toward Angela, Calleigh leaped between them and raised her hands, breaking her bonds.

And then she raked her hand across his face, her nails leaving gashes and long ribbons of blood that drizzled down his cheeks.

Chapter 6

Carl Bailey let out a cry of rage that seemed to shake the walls.

He changed·then, for long seconds becoming some horrible parody of both wolf and man. There were split seconds of horror-movie recall in which it seemed he was nothing but bones, teeth and a macabrely grinning mask, sheets of sinew and muscle, and then...

Then he became the biggest, most vicious-looking silver wolf ever to walk the earth.

He cast back his head and let out a howl that seemed to shatter the earth.

Saxon dug in his pocket for his phone and hit speed dial, praying he would get a signal this deep underground. He knew that if the call went through, his fellow cops would have his location and hear the terrifying cacophony.

No more waiting.

Saxon leaped into the fray, aiming his gun and its specially made silver bullets at the crowd.

"Stop!" he demanded as the room went still. "Do you all want to die?"

"Take him, you fools!" Carl Bailey roared, back in half-human form. "He can't kill you!"

"This gun is loaded with silver bullets—I sure as hell can kill you!" Saxon responded.

One of the half-changed wolves stepped toward him. "Silver bullets? Sure!" He laughed.

Saxon shot him.

He dropped.

The crowd surged forward and Saxon shot indiscriminately into the wall of fur and flesh.

Carl Bailey took a standing leap that carried him over Saxon's head to take up a position behind his acolytes, where their flesh protected him from harm. His followers howled and screamed, shifting between forms in their fury and terror and pain.

"Control yourselves! He can't kill all of us!"

Saxon shouted to be heard above the din. "Let the women walk out of here with me and there will be no more death!"

For a moment there was silence except for the whimpers of those who had been wounded.

Several others lay dead on the floor.

"Stop this!" Saxon shouted. "Stop this cycle of death!" He walked into the center of the room, despite knowing that this action left his back exposed and that he didn't have enough silver bullets to take them all down.

But this was wrong.

It was wrong any time any race or religion set out to destroy or enslave another, to take all the power and use it without mercy.

"You are powerful," he exhorted them. "And because you're powerful, your responsibility is to protect others, not use them and destroy them. What is the matter with you? There has never been a force so great in the history of the world that it has managed to subjugate all men, all races, forever. They will rise against you—and you will be exterminated. Follow Carl Bailey and they will find a way to hunt you down and kill you. All of you. Even the mortals—frail as they may seem—will show you abilities you never dreamed they possessed. What they lack in strength they make up for in cunning. They, too, are capable of cruelty—but they're also capable of laws and compromise and governance to protect the weak among them."

He heard growling...but he also heard whimpering, a sound that could mean pain—or a fierce desire to heed his words held in check only by fear.

"Stop the death—including your own," he commanded them.

"Saxon!"

He heard Calleigh cry his name in warning and whirled to see one of Carl Bailey's die-hard lieutenants leaping at him.

He fired at point-blank range, and the wolf went down like a rock.

"Fools! He can't shoot all of you at once!" Carl shouted.

Saxon was grateful for his acute Elven hearing.

Grateful that he knew one of the wolves was nearly on his back. He spun, thrusting an elbow into the creature's side with a force that sent his attacker flying back against the wall.

"The women! He can't shoot the women!" someone—apparently brighter than Carl—called out.

Damn! The creature was right. He had to reach them before the werewolves did.

He swung around, shooting the two creatures separating him from Calleigh and Angela. Then he leaped to join the women, who immediately flanked him. He quickly handed Angela his knife so that she could cut herself free.

"We're getting out," he told them quietly. "We need to back up along the hall and around the corner. Block the way so they can't surround us. It'll force them to come at us a few at a time."

Their barely perceptible nods assured him that they'd heard him, and as a group they moved backward along the passageway.

He kept his gun on the crowd, and they moved as quickly as they dared.

"You'll never get out—this place is a labyrinth!" Carl warned. He was making his way through what remained of the hesitant crowd, but he kept two of his followers in the lead as lupine shields.

"You're killing your own people, Bailey," Saxon persisted. "Doesn't that matter to you?" Carl responded in growls, so Saxon addressed the throng. "Don't you see? You're expendable to him. He calls you magnificent creatures, tells you you're poised for greatness, but he treats you as puppets, as tools in his rise to power!"

"Stairs. Stairs behind us," Calleigh whispered to him.

His feet touched something.

He looked down, and his stomach rebelled.

He was very much afraid that he'd found the craps dealer.

He was a pile of bones and ripped clothing, broken and gnawed limbs, blood and death.

He heard Angela moan softly.

"Hold yourself together. You can do this," he told her. "You are Elven."

He sensed rather than saw her nod. She swallowed and kept moving with him. One by one, with Saxon going last, they backed their way up the narrow stairway.

"The door," he whispered to Angela, who was first to reach the top. "Just push it up."

He caught Calleigh's eyes. Beautiful eyes. They were wolf eyes, that extraordinary glittering gold shot through with green.

He'd known that werewolves could be remarkable, just as he'd known that all sentient beings came with a capacity for evil. But overall they were good, driven by the desire to live and let live. The fight for survival had made monsters of many in the past, humans included. But laws and rules created a world where everyone could live and prosper.

Until you threw a Carl Bailey into the mix.

Saxon kept his eyes trained on the wolves that were still stalking them, step by step.

He heard Angela open the hatch at the top of the stairs and climb through.

"Go!" he shouted to her. "Run!"

He felt Calleigh behind him.

"Go," he ordered her. "Take your sister and get out of here."

The minute she was through, he followed, slamming the hatch down and jamming the latch with a nearby rock. He felt Calleigh next to him and knew from the tension in her body that something was wrong.

He spun quickly...

...and found himself facing the captain.

Captain Clark Bower. The man who was so near to retirement—the man who had ordered Saxon to put an end to the chaos.

And he had a semiautomatic trained on the three of them.

Saxon stepped onto the wooden hatch to further delay the werewolves and weighed his odds.

Elven could heal almost magically, but they weren't immune to bullets, silver or otherwise. Elven had tremendous strength—but a bullet in the heart trumped the strongest muscle.

"Captain," he said, his shock evident in his voice. "You're in on this? You're human, for God's sake."

"Human, hardworking and tired as hell. I've watched monsters—human monsters—do terrible things, go to court, blame it on a video game and be acquitted. I've been shot, stabbed, beaten and nearly ripped to shreds by a junkie running on coke and adrenaline. And now—now I have a retirement package that wouldn't support a poodle for a month. Sorry, Saxon. You're a good cop, a good guy. But I'm ready to savor the fruits of a long career as provided by those with the true power. Carl Bailey will set me up in a penthouse for life with a monthly allowance that will keep me well into my twilight years."

Saxon could hear the wolves banging at the hatch beneath his feet.

"Step aside," the captain told him.

He held his ground. "Why is it that we can all be so incredibly stupid when we want to be seduced?" he asked. "Carl Bailey used Monty Reilly and dozens of others, and he's using you. He tricked a weak young man into doing his bidding tonight, and he's tricking you. He intends to kill everyone who helps him as soon as he's done using them."

The captain's gun remained on Saxon; his hands were steady.

"I'm an old man, Saxon. Old and tired. I know you. I know all about you. You can afford to let the years go by. You can grow very, very old and still be in your prime."

A board burst beneath Saxon's feet. The pack would be bursting free any second.

"Let the women go," he said to the captain. "Let them go—give them a chance to escape—and I'm yours."

"No!" Calleigh cried. "No, listen, Captain, please… please, look at me!"

Saxon frowned, about to protest, but Calleigh had already drawn the captain's attention.

Yet she just stared at him, hopefully, searchingly, as if speaking to him through the changing expressions in her eyes. What was happening? Suddenly Saxon remembered how he had watched her dancing in that glass enclosure, remembered how their eyes had met, the way she had watched him with complete disdain—and yet he had kept staring at her...hypnotized.

Just as the captain now seemed to be under her spell, his gun hand down by his side, his expression slack.

But before the captain relaxed so fully that he dropped his gun, there was a massive bang as the hatch shuddered beneath Saxon's feet, and the sound broke the spell.

The captain realized his imminent danger and pointed his gun directly at Saxon's chest....

The crack of a bullet split the night.

Time seemed to slow as Saxon braced himself for the pain. Yet nothing ripped into his flesh. Instead, as he watched, a red stain spread out over the captain's chest and he fell forward.

"Dirk!" Angela cried. An angelic smile illuminating her face, she rushed forward into the arms of the man who had come to her rescue.

Saxon stared in surprise. Dirk stared back. He was shaking, but his arm was around Angela, holding her close. His voice was barely a whisper. "I had to come. I love her."

"Great," Calleigh said. "Now get her out of here."

"Get them both out of here," Saxon snapped at Dirk.

The wood beneath his feet was splintering. "For the love of God, get them both out of here now!"

Everything seemed to happen at once. Calleigh shoved her sister and Dirk, pushing them away.

The hatch shuddered as it started to give, and Saxon moved to the side, ready to fight for his life.

Then the wailing of sirens resounded in the night, and flashes of headlights cut erratically through the darkness.

The cavalry was arriving at last.

Dirk finally grabbed Angela's hand and raced with her toward the road.

The hatch burst open.

Calleigh stood shoulder to shoulder with Saxon as the werewolves surged forth in full, vicious splendor. He started shooting and didn't stop, and they began to fall, the dead delaying the living and buying him time. But there were just too many of them, and one injured wolf hurtled into him, nearly dragging him down.

Calleigh whirled and shoved, using her strength to send the wolf flying.

They backed away from the hatchway, Saxon still shooting, but there were so many of them. Too many.

For every werewolf that fell, at least two more came.

But then he felt the ground tremble as the squad cars came roaring up, and dust rose around him as he was joined by Keeghan McMurtree and a horde of men in uniform, guns blazing.

"Werewolves... Your bullets..." Saxon began.

"Silver, of course," McMurtree said with a grin.

The wolves fell by the dozens then, dying as animals,

twisting in their death throes, becoming human again. Someone rushed past Saxon, and he realized that it was Calleigh. She was carrying a tear-gas grenade that she'd taken from one of the cops, and she was streaking toward the open hole in the desert floor.

"Calleigh!"

He called her name just as Carl Bailey appeared in his mammoth silver glory. He raked out a massive hairy paw and brought her down, then dragged her against his massive chest and open, slavering jaws. The grenade fell into the hatch.

Choking fumes rolled out and filled the night air.

Saxon couldn't fire: he might hit Calleigh.

Saxon shoved his way through the stragglers still coming at him and pitched himself atop Carl Bailey's shimmering silver back. He clawed at the wolf with a strength he'd never even suspected he possessed. His gun went flying as he wrapped an arm around Carl's massive neck and tightened it in a choke hold.

Distracted by the attack, Carl loosened his grip on Calleigh, who slipped free as Saxon and the wolf rolled together through the dust and dirt. Cacti pierced Saxon's flesh, but he didn't feel a thing.

Finally Carl pinned the Elven cop beneath him, and Saxon looked up and saw Carl's predatory eyes on his. Saw his gaping maw. Saw his canines as he bent down, saliva dripping, to savage Saxon's throat.

Elven had strength, Saxon reminded himself.

And cunning…

He waited, then rolled at the last second.

The werewolf took in a mouthful of dust, and Saxon leaped to his feet.

Carl made a quick recovery, rising and standing for a moment silhouetted against the moon, a giant silver-haired man-wolf in all his strength and glory.

And then a shot rang out and he fell.

Blood soaked the ground beneath his body as he melted back into human form.

Saxon turned and saw Calleigh holding his gun in a two-handed grip, arms still outstretched, ready to shoot again. And she was shaking.

He walked over and wrapped his arm around her. She was beautiful, tall, slender, vulnerable there in the darkness.

He didn't speak; he just held her. He could hear Mc-Murtree and the others finishing their cleanup of the remaining combatants.

Calleigh pressed closer to him. "I've just killed my own kind," she said softly.

"You had to," he said. "You saved my life."

She flashed him a smile. "No, you saved all our lives. I'm not sure he would have been a match for you, but…"

"But?"

Her eyes met his. The same eyes that could seduce, that could kindle with pure wickedness, were, at this moment, completely giving, and as bright and beautiful as the sun.

"I don't like to take chances, you know?" she whispered.

McMurtree walked over to them and gestured at the bodies strewed across the desert. "How the hell are we going to explain this?" he asked.

Chapter 7

The City News and Herald
Las Vegas

Desert Raid Puts End to Militia Threat

A violent militia group with an underground stronghold and vast cache of weapons was brought down last night in the desert outside Las Vegas.

Inside the secret underground complex, police found evidence connecting the dissidents to the recent deaths and disappearances in the city. Police speculate that the militia leader orchestrated the violence to destabilize the city and facilitate an attempt to take control.

The death toll is still being determined, but police have revealed that two prisoners being held by the cult were freed in the raid. The names of the dead are presently being withheld, pending notification of next of kin.

Captain Clark Bower of the police is among the dead; his position is being temporarily filled by Lieutenant Keeghan McMurtree, one of the officers who led the assault.

Further information will be made available as it is released to the press.

"Not bad," Calleigh said, putting down the paper.

She and Saxon had escaped the frenzy in Vegas and taken a suite in a luxury hotel in Reno. Calleigh was curled up next to Saxon on a deeply upholstered love seat. He was staring out at a view that, unlike what every window in downtown Vegas offered, was not of neon lights or man-made towers.

These plate-glass windows looked out over the majestic splendor of the mountains.

Calleigh touched his cheek. "Good story, don't you think?"

He nodded and opened his mouth to speak, but she kissed him, and that was the end of the conversation.

She was sleek and beautiful. She had skin like silk, radiated heat like the sun and demonstrated a range of passion to match the golden fires that burned in her eyes.

Her kiss had the power to turn his blood to lava. She could move as if making love were the most exotic dance known to man, and she had the ability to make him forget himself and the world, leaving him absorbed in a feeling of wonder that they were alive and together.

They lay in each other's arms on the floor in front of a leaping fire, sated and spent.

She turned and looked at him, stroking his face as he stared back at her in wonder.

She smiled slowly. "News flash. Elven cop seen with Vegas entertainer. Can a true Elven find happiness with a half-breed werewolf?"

He smiled. "I seem to be too worn out to think of an answer."

She smacked his shoulder lightly. "Cut me some slack. I'm laying my heart at your feet."

He grinned and rolled on top of her. "You are half-Elven," he reminded her. "Making love… It's a pretty amazing deal for the Elven, you know."

She touched him intimately. Even now she could get him sizzling again, kindle another fire in his loins—and fingertips, muscles, tendons, blood, toes…

"I know," she told him wickedly.

"I know I won't ever let you out of my sight again," he told her.

They both jumped at a thunderous knocking at their door.

"Get dressed," he said to her, reaching for his jeans.

A moment later he checked to make sure she was decent, then made his way to the door, checked the peephole and opened it, his expression a mix of welcome and surprise.

Keeghan McMurtree smiled and walked in, accompanied by an entire group of Keepers. He immediately started making introductions. "This is Brad Thierson, Keeper of the New York City werewolves."

"And we're all appalled by what Monty Reilly let happen in Vegas," Thierson said.

"I'm Eamon MacDonald, leprechaun Keeper, Dublin," another man said.

The introductions went on, with Calleigh standing behind Saxon, both of them confused as to what the hell was going on.

"Think we can sit down?" McMurtree finally asked.

Saxon nodded, and Calleigh led the way, seating them and asking if she could get them something to drink.

"I'm not going to waste time here," McMurtree said to Saxon once everyone was settled. "You've been chosen to head a new council."

"What? Why me? And what kind of council?"

"A council of Keepers," McMurtree explained.

"But I'm not a Keeper," Saxon said.

"Doesn't matter—hell, maybe your independence makes you an even better choice," McMurtree told him. "You see the need for a centralized system of regulations, of checks and balances, the one to insist that the Keepers need to have the power to maintain control so that they don't fall prey to the powers of the very beings they are born to control." McMurtree grinned. "All you have to do is set the date and the place, and Keepers from all over the world will be called to a summit. Bailey wanted a New World

Order—well, we're going to create one, and it's going to be based on a code that's fair and rational and backed up by the power of a worldwide network of Keepers. It's complex. I realize that. But we need you—not just as a figurehead but because of your ethics and your beliefs, your strength and your courage."

Saxon looked at Calleigh, awed, uncertain, even a little bit afraid of the responsibility that was being handed to him.

"Put your money where your mouth is, big boy," she suggested softly.

He stood. He was being given the opportunity to be part of something that could change the world—and not only his world—for the better.

"When do we begin?" he asked huskily.

"In the morning," McMurtree told him. "Invitations will go out across the world, and a true governing council for the underworld races will become a reality."

With that announcement, McMurtree stood and pulled Saxon in for a hug.

Moments later the visitors were gone, and Saxon looked at Calleigh. "Is it possible?" he asked.

She slipped into his arms. "All things are possible," she whispered, her eyes meeting his. "All things. Because I'm here, with you."

He took her into his arms. When she was with him, he realized, he did indeed believe that all things were possible.

"News flash," he said. "Elven cop finds life, purpose and everlasting happiness in the arms of a half-breed werewolf."

And just in case she wasn't sure he meant what he'd said, he proceeded to demonstrate exactly how true his words had been.

* * * * *

When Vampire Keeper Rhiannon Gryffald moves to L.A., she finds herself in the middle of a vampire's killing spree. Joining forces with Brodie McKay, a gorgeous Elven cop, may be her only hope of survival as they discover a conspiracy that shakes the Los Angeles theater scene to its core...

Read on for a sneak peek of
KEEPER OF THE NIGHT
by New York Times *bestselling author*
Heather Graham.

Hollywood, California

City of dreams to many and city of lost dreams for too many others. A place where waiters and waitresses spent their tips on head shots, and the men and women behind the scenes—the producers—reigned as the real kings.

So many of the paranormal races—the vampires, the shifters, the elven and more—traveled there, and many stayed, because where better to blend in than a place where even the human beings hardly registered as normal half the time? With so much going on, no one set of Keepers could control the vast scope of the Greater Los Angeles underworld, and so it was that the three Gryffald cousins, daughters of the three renowned Gryffald brothers, were called to take their place as pcacekeepers a bit earlier than had been expected.

And right when L.A. was on the verge of exploding with underworld activity.

Hollywood, they were about to discover, could truly be murder.

There was blood. So much blood.

From her position on the stage, Rhiannon Gryffald could see the man standing just outside the club door. He was tall and well built, his almost formal attire a contrast to the usual California casual and strangely at odds with his youth, with a Hollywood tan that added to the classic strength of his features and set off his light eyes and golden hair.

And he was bleeding from the throat.

Bleeding profusely.

There was blood everywhere. It was running down the side of his throat and staining his tailored white shirt and gold-patterned vest.

"Help! I've been bitten!" he cried. He was staggering, hands clutching his throat.

No! she thought. *Not yet!*

She had barely arrived in Los Angeles! This was too soon, far too soon, to be called upon to take action. She was just beginning to find her way around the city, just learning how to maneuver through the insane traffic—not to mention that she was trying to maintain something that at least resembled steady employment.

"I've been bitten!" he screamed again. "By a vampire!"

There were two women standing near him, staring, and he seemed to be trying to warn them, but they didn't seem frightened, although they were focused on the blood pouring from his wound.

They started to move toward him, their eyes fixed on the scarlet ruin of his neck.

They weren't concerned, Rhiannon realized. They weren't going to help.

They were hungry.

* * * * *

Don't miss the dramatic conclusion to
KEEPER OF THE NIGHT by Heather Graham.
Available January 2013,
only from Harlequin Nocturne.

COMING NEXT MONTH FROM
HARLEQUIN® NOCTURNE™

Available December 18, 2012

#151 KEEPER OF THE NIGHT • *The Keepers: L.A.*
by Heather Graham

When a series of gruesome murders rocks the Los Angeles theater scene, Elven cop Brodie McKay suspects a vampire serial killer is responsible. Going deep undercover as an actor, Brodie knows nothing—or no one—can distract him from the case. Until he meets Rhiannan Gryffald. Having recently given up her rock-star dreams to fulfill her destiny as a vampire Keeper, the gorgeous former musician may be his best ally—and his ultimate temptation.... Don't miss this first book in The Keepers: L.A.

#152 DARK WOLF RISING • *Bloodrunners*
by Rhyannon Byrd

"Dark wolf" Eric Drake has never trusted himself with a human, dating only pack females—and then the night comes when he finds a woman, Chelsea Smart, mistakenly trespassing on Silvercrest pack land. Chelsea has dedicated her life to the belief that a woman doesn't need a man by her side to make her complete. She's always done her best to avoid arrogant, overbearing, gorgeous alpha males...until the search for her missing nineteen-year-old sister brings her face-to-face with a mysterious man she finds impossible to ignore...or resist.

REQUEST YOUR FREE BOOKS!

2 FREE NOVELS FROM THE PARANORMAL ROMANCE COLLECTION PLUS 2 FREE GIFTS!

YES! Please send me 2 FREE novels from the Paranormal Romance Collection and my 2 FREE gifts (gifts are worth about $10). After receiving them, if I don't wish to receive any more books, I can return the shipping statement marked "cancel." If I don't cancel, I will receive 4 brand-new novels every month and be billed just $21.42 in the U.S. or $23.46 in Canada. That's a saving of at least 21% off the cover price of all 4 books. It's quite a bargain! Shipping and handling is just 50¢ per book in the U.S. and 75¢ per book in Canada.* I understand that accepting the 2 free books and gifts places me under no obligation to buy anything. I can always return a shipment and cancel at any time. Even if I never buy another book, the two free books and gifts are mine to keep forever.

237/337 HDN FEL2

Name	(PLEASE PRINT)	
Address		Apt. #
City	State/Prov.	Zip/Postal Code

Signature (if under 18, a parent or guardian must sign)

Mail to the **Reader Service:**
IN U.S.A.: P.O. Box 1867, Buffalo, NY 14240-1867
IN CANADA: P.O. Box 609, Fort Erie, Ontario L2A 5X3

Not valid for current subscribers to the Paranormal Romance Collection
or Harlequin® Nocturne™ books.

Want to try two free books from another line?
Call 1-800-873-8635 or visit www.ReaderService.com.

* Terms and prices subject to change without notice. Prices do not include applicable taxes. Sales tax applicable in N.Y. Canadian residents will be charged applicable taxes. Offer not valid in Quebec. This offer is limited to one order per household. All orders subject to credit approval. Credit or debit balances in a customer's account(s) may be offset by any other outstanding balance owed by or to the customer. Please allow 4 to 6 weeks for delivery. Offer available while quantities last.

Your Privacy—The Reader Service is committed to protecting your privacy. Our Privacy Policy is available online at www.ReaderService.com or upon request from the Reader Service.

We make a portion of our mailing list available to reputable third parties that offer products we believe may interest you. If you prefer that we not exchange your name with third parties, or if you wish to clarify or modify your communication preferences, please visit us at www.ReaderService.com/consumerchoice or write to us at Reader Service Preference Service, P.O. Box 9062, Buffalo, NY 14269. Include your complete name and address.

HARLEQUIN®

NOCTURNE

Discover

THE KEEPERS: L.A.,

a dark and epic new paranormal quartet
led by *New York Times* bestselling author

HEATHER GRAHAM

New Keeper Rhiannon Gryffald has her peacekeeping
duties cut out for her. Because in Hollywood, it's hard
to tell the actors from the werewolves, bloodsuckers and
shape-shifters. When Rhiannon hears about a string of
murders that bear all the hallmarks of a vampire serial
killer, she must unite forces with sexy undercover
Elven agent Brodie to uncover a plot that may forever
alter the face of human-paranormal relations....

KEEPER OF THE NIGHT

by **Heather Graham,**
coming **December 18, 2012.**

And look for

www.Harlequin.com

HN0113HGST

Special excerpt from Harlequin Nocturne

*Could a play about vampires be the perfect cover-up for
a serial killer—and the first test for L.A.'s
new Keeper of the vampires?*

*Enjoy this sneak peek at KEEPER OF THE NIGHT
by New York Times bestselling author Heather Graham,
book one in the dark and epic new paranormal quartet
THE KEEPERS: L.A.*

Hollywood, California.

City of dreams to many, and city of lost dreams for too
many others. A place where waiters and waitresses spent
their tips on head shots, and the men and women behind the
scenes—the producers—reigned as the real kings.

So many of the paranormal races—the vampires, the
shifters, the elven and more—traveled there, and many
stayed, because where better to blend in than a place where
even the human beings hardly registered as normal half
the time? With so much going on, no one set of Keepers
could control the vast scope of the Greater Los Angeles
underworld, and so it was that the three Gryffald cousins,
daughters of the three renowned Gryffald brothers, were
called to take their place as peacekeepers a bit earlier than
had been expected.

And right when L.A. was on the verge of exploding with
underworld activity.

Hollywood, they were about to discover, could truly
be murder.

* * *

HNEXP0113HG

There was blood. So much blood.

From her position on the stage, Rhiannon Gryffald could see the man standing just outside the club door. He was tall and well built, his almost formal attire a contrast to the usual California casual and strangely at odds with his youth, with a Hollywood tan that added to the classic strength of his features and set off his light eyes and golden hair.

And he was bleeding from the throat.

Bleeding profusely.

There was blood everywhere. It was running down the side of his throat and staining his tailored white shirt and gold-patterned vest.

"Help! I've been bitten!" he cried. He was staggering, hands clutching his throat.

No! she thought. *Not yet!*

She had barely arrived in Los Angeles! This was too soon, far too soon, to be called upon to take action.

"I've been bitten!" he screamed again. "By a vampire!"

There were two women standing near him, staring, and he seemed to be trying to warn them, but they didn't appear frightened, although they *were* focused on the blood pouring from his wound.

They started to move toward him, their eyes fixed on the scarlet ruin of his neck.

They weren't concerned, Rhiannon realized. They weren't going to help.

They were *hungry*.

Pick up KEEPER OF THE NIGHT by Heather Graham on December 18, 2012.
Available only from Harlequin® Nocturne™.